Paradise for a Sinner

by

Lynn Shurr

The Sinners Series, Book Four

Paradise for a Sinner

Cover Art by *Diana Carlile*

The Wild Rose Press, Inc.
PO Box 708
Adams Basin, NY 14410-0708
Visit us at www.thewildrosepress.com

Publishing History
First Champagne Rose Edition, 2014
Print ISBN 978-1-62830-219-6
Digital ISBN 978-1-62830-220-2

The Sinners Series, Book Four
Published in the United States of America

He helped a tall, slim, very light-skinned woman alight from the rear. She possessed large, green, slanted eyes that marked her as a relative of the Rev's Mintay, but had better hair than the esteemed doctor's straightened black bob or Adam's frizzy mane for that matter. Hers, light brown and parted in the middle, fell in soft, golden edged waves around a perfectly oval face and down her chest to the tops of two firm, upturned breasts encased in a tangerine-colored clingy top. Not large but alluring, those tits tilted as if they offered themselves to a man's mouth. All she needed to set off that face, that body, was a red hibiscus flower tucked behind an ear and a brightly colored lava-lava dress. Adam stood to greet her—and Mintay and the Rev of course.

Mintay reached him first and gave him an affectionate hug. "So good to see you, Adam. This is my sister, Edwina, but we call her Winnie. She's a registered nurse, and I thought she could help out with Teddy's needs until Miss Wickersham is free. Winnie will be staying here for a while. She's newly divorced."

Winnie cheeks flushed lightly. "Sister, I do not believe you just said that to this man."

Adam smiled a grin so broad he thought his face might stay that way permanently. "Lovely lady, there is a saying in Samoa that the best cure for a lost love is a new love." He offered his hand.

Praise for Lynn Shurr

"Shurr is a wonderful storyteller."

~The Romance Studio

"Very easy reads, well written, combined with conflict, believable plots and secondary characters that make the story come alive."

~Jane Lange, Romance, Reads, and Reviews

"Lynn Shurr's stories have that distinctive flavor…and make you eager for another taste."

~J. L. Salter, author

Dedication

For Fiona and Kelly Jacoby,
who shared their knowledge of spina bifida with me.

Chapter One

Joe Dean Billodeaux, star quarterback of the New Orleans Sinners, finished rubbing down his quarter horse, Lazy Boy. He and the big stud had a lot in common: getting older, being as good as ever, and having a whole bunch of offspring. Glad last winter's surgery had healed well and loosened up nicely, Joe flexed his shoulder. His arm remained great enough to get the Sinners as far as the last game of the playoffs, lost by single point on the scoreboard. Right after his triplets came into the world and he saw how hard they fought to survive, he'd been inspired to win his fourth Super Bowl. Now he wanted a ring for his thumb, but this would not be the year.

Exercising his horse on a long ride was not exactly how he planned to spend the first day of his off-season. Nell knew that. Still, his wife had gone running off to the clinic where she volunteered her services as a psychologist to keep an early morning appointment. Giving L.B. an affectionate swat on the rump, Joe put away the curry comb and brushes and headed for the house, a recently expanded mansion really.

He wanted to spend the whole day in bed with Nell right after all eight of their kids left for school. Dean, twelve, Tommy, eleven, the twin girls and Xochi, aged ten, pretty much got ready themselves, but the triplets, only five, still needed help to get out the door. With their housekeeper, Corazon, shoving breakfast down little gullets, and her husband, the ranch manager, Knox Polk, doing a uniform inspection and backpack check before driving the brood and his own son to school in the van, they did have plenty of help. But as the old TV show claimed, eight is enough.

Still, the ancient *traiteur*, Madame Leleux, predicted he and Nell would have twelve children, this way, that way, all ways. In that she had been correct with Dean being his natural son, Tommy and Xochi adopted though related to his family, and the rest conceived by in vitro. Joe did not consider himself superstitious—much, no more than other athletes. Sure, he wore lucky number seven on his uniform and never played a game without his holy medal around his neck. It just seemed wise to add four more bedrooms and two baths to the house, he told Nell. Putting a small movie theater beneath the extra rooms made sense, too, as anyone attempting to take a tribe of eight to a show must realize. Saying it would get hot inside during a Louisiana summer and just tempt paparazzi, Nell vetoed an exterior glass elevator to the second floor. They compromised on a regular lift. After twelve years of marriage, Joe thought he'd gotten pretty good at compromising, but Nell didn't agree with that either.

She knew how he liked to spend his first day off entirely alone with her. He'd given Corazon and Knox a free day, *mais* yeah, but she'd gone to that appointment anyhow. Nell said kind of sassy, "Well, I expected you to be in training for the Super Bowl, so don't blame me. This woman is in crisis and needs my help more than you need me in bed."

She softened that statement with a deep kiss and a promise to hurry home. Maybe during his long ride and time in the barn, she'd come back and waited naked upstairs right now. He smelled like horse and needed a shower. Shower sex or tub sex, her choice. See, he could compromise. The very thought of Nell and lots of lather made his jeans feel tight.

Good, her little red car, the one she zipped around in when the children weren't along, sat in the driveway. Unfortunately, a huge black Escalade filled the space next to it. Not the one belonging to his old teammate, Revelation Bullock, either. Since becoming an ordained minister, the Rev had ordered his latest vehicle with a gold cross on the back, not the team's red devil logo. A red imp winked on the rear of this one. Which team member possessed the nerve to violate Joe's first day off ritual? A little steamed and very frustrated, he entered by the kitchen door and slammed it shut.

Two pairs of eyes turned toward him. The large, brown ones in the broad mocha face belonged to his terrific Samoan cornerback, Adam Malala, the man who replaced the Rev on the Sinners' defense. The other pair, wide and baby blue, resided in the face of a small boy with a shock of pale corn silk hair hanging down to his blond brows. The child hunched forward in a scratched and dented red wheelchair. Joe's guests appeared to be sharing a gallon jug of milk and a stack of peanut butter and banana sandwiches with a side of oatmeal cookies.

"Hey, Adam. I thought you were on your way to the islands. Aren't you getting married in May?"

The big shoulders of the Samoan heaved. "Change of plans. I thought I'd hang out with you for a while."

3

Without calling first, without an invitation? Joe held in his thoughts because he liked the easygoing guy and sure could not fault his ability on the playing field. Malala tended to be kind of casual about his visits. Most times that didn't matter, but today…

Joe turned to the boy. "Who might you be, young man? Don't your parents know Camp Love Letter isn't starting for a few more months?" He referred to his charity for sick and crippled children.

Far from being intimidated in the presence of the famous quarterback, the kid beamed at him. His small voice twanged like a tightly tuned country banjo as he held up a folded piece of notebook paper. "I'm your son, Teddy. My mama says so in her letter."

"Nell! Nell, where are you?" Joe shouted.

Adam inclined his head on its thick neck toward the hall. "She's on the phone. Your wife said to make ourselves at home so I put together some lunch. You want a sandwich?"

"No, no, I do not." He strode to the base of the staircase in the high vaulted foyer and shouted strong enough to be calling a desperate audible play in a noisy stadium, "Nell, where are you?"

"Upstairs," she yelled back.

Amazing how loud such a small woman could be when necessary. Ordinarily, Nell did not approve of yelling, but when you had eight children to command, that rule sometimes went by the wayside. Joe suggested she wear a whistle, but she said she refused to be like the father in *The Sound of Music*. Taking the stairs two at a time, he tried to decipher if that one shouted word held any anger directed at him. He would know in a minute.

There she sat out of her psychologist clothes and wearing exercise attire on their king-sized bed with her legs and bare feet curled under her and the phone in her hand. Not exactly sexy, but cute. She still wore her dark brown hair in a practical pixie cut and her face remained gamine despite her thirty-five years. Her breasts and hips were fuller now, and she bore a C-section scar on her belly, his fault for wanting her to have the triplets. Despite that, she was still his Tinker Bell, his Tink. At the moment, her beautiful and usually understanding brown eyes held a peculiar expression. She did not smile when he entered the room.

Only one thing to do. Joe fell to his knees by the bed, took her hand, and swore, "Cross my heart and hope to die, that boy is not mine, Nell."

He dropped her hand and made the sign of the cross for emphasis. "I made a vow to be faithful to you, and I have been for true. What age is that boy? Around eight judging by the size of those big front teeth. Sounds like he's from Tennessee or somewhere in the mountains. We played the Titans at home that year, and I came directly to you after the game. My mama had the boys, and your parents were taking care of the girls. We had our own very special victory party. Remember? A night on the town in the French Quarter, that hotel suite with room service, and sex all night long with our cell phones turned off, no interruptions. We skipped church and had his and her massages."

He flashed that sure-to-get-you-laid smile of his, especially effective from his position of supplication. Nell nodded against the phone. "Yes, that's Joe. I understand you have a problem of your own, Mintay. We'll deal with it. Just wanted to let you know what happened. Bye." Nell disconnected from Dr. Arminta Green Bullock, the Rev's wife and her partner at the clinic, but her soft, generous mouth stayed strangely puckered.

Joe tried again. "By Jesus, Mary, and Joseph, that boy is not my son."

His little wife burst out laughing. "Of course he isn't. Every child you father has the mark of the Billodeauxs on them in one way or another. Seeing you on your knees like that reminds me of the first time you said 'I love you' and wanted to marry me the very next day so Dean would have a mother. Too irresistible not to want to see that again."

Nell patted the space next to her on the bed. Joe vaulted into it and wrapped his arms around her. Only took a few seconds to coax that smiling mouth open and insert enough tongue to imitate the act of love. Nell cooperated for a minute or two, but when he reached for his fly, she held him off by placing her dainty hand on his crotch—as if that helped to put out the fire.

"We have two people sitting in the kitchen who need our attention, Joe."

"Sorta forgot that. What's the story on the boy?" Joe rolled back on a pillow with a groan.

"Teddy's mother abandoned him at the clinic today. She hands him a letter to show me and says she is going out to get him a breakfast sandwich. Never comes back. The child isn't stupid, and he reads very well. I gather that is his favorite pastime. Naturally, he read the note before I got there. I think the only thing holding him together right now is the belief he is the son of the second most famous man in Chapelle, Louisiana."

"Second most?" His vanity pricked, Joe frowned.

"I do think billionaire techno-geek Jonathan Hartz might top you."

"In some circles, maybe. What a rotten thing to do to a kid, any kid, not just one in a wheelchair. She deserts him and piles a big, fat lie on top of that. Why did she pick on me?"

"I've been seeing Maydell Wilkes for several months. You pegged the Tennessee accent. She came to Louisiana two years ago with a boyfriend looking for work—not the boy's father. She never said who that was. I sensed incest, an uncle, a cousin, might have been the case since she had Teddy at fifteen in some backwoods town. Her father died a few years before that in a hunting accident. The child comes into the world with a handicap, spina bifida, his spinal cord exposed between his vertebrae. Several churches and charities see the baby gets the surgeries he needs to survive. For a while, Maydell and her mother cope. The grandmother dies, and she takes off with a man who will support her and the child—she believes. The boyfriend can't handle a handicapped child and threatens to leave her. Afraid of being alone, she skips and leaves her burden behind in the clinic's waiting room."

Joe, hands behind his head, asked again, "Why me?"

Nell brushed back the dark curl that always escaped onto his forehead and replaced it with a light kiss. "Because she heard about your work with crippled children at Camp Love Letter. She knows we have a bunch of children, some of them adopted, and we have the means to give Teddy a good life. He'll need more surgeries as he grows and special care."

"But she lied about me."

"For heaven's sake, we'll do the DNA test and clear your good name!" Not so gentle now, Nell punched his arm. "Until then, he needs a home and people who can take care of him. We were cleared for foster care when Xochi came to us. I've already spoken to the child welfare people. They will send someone over to check out the situation and put the process in motion. Nurse Wickersham is available to help with his bodily needs as soon as her current job ends. She is caring for a terminally ill patient at the moment and says he doesn't have long."

Her physical punches packed no wallop, not to a guy who sometimes got taken down by three-hundred pound linebackers, but Nell's emotional blows were always weighty. Joe considered. He rarely waffled about decisions on field or off.

"Okay, we'll keep him."

"Temporarily of course. His mother will have a change of heart, I'm sure. You aren't concerned about having a special needs child in the house?'

"Nope. The kids that come to Camp Love Letter helped me get over whatever hang-ups I had about diseases and such years ago."

"You aren't bothered that I set this up without asking you first?"

"Did I ask you when I brought home Xochi and a dog that just kept getting bigger? This only makes us even."

"Joe Dean Billodeaux, I love you."

This time her hand reached for his zipper, but she stopped and wrinkled her nose. "You reek of horse."

"Just noticing now?"

"Yes. The bedspread will have to be washed."

"Later, Tink. Can you spare ten minutes? I need to shower."

"Sure." She started to rise. He pulled her back by the loose waistband of her gray yoga pants, so much easier to get into than tight jeans.

"With you. A quickie, I promise."

"You deserve more, but we cannot linger. Promise?"

"Absolutely. Don't worry. Adam will watch Teddy. He told me once he used to take care of the little children in his village when he was a boy. He'll keep the kid occupied."

"Any idea why Adam is here and not in Samoa? He drove up behind me as I was opening the gate, followed me to the house, and helped me with the wheelchair. Only said he wanted to talk to you."

"Could we not think about Adam now?"

Joe untied the string of the yoga pants and nearly upended her peeling them off. No panties beneath. She had been waiting for him after all. He stripped off her hot pink sports bra and released those suppressed breasts into his hands. They would never be huge, but motherhood had made them larger, softer, so nice to squeeze gently and stroke lightly. He almost forgot they were on short time until Nell said, "To the shower."

He carried his wife into the bathroom and sat her on the closed lid of the commode while he stripped down and adjusted the water. The shower in the gym might have been better with its many sprays and nozzles, but this would have to do for now. Water thundered from the showerhead into the vast two-person tub with the view of the bayou. He ripped the curtain closed and in his haste, bumped his head on the dangling crystals of the chandelier that provided light over the basin.

Joe beckoned to his naked wife. "Let's get the horse smell off me first, then on to the good stuff."

Nell obliged by soaping his back, but then she got frisky, running her hand between his legs, massaging the root of his cock and giving his balls a very thorough washing. When he turned around, Joe had to stop her fingers from slicking along a very urgent erection. "I won't last if you do that, sugar."

One nice thing about standing six-foot-three and having a pint-sized wife was the easy lifting. He raised her on his hips and braced her against the tiled wall away from the spray of the water. As he entered her deep, Nell wrapped her legs around his waist and clutched his broad shoulders. Holding back as best he could, Joe ran a slippery finger into her cleft repeatedly until she began to arch and push back. He drove hard for the goal line. Score!—and an extra point for making Nell come, too. No one, not even the many women from his man whore days, could say Joe Dean Billodeaux failed in being a generous lover.

Nell slid down the wall and rested her head on his still soapy chest. "Wobbly," she said. "I think I was as ready for that as you were. And I'm sorry we won't be alone today. Rinse. We have to take care of a few problems downstairs."

She already had her clothes on by the time he dried off and pulled on clean garments, the hell with shaving. Nell put on a pink and white checked shirt over the sports bra and tied it at the waist. Sure, she'd had a nip and a tummy tuck after giving birth to the triplets, but she worked hard in the gym to keep her waist slim and sexy. Joe appreciated that. Running after all those children kept her trim, too, he guessed.

As Nell drew a comb through her short, practical hair, the doorbell sounded its mellow chimes. Macho, their oversized ranch dog, began barking in a mean basso that only fooled strangers. Quickly, she glossed her mouth with a little pink lipstick. No time for makeup. Shoving her feet into flip-flops, she headed to the bedroom door.

Joe stopped her. "Nell, I just had a frisson, me."

"No time for the cute Cajun routine, Joe. Someone let Macho in, and he'll scare Teddy to death, not to mention whoever is at the front door."

"We should stay in bed like we planned and not go down there. I got this bad feeling it's going to be another one of *those* off-seasons, the kind with bad problems we have to fix."

"Are you telling me the great Joe Dean Billodeaux is afraid to face an off-season?" Nell raised her eyebrows at him.

"No way. Okay, we move on the count of three." They went through the doorway together.

Chapter Two

From the top of the stairs, Joe and Nell gazed down on chaos. Macho, huge, yellow-furred, curly-tailed, black-muzzled, and white-pawed, dragged Teddy's red wheelchair back and forth across the shining burgundy tiles before the front door. The boy, strapped into his chair, had a tight grip on the dog's wide leather collar and a large smile on his small face. The mutt stopped barking and paused to snuffle along the sill. The bell rang again setting off more furious woofing and pacing. The people on the other end of the onslaught had no way of knowing Macho would embrace them, paws on their shoulders, and slurp their faces once he got loose.

"Teddy, let go of the dog's collar!" Nell cried. "He'll tip you over. How did Macho get in here?" Fearlessly entering the maelstrom, she headed rapidly down the stairs. The toe of her flip-flop caught the edge of the runner, but Joe grabbed her elbow before she tumbled.

Adam's broad face looked up apologetically. "My bad, Mrs. Joe. He was scratching the H out of your kitchen door so I let him inside. He went right over to the kid to get his ears rubbed. No problem. They were getting along great. Then the bell rang, and they both took off. Want me to kick the mutt out?"

"Just put him in the kitchen and close the door for

now."

"Aaah, we was having fun," Teddy said as Adam wrested the collar from his grip and attempted to drag the dog to the kitchen. Macho dug in his rear paws. His claws scraped the waxy surface of the tiles. Finally, the cornerback grasped the canine under the forelegs, pressed him to his broad chest, and walked the dog to the other room to be confined. The barks turned to pleading whimpers.

"That's better," Nell said. "This can't be the Rev or Mintay. Macho recognizes them. Besides, they are dealing with their own situation this morning. Knowing them, they'd come to help anyway." Nell placed her hand on the deadbolt to open the door.

"Wait." Joe peered out a curtained sidelight. "Airport limo. How did it get up the drive?"

"Sorry," Adam said, this time hanging his head and showing them the part in his outrageous mane of frizzy, black curls that extended well below his shoulders. "The guy said their need to see you was most urgent, his exact words. I buzzed them in since you were—um, busy upstairs. I mean we all know how you like to spend the first day of your off-season. I shouldn't have come."

Nell looked at her husband with astonishment and measured her words carefully in front of Teddy. "You told the team what we do to celebrate the off-season?"

"Might have slipped out," Joe admitted and stepped out of the range of her fist. "Let me get the door in case it's some new paparazzi trick."

The bell chimed again almost apologetically. "Please, sir, call off your hounds and allow us to enter. I have grave news to relate," a very proper British voice implored on the other side of the heavy, dark oak door.

"He thinks our mixed breed Texas cur is hounds," Joe snickered. He raised his voice and asked, "What do you want here?"

A tall, long-faced form with an impressively large nose placed itself before the sidelight. His hands rested on the shoulders of a beautiful female child. Nell took a peek.

"Good Lord, I think that's my niece. At least, she looks like the picture on the Christmas card Emily sent last year. Open the door."

Joe did. The odd pair entered. Nell held out her hands immediately in greeting. "I know you must be Anastasia. That would make you Prince Stefan. Where is my sister?"

"No, madam, I am not the prince. So sorry to confuse you. This, however, is the Princess Anastasia Marya Polasky, his daughter. I am Clive Brinsley. I served the prince as both valet and butler."

"So happy to have you both here. I've asked Emily to send Anastasia to visit her cousins often, but I wish she had let us know you were coming. We would have met you at the airport."

The child declined to step into Nell's embrace. Instead she stared at her aunt with blue eyes like Teddy's, but hers were narrowed, sharp and bright as broken bottle glass. A pert nose and pouty lips made up the rest of her face. Dark blonde curls held back by a pink ribbon cascaded around her thin shoulders and down her back nearly to her waist. She wore a pair of tan suede boots with fringe around the top, pink leggings, and a short pink and white polka-dotted dress belted low on her childish hips. The twins would be envious of the clothes their cousin sported, hipshot like a model poised at the end of a runway.

"What a pretty outfit," Nell said. Still trying to lure the child closer for some affection, she stepped toward her. The girl put her off with a remark.

"Mommy said you didn't know how to dress. I can see that is true." Anastasia eyed the yoga pants and flip-flops.

Behind Nell, Adam Malala sucked in his breath and issued a rebuke. "You do not talk to your elders that way."

"Golly, yes. That woulda got my mouth washed out with soap or a pretty good slap from Newt," Teddy chimed in.

"Is this one of my cousins? Mommy said they were backwater Cajun hicks with a rich daddy who got lucky playing American football."

Nell reined in her outrage for her children. A cruel statement like that defined Emily's personality. No matter that her sister had put the moves on Joe more than once and would gladly have married him or anyone else on the Sinners team. Joe placed his hands on her shoulders and both looked out at the limo where the driver unloaded a pyramid of pink luggage with a tan leather trim and one large, black suitcase. A small curly heap of a dog pressed its nose to the door of its carrier on top of the baggage and yapped in sharp, little barks.

Joe's fingers dug into Nell's flesh. "Compared to a smart-mouthed brat like you, my kids are angels. Since we're so *basse classe,* why don't the two of you get back in the limo and return to Italy and mommy dearest right now. I'll pay your way with some of my lucky money."

The butler's long, serious face became grim as his thin lips turned downward. "Please, sir, allow me to address the situation." He bent over Anastasia. "Princess, a cultured person does not repeat what they have overheard, especially if hurtful and rude. I cannot remain in the service of one who does."

Instantly, the superior blue eyes released a waterfall of tears that cascaded down the dimpled cheeks and onto the dress to mingle with the polka dots. Anastasia buried her face in the dark pants leg of the servant and cried as if her world had come to an end.

Joe shifted with discomfort. Nell knew he had a weakness for crying children. Heaven knew his own daughters tried that ploy often enough, but the girl's emotion seemed genuine.

"I didn't mean to make her cry," Joe said. "You are welcome to visit, but no more mouth about your cousins or Aunt Nell, you hear."

"Perhaps, the princess could take Titi from her crate and give her some water and a short walk while we talk," Clive Brinsley said. "Go along, Anastasia. Get her lead and let her out. Think of something other than yourself."

Anastasia accepted a clean handkerchief from her butler and patted her face dry. She turned to the mound of luggage. Teddy wheeled up beside her. "I can help you."

"What could you possibly do?" The girl, a trifle older, looked down on him.

"Lots of things. I can already read Harry Potter. We could tie her leash to my chair and just roll along together—if someone will help me down the front steps."

Adam simply lifted the chair and the boy and set them on the ground, only two easy steps for him, one from the doorway and one off the verandah, but impossible for Teddy. "Thank you, sir," he said politely.

"You're a good kid, Teddy," Adam replied gruffly, implying by his expression that the other child was not.

The girl took a leash, a plastic dish and a water bottle from a carry-on bag and opened the little dog's crate. The animal bounded into her arms and lavished affection with a small pink tongue, wiping away the remnants of the salty tears.

"Can I hold her while you pour the water? I'm a good holder."

"I guess so." Anastasia placed the pup into his lap where Titi gave him an identical welcome.

The limo driver lurked beside the passenger door of his black vehicle. "I guess that's all the luggage." He made no move to leave.

Adam glanced back at the mansion with its tall, white pillars a la Scarlet O'Hara. None of the other adults still stood in the open doorway. Apparently, his babysitting days were not over. He took out his wallet and plastered two twenties in the driver's hand. "That do it?"

"Yes, sir. Thank you, sir. Aren't you Adam Malala? I know this is Joe Dean Billodeaux's place. They use our service sometimes, but this is my first trip here. These your children or his?" He held out his receipt book hopefully, and Adam gave him an autograph.

"No and no. Guests." As if his own children if he

ever had any would be so light-skinned.

"Oh, must be one of the crips Joe works with, but that other one is a piece of work, let me tell you." The driver made that statement as if little kids had no ears.

That irritated Adam no end, especially on Teddy's behalf. "You'd better get going," he said in a way that caused opposing players to beware and made the man step lively to the other side of the car.

"I need someone to open the gate again."

"I got it. You two don't go anywhere until I get back, okay?"

Both children nodded as they watched Titi lapping water as if it were dog ambrosia. Adam headed straight for the kitchen as the limo sailed down the long drive. He forgot about the dog, the huge one. Macho bowled him over and skittered for the open front door. How humiliating for a Pro Bowl cornerback. Adam dashed across a devastated kitchen: milk jug spilled on the floor, cookie packet empty, sandwich plates, one broken, knocked down and licked clean. He hit the button, swiveled, and turned on the speed as he raced back to avert another disaster.

Macho beat him to the entry and plummeted down the steps right to the water dish. Titi squeaked. Macho barked once sharply. He sniffed under the intruder's feathery tail, then moved to the other end of the little fur ball and touched his big, wet nose to the little black button that protruded from the mound of fluffy hair. Adam stooped to pick up a landscaping stone from the flowerbed. Seeing that monster eat the bit of fluff would not be good for the children. Before he could chuck his rock at Macho, the top dog nudged the other aside and finished off the water in several slurps of the bowl. Evidently, peanut butter and cookies made him thirsty and spilled milk did not do the trick. Finishing his drink, Macho trotted off to raise a leg against the trunk of one of the massive live oaks that dotted Joe's property. The toy dog followed and sniffed, obviously impressed by the aroma and output. Both lay down in the shade.

Anastasia went to sit by her puppy and spread her skirt out on the layer of brown fallen oak leaves as neatly as if she were on a picnic in Tuscany. Teddy gamely pushed his wheelchair through the duff and took up a place next to Macho. The dog placed his huge head in the boy's lap and offered his ears for scratching.

Adam sank down on the porch step and rested his elbows on his knees. He wondered how long he would have to wait to have that heart-to-heart talk with the man the team called Daddy Joe. He could not go back to Samoa without some sound advice about women. On that topic, Joe Dean Billodeaux was the acknowledged expert.

Chapter Three

In Joe's vast den, actually now the family room since the children came along, Clive Brinsley perched on the very edge of one of Joe's leather recliners. Joe relaxed into a matching chair while Nell seated herself on the long sofa.

"Now, Mr. Brinsley, what is the problem?" Joe began.

"Simply Brinsley, sir. A butler is addressed by his last name only. I bring grievous news." He turned to Nell. "I am so sorry to report that your sister and her husband perished in an automobile wreck two weeks ago. While the prince and Mrs. Polasky were not given to planning ahead, they did leave a will naming you as guardian of their only child. Rather than pay a solicitor, they asked me to be their executor. I've brought Anastasia here at my own expense."

Nell, stunned and thrust suddenly into the disbelieving stage of grief, said, "How could that be? No one called us. Do my parents know, my brother and his family?"

"No one. A matter of misplaced pride, I believe. The madam specified if she should die in Italy, she wanted a cremation and her ashes scattered privately in the Adriatic Sea from the terrace of the palazzo. Only afterward was her family to be informed. You see, the creditors were at the door ready to strip the place down to the mosaic floors."

Nell rubbed her forehead as if shoving the facts inside her brain. "Do you think they committed suicide?"

"Not your sister. She had too much spirit for that, but the prince, perhaps. He was given to mercurial moods, charming one moment, morose the next."

"Yes," Nell agreed. "I doubt Emily would leave this earth willingly. She'd go out kicking and complaining. When my parents visited after she gave birth to Anastasia, they had doubts about the prince and his temperament."

"That's not all," Joe said. "I paid to have this Prince Stefan investigated to ease their minds. The report found his royal lines to be completely faked. He made his living gambling and escorting rich women. By the time the child came along, too late to do anything much about it unless Emily divorced him by her own choice."

Brinsley nodded sadly. "I suspected as much. The madam often jested that she met the prince in Monaco when she'd gotten down to her last million. He used her funds to restore her fortune in the casinos—and his. Until recently, he played adeptly at cards."

"My fortune, you mean. We paid the damn—Nell's sister that money for a donation of eggs to make our family. She took the cash and ran for Europe. Never came home. We got her wedding announcement, another one for the baby's birth, and an annual Christmas card. She didn't stick around to see Nell through any of the difficult births, had no interest in meeting the children. That's how much she cared about family." Joe socked a fist into his palm.

"Please, Joe. Emily is gone now. She did save my life with a bone marrow transplant when I was a teenager. Remember that. We wouldn't have most of our children without her donation either." Nell went over to his chair, pried open his fist and placed her hand inside.

"Yeah, right."

Brinsley continued. "I can tell you on the day of the accident, they went to visit a vineyard and imbibed a great deal. Witnesses said they argued about their circumstances. On the return home, the Maserati went over a cliff and burst into flames. Cremation was the only option regardless. I allowed Anastasia to help me scatter the ashes as we all need closure. Not long after, the *banca* seized the house, and the rest of the creditors, the furnishings. One vile specimen attempted to take Titi from the child. He thought he could get money for the dog, but I would not allow that. Other than the pup, we left Italy with only our personal belongings. I paid for our fare from my savings."

"I see what you're getting at, Brinsley. How much do we owe you? Add in some extra for your trouble." Joe rose to get his checkbook.

"Not necessary, sir. Anyone who would abandon a child in need would be a very low creature indeed. My expenses should have come out of the estate, but the estate vanished in a matter of days. Being butler to the Polasky family was not an ideal situation, but I have always stood by my employers. Having saved prudently over the years, I had the means to help, and did so. However, I would ask one favor. I would like to stay on with your family for a short time until Anastasia has settled. The dog and I are all she had left of her former life besides her personal possessions."

"She's got a heap of those along with a bad attitude. I'm not so sure she'll be staying here after those remarks she made. Maybe your parents will take her, Nell, or your brother."

Nell stroked Joe's arm. "My parents are too old to raise another child, and my brother has three boys. Besides, she is a half-sister to both the twins and the triplets."

"Maybe your sister-in-law would like to have a daughter. This kid doesn't look anything like Emily, but she for certain has the same sorry nature. She won't fit in here."

"I could have said the same of Xochi when she arrived, but she has thrived."

Brinsley looked from one to the other and finally inserted his plea. "Anastasia greatly resembles the prince who was a handsome man, but a child will reflect the parent she is with most often. Her mother did not permit her to play with the village children. She had only an Italian girl and a private tutor to see to her. They left as soon as the first paycheck bounced. No loyalty at all. Now if the child had a professional English governess things might have been different, but instead, she was her mother's confidant. Mrs. Polasky became an embittered woman, well aware of her mistakes and refusing to admit them. I have been working with Anastasia to improve her behavior, but it will take time and patience to undo the damage, I fear. If you are not up to the challenge, I could seek the Polasky side of the family, but I am afraid they don't exist, and certainly not as Polish royalty."

"We figured as much. I guess she must stay. Be glad to have you remain a while, too," Joe conceded. Nell hugged his shoulders, and he knew he'd done the right thing deep down no matter how difficult it would be. He and Nell had faced hard issues before and could handle them together.

He clapped his hands together. "Okay, so let's get that load of luggage moved upstairs. Where do you want to put the children, Nell?"

"Let Anastasia pick her room. Teddy can go along and decide where he wants to sleep, too."

"I can handle the luggage, sir," Brinsley offered.

"The hell you can. It will take you, me, and Adam to move that mountain. Good thing we put in an elevator, huh, Nell? You coming along?"

"No, I have to break the news to my family. Close the door when you go out, please."

"Should I stay?" Joe noticed the tears forming in the corners of her brown eyes.

"No. Taking care of the children will be the biggest help right now."

"If you say so."

He left his wife in the closed room and went out the front to tackle the baggage with Brinsley. He saw Adam's broad, hunched shoulders first, then the rather charming tableau of the two children and the dogs under the oak tree. Maybe this could work.

"Ah, Joe, you got a minute now?" Adam asked.

"As soon as we move Anastasia's things into her room, bro. Grab a few bags."

Picking up two of the pink suitcases and shoving a hatbox under one muscular arm, the big Samoan complied. Brinsley extended the handle from his black, wheeled luggage and piled two smaller cases on top.

"Princess, bring along Titi's carrier, please," the butler directed his charge.

Anastasia snapped the leash on to the dog's rhinestone collar and took up the small crate now sitting on the ground. Teddy wheeled up after rocking a little to free his chair from the oak duff.

"I can help. Put a little one on my lap."

Joe placed him on the porch first before setting smallest case on the boy's lap. He tipped the wheelchair up the steps into the house and went back for what remained of the baggage. Like a caravan of overloaded camels, the men followed the high plumed tail curled over Titi's back and the equally head-held-high form of Anastasia. Macho attempted to join the march. Joe kicked the door shut in his snout.

"Make a right at the end of hall to the elevator," he called from the rear.

"Golly, you got an elevator. I never lived in a two-story house before or one with an elevator neither. Can I push the button to make it work?" Teddy did the honors.

"I guess we knew you were on the way," Joe said as he motioned the children inside and got aboard himself. "We'll have to make two trips." Leaving Adam and Brinsley behind, they ascended to the second floor.

"We have four bedrooms with shared baths between them. Pick your place."

Anastasia wrinkled her nose. "I do not share a bath."

"Well, you do now."

The girl opened one door after another. "None of them is pink. Pink is my color."

"The twins have the pink room and aren't likely to move out for you. Choose something else," Joe ordered with his dislike of the child creeping into his voice. He choked it back and turned to Teddy. "Which one do you want? Now you get first choice because the princess here can't make up her mind."

"Hey, ladies first!" Anastasia objected.

"You snooze, you lose. Go on, Teddy."

Teddy peered into the first room by the elevator. "This 'un's fine. It's green. I like green. I never had such a big room before. Thanks, Dad."

"About that business. I don't think your mom and me ever…I mean she had you at fifteen, and I'd never do… Forget it for now." Joe let the two pink suitcases fall to the floor. "Where's your luggage. Let's get you moved in."

"My duffel bag is in the kitchen. I hope Macho didn't eat my meds 'cause I really need them."

"Only if they smell like food."

The elevator slid open and disgorged Brinsley, Adam, and the rest of the luggage. Anastasia stamped her foot and addressed the butler. "Uncle Joe says his twins have the pink room. Teddy took the green one, but it's by the elevator and I didn't want it anyhow. The worst rooms in a hotel are always by the elevator. *And* I have to share a bathroom."

Brinsley appeared to reflect for a moment. "However, this is a very nice house and will not be quite as noisy as a hotel. Let's see what we have left: a very lovely lavender, pale gray, cream and white with gold accents. Why this last is fit for royalty and away from the lift. White and gold furniture in the French style, a beautiful lamp with crystal drops, a padded headboard, superb! What do you think, Anastasia?"

"Then it should be mine. Where will you stay, Brinsley?"

"In the servants' quarters, I imagine. If you will point the way, I will dispose of my baggage and return to assist the princess in her unpacking." He addressed Joe and awaited directions.

"We don't exactly have servants' quarters. Take the gray room. Our housekeeper and ranch manager have one of the cottages, but that's a lot of room for one person. I think you should stay by Anastasia for now."

"As you wish."

Adam let his burdens fall to the floor with a thunk. "Joe, do you think now…"

"Would you go downstairs and get Teddy's duffel bag?"

"Sure, but then…"

"Absolutely."

Adam gave up and headed for the sweeping staircase. He needed to burn off some frustration. Cleaning up the mess the dog made helped. Placing the broken plate in the sink, he sopped up the spilled milk with paper towels, put the jug back into the refrigerator, and the dog-licked dishes in the washer. Shouldering the duffel, he ran up the flight of stairs only to find Joe gone and Teddy alone in his room.

"Thanks, Mr. Adam. I don't got much. Set it down by the dresser, and I can put my stuff away by myself."

"You sure?"

"Yep."

Across the hall, Anastasia's shrill voice corrected, "Not there, Brinsley! My undies go in the upper right hand drawer."

Glad to escape, Adam jogged down the stairs again. In the hallway, Joe held a sobbing Nell to his chest.

"I know Em could be mean and vindictive. She resented all the attention I got because of my illness, all the sacrifices she had to make. We weren't close, but still she was my only sister and now she's gone."

Over his wife's head, Joe mouthed, "Not now."

Adam nodded and went out the front door. He took his seat on the step again. Macho came over, put his big head in Adam's lap, and dusted the sidewalk with his tail.

"You know, I don't like dogs very much. They bark too often and leave shit everywhere. They make big messes like the one in the kitchen. In America, you can't eat them, but you'd make a pretty good-sized roast. Still, you seem like a good listener. Here's the problem. My girl told me she is going to marry my best friend, not me. She held off until we lost the playoff game. Didn't want to upset me. Ha!"

Macho tilted his head and scratched his side with a rear paw. He appeared ready and willing to offer comfort and support in time of need. Adam continued with his tale.

"How can I go back to Samoa when all I want to do is find Sammy Tau and squeeze his neck until he dies? He stole my *taupou,* a real island princess, not like that kid upstairs who thinks she's royalty. Where am I going to find another one of those, huh? Everyone in Pago Pago must be laughing at me by now. I mean you can be a big deal in the U.S. of A. and still be nothing in Samoa. I can't go home. Not now."

Adam buried his broad face in his huge hands.

Macho tongued the part not covered, then pricked his ears and, barking ferociously, raced toward the front gate.

"Even you desert me, Macho," Adam muttered.

Running alongside another black Escalade, the dog escorted the new arrivals to a parking space and waited eagerly for a door to open. Adam recognized the vehicle and knew it bore a gold cross and a chaplain's license plate on the rear rather than a red devil. Revelation Jeremiah Bullock, the man he had replaced on the Sinners' team, had come calling. Adam brightened. Maybe he needed a man of the cloth to listen to his woes more than Joe Dean's advice.

Huge, black, and ponderous, the Reverend Rev got out from behind the wheel, and being the consummate gentleman, moved around the front of the SUV to hand his pretty and svelte wife, Dr. Arminta Green Bullock, down from the front seat. She carried a medical file under one arm and smiled brilliantly when she recognized Adam. The Rev opened the backseat door, probably to release his three children, but no.

He helped a tall, slim, very light-skinned woman alight from the rear. She possessed large, green, slanted eyes that marked her as a relative of the Rev's Mintay, but had better hair than the esteemed doctor's straightened black bob or Adam's frizzy mane for that matter. Hers, light brown and parted in the middle, fell in soft, golden edged waves around a perfectly oval face and down her chest to the tops of two firm, upturned breasts encased in a tangerine-colored clingy top. Not large but alluring, those tits tilted as if they offered themselves to a man's mouth. All she needed to set off that face, that body, was a red hibiscus flower tucked behind an ear and a brightly colored lava-lava dress. Adam stood to greet her—and Mintay and the Rev of course.

Mintay reached him first and gave him an affectionate hug. "So good to see you, Adam. This is my sister, Edwina, but we call her Winnie. She's a registered nurse, and I thought she could help out with Teddy's needs until Miss Wickersham is free. Winnie will be staying here for a while. She's newly divorced."

Winnie cheeks flushed lightly. "Sister, I do not believe you just said that to this man."

Adam smiled a grin so broad he thought his face might stay that way permanently. "Lovely lady, there is a saying in Samoa that the best cure for a lost love is a new love." He offered his hand.

Chapter Four

Winnie Green—Green because she'd taken her maiden name back with a vengeance—stared at the outstretched hand and all the rest of Adam Malala. Being sister-in-law to the Rev, she'd seen pro football players up close at various family events, but at the time she'd been married and following the advice of her grandmother and mother. Nana, the original Arminta and wasn't Winnie glad she'd escaped being *her* namesake, always pounded home the age old wisdom. Marry lighter than yourself. Raise up your family. Better opportunities come to the light-skinned.

Her mother, a beneficiary of the Civil Rights movement, who held a doctorate in sociology and possessed a husband who matched her in intellect, degree, and fair complexion, simply said, "Marry white because you can." When Mintay accepted a proposal from the Rev, considerably darker than the Samoan who stood before Winnie today, her family erupted like a volcano in the South Seas.

"Do you know what you are doing, girl? We don't care how rich he is, how can you marry that big, black brute of a football player?" By the time the wedding rolled around, the Rev had won them over with his outsized personality, kind heart, and in the case of Nana, his love of the Lord. It could happen again, especially since Winnie, the pliable baby sister of the family, had failed to keep her white man.

As of today, Winnie Green was done with skinny white boys. She desired someone big and warm and brown, as delicious as hot fudge topping. She wanted to rake her fingers through the mass of soft curls surrounding Adam's face and enjoy everything broad about him, his nose, his cheekbones, his lips— especially his lips. Then on to his chest stretching the red knit Sinners shirt over a mass of muscles and down to an ordinary pair of khakis made extraordinary by the way they pulled over his large, hard thighs.

She took Adam Malala's hand. "Very happy to meet you."

"Me, too." Without releasing her hand, Adam guided her into the house with the Rev and Mintay following, and Macho being shut out again to whine for entrance. "I'll take you to meet Teddy. I think the doctor and Rev should go see Mrs. Joe. She just learned her sister died."

Mintay thrust the medical file at her sister. "This is Teddy's information for you to study. I need to comfort Nell. You two go ahead."

In the elevator, Adam stood close enough to Winnie catch a whiff of light perfume. The scent of her shampoo in that golden brown hair exuded the fragrance of coconut and papaya that reminded him of the islands, palm trees, and ripe fruit for the picking. When the door opened on the second floor, the complaints of Anastasia ordering Brinsley about filled the air, and not in a good way.

"A niece and a butler the Billodeauxs inherited," Adam explained.

"I would have been surprised if Nell allowed any of her children to act like that. Where is Teddy?"

They found the boy sitting near the window facing the front of the house. Although his Harry Potter book lay open on his lap, Teddy gazed outside at the tops of the oaks and Macho beneath them snuffling in the dirt and barking at a squirrel that darted up a trunk. He wheeled around to face them with a big smile. "Hi, Mr. Adam. I put my all clothes in the middle drawers so I can reach them and my medicine bag is in the bathroom. Is that okay?"

"Not my house, but it sounds good to me. This is Edwina Green. She's a nurse who will help you out for a while. Teddy and me are buds. We met at lunch."

"Mr. Adam made me a peanut butter and banana sandwich, Miss Ed—ed—ina."

"Call me Winnie. That's short for Edwina. I was named after my father, Edwin. That's kind of funny, huh?" She sat on the bed to be more on the boy's level.

"You shouldn't laugh at people's names, Mama said. She went away today and left me to be raised by my dad. Winnie is a nice name like the sound horses make."

Faced with this bald statement of abandonment, she fell back on the mundane. "Did you eat all your lunch?"

"Most of a sandwich and some milk and an oatmeal cookie, but Mr. Adam ate four sandwiches and a big glass of milk. I guess Macho got the rest of the cookies," he said regretfully.

"I'm sure you can have a snack when the other children get home from school."

"Miss Nell said she has eight kids. That's a lot. Do

33

you think they will like me?" His small, pale forehead wrinkled with concern.

"I think they will. Adam and I like you already. Right now, do you need help using the bathroom or need anything else?"

Winnie added a warm smile to her statement that made Adam wish she'd directed it at him. He could have sworn he'd seen some heat in those green eyes when they met, but now all her attention had gone to the patient. He counted that as a good thing even if it bruised his ego some.

"No, I can cath myself," Teddy said with some pride. "But I need help with doing a number two at night."

"We'll take care of that this evening. I see you like to read."

"Yes, ma'am. I can't take PE in school. Mostly I read during that time."

"Reading is great, but you need your exercise, too. Are you using crutches yet?"

"Yes, ma'am. They are in Miss Nell's car, but I don't like them. They slow me down. In my chair I can go fast as I want." Teddy swirled his chair in a quick circle on the hardwood floor to make his point.

"Still, you need to practice with your crutches every day to get better at it and do some upper body exercises to make you strong." Winnie made a note in the folder. "I need to look over this big, fat file that tells me all about you. Why don't we just sit here and read for a while?"

"Okay." He opened his book, but stared out the window again. "I bet heaven is like this—way above the treetops. I bet my granny is there, and Jesus gave her a room just as nice as this one. And dogs. There would be dogs running around in heaven."

"I'm sure you are right about that." Winnie shared her smile with Adam now.

He smiled back, maybe a little too broadly. "Guess you don't need me here."

"Not at the moment, but I think I'll want some help lifting him into the bath and bed if you are staying overnight."

"I hope I am. I want to stick around for a while if Nell and Joe will let me." More reason now than ever.

"You know they always have room for one more."

"True, they are full of *alofa*. That's a giving kind of love in Samoan."

"I'd like to learn more about Samoa."

"I would love to teach you. I wish we had a few palm trees and a beach for our lessons."

Even Teddy felt the sexual tension invade the air. He asked, "Is Mr. Adam your boyfriend?"

Winnie laughed, a low and lovely sound. "No, we just met."

But Adam said, "Not yet."

Chapter Five

Mintay held Nell's hand and gave Joe's shirt some time to dry. They'd been over the ambivalent feelings Emily's death caused, and the Rev had offered a prayer for the soul of the departed. Their attention turned toward the two children upstairs who must be foremost in their minds.

"We have to keep Anastasia and try to teach her how to fit into the family. That won't be easy after nine years in Emily's hands. As for Teddy, I know Maydell will come back for him when she's less stressed and leaves that boyfriend of hers. In the meantime, we'll see Teddy has all the care he needs. Good idea bringing Winnie over to help us. I worried if I could handle his schedule. His mother left a long list in his medical bag." Nell squeezed Mintay's hand and let go.

"Two birds with one stone as they say. Winnie's divorce went through last week. She packed her bags, left Shreveport, and landed on our doorstep last night. Says she is so humiliated she is never going back. Can you believe she gave up medical school and took nurse's training instead to help her husband become a doctor, and that bastard drops her for a busty blonde he met while my sister worked double shifts at the hospital? The asshole!"

"Language," the Rev reproved gently.

"You are the minister, not me, honey bear. Anyhow, Winnie is at loose ends now. I think she should go back to med school and finish. She says she will look for another job in this area and not impose on us any longer than necessary while that lowdown slime she married sets up a practice and a household with his mistress who is going to be his receptionist. We should sue for all the money my sister earned to put him through school. That's what we should do."

"Vengeance is mine sayeth the Lord," the Rev quoted. At a glare from his doctor wife, he added, "We'll cover her tuition if she wants to go back to med school, and she is welcome to stay with us as long as she likes. You know that, sweet thang."

"Look," Joe said. "We'll pay her for taking care of Teddy until Nurse Wickersham is available. Anything else we can do to help?"

"You might have already done that. When I heard Adam showed up here, I thought exactly what that Samoan said. She needs a new love, and pretty quickly to get over that skinny-assed white boy. I mean Adam is just mouth-watering delicious, don't you think, Nell?" Mintay appealed to the only other woman in the room.

"Fairly scrumptious, yes."

"Hey! Sure, he's a good-looking young man, but he is supposed to be getting married in a few months. Besides, the two of you have the best men the Sinners ever produced, past or present," Joe insisted.

"Shit!" Mintay exclaimed. "Forgive me, this sorry affair has me all worked up. I forgot about his engagement, but I could have sworn I saw a spark when Adam and Winnie touched hands. Maybe he is having second thoughts about the wedding and that's why he is here."

"No, that's not the reason," Adam said, standing in the doorway. "Joe, Rev, you got a minute now, maybe without the ladies? Sorry for your loss, Mrs. Joe."

Mintay stood up and grabbed a black purse big enough to be an old-fashioned doctor's satchel from the coffee table. "I brought a DNA test kit along for Teddy. Nell, why don't we take care of that right now?"

"I should get the note his mother left to show to the social worker when she comes." Nell stood also, embarrassed along with Mintay wondering how much Adam overheard.

"It's in the kitchen trashcan. Macho made kind of a mess in there, and the note got all soaked with milk. I cleaned up, but it should be right on top under the cookie bag," their scrumptiously delicious guest said.

"Good. I'll fish it out and let it dry. Come on, Mintay. Help me find it, then we'll go see Teddy." Nell fairly jerked her friend from the den.

"Women! If we said that about some babe, they'd be all over us like flies at a crawfish boil. Sit down, Adam." Joe gestured to the sofa the women recently vacated.

"Said what?" Adam asked, acting perplexed.

"Nothing you need to know. So what is the problem? Why are you here and not on the road to your island honey?"

"Pala broke off the engagement right after we lost the playoff game. Here I think she is calling to console me, and bam! She tells me she is marrying my best friend, my *soa,* the guy who was supposed to keep an eye on her and sing my praises while I'm away playing football."

Adam rammed a fist into the leather of the sofa and left a sizeable dent. "Sammy Tau, we were on the same team in high school, but he wasn't good enough to earn the college scholarship and get off the island. So he stays behind and steals my *taupou*, my princess, a real one, not like that crazy kid upstairs, but a beautiful, nineteen-year-old virgin who represents the very best of Samoan womanhood. You know how rare that is? I could break Sammy's neck."

"Yep, nineteen-year-old virgins are pretty thin on the ground," Joe said. "Now that's your problem. I never did virgins. Too much trouble. You need to forget her and concentrate on your game because I do not want to go through that broken heart crap again with any of my players. First Connor Riley, then Howdy McCoy. Not again, never again! Find someone else. Move on."

"Well, the guys did tell me you were the man when it came to the ladies back in the day. That's why I came to you for advice. I should take it."

"Back in the day," Joe spluttered. "I only have ten years on you, maybe a couple more."

Adam turned to the Rev. "You think Winnie and me threw sparks?"

The Rev held up a pair of hands as big as Adam's. "Not me who saw those sparks, son, but you did hit on her. Now look here, you don't seem as cut up over losing the girl as you do about your friend betraying you. Could be having a *taupou* meant more to you than the woman herself. Now, you think about that before you start connecting with my sister-in-law because I can still take you on."

Adam bowed his head over his clenched hands and considered the Rev's words. "Maybe you are right. Pala was only twelve when I left for college on the mainland. I never noticed her before she became the *taupou,* but you know, she kind of ripened last summer. By the time I came back here for summer camp, we were engaged. I'm not so sure if that was my idea or hers or our families. One thing for certain, I wasn't getting under her *puletasi* without putting a wedding ring on her finger."

"As it should be," the Rev intoned.

Joe tweaked his friend. "Like you and Mintay?"

"I was a football player, not an ordained minister, back then. I'm trying to give Adam some good Christian advice here. Do not jump into another relationship right away. If you have any interest in my sister-in-law, get to know her first. You take things slow. You court her, you hear."

Adam nodded solemnly. "I understand you stand for her as a brother. I must respect your words. Say Joe, can I hang around for a while? I'm not going home until I am sure I won't kill Sammy Tau on sight, and most of the guys have left New Orleans already. Is Winnie going to stay here?

Joe shook his head. "I don't know, Rev. Maybe they both just need a good f—"

From behind the men, Nell answered. "I'll put her in the lavender room next to Teddy in case he needs her during the night. Adam, of course you are welcome to visit."

"I told Brinsley he should sleep in the gray room by Anastasia for the same reason," Joe said. "I guess you can stay in one of the cabins as long as you like,

Adam."

The Rev's dark face broke into a big, happy smile. "Great idea. Privacy and lots of room in those cabins. Just remember, once Joe sets the alarms at night, you can't get back into the main house. That would be humiliating to set off those alarms."

Nell sat down by Adam and smoothed out Maydell's limp note on the coffee table. "The social worker will be here shortly. I'd like Mintay to sit in with us. Rev, Adam, you know your way around the property. Why don't you collect Anastasia, Teddy, Winnie, and Brinsley and give them a tour of the grounds. It's a lovely, mild February day for a walk. Joe, are you hungry? We never did get lunch."

"I'm starving in more ways than one, sugar, but I'll settle for a sandwich and a cold drink. Yeah, you guys, give Teddy and the princess the grand tour."

Chapter Six

Joe's Lorena Ranch, a former dairy farm, abounded with acreage, and a good thing, too, as Camp Love Letter kept expanding along with his family. As the Rev explained, if Joe heard of something the children would enjoy, he bought it. Once on the smooth, concrete paths winding to various recreation spots, Teddy spun along in his wheelchair without help. Anastasia, not an outdoors kind of girl, complained about the long walk and the inferiority of the facilities. No wonder Brinsley had elected to take a "bit of a lie down" after the ordeal of getting his charge unpacked instead of going along on the tour. Her excess possessions overflowed into his closet and dresser. He did not complain, but Winnie, noting the strain in the man's face, insisted he needed a break after his travels. The suggestion was most gratefully accepted.

At the basketball court, the men and Teddy practiced free throws. The boy with a mighty effort put two through the hoop. Though Winnie took a turn and got one ball in, Anastasia refused to participate. Foot tapping with impatience, she and Titi, joined by the roving Macho, watched from the sidelines.

"I want to see the horses."

They went to the barn next where Teddy petted Lazy Boy's inquisitive, velvet nose and laughed when the stallion sneezed on him. Uneasy around horses and their big teeth, the Rev stayed away from the stalls, but Anastasia inspected them all.

"I'll want to ride the white mare. Is she English trained?" she said, referring to Fatima whose dapples had faded away with age.

"Hmmm, I think the twins and Xochi share her. You sure better ask them first. The older boys ride Drummer Boy and Copperhead, and the little ones stay on the ponies. I know Lorena likes Buttercup best. That still leaves a pony for you, and they all use western gear." Still staying clear of the animals, the Rev told as much as he knew.

"Two of those ponies are so old they have gray hairs. I am used to a more spirited mount, but I suppose I must learn to ride western if that is all that's available." With a great put-upon sigh, Anastasia asked, "What else is there to do here?"

"Fishing, canoeing, boating, swimming," Adam listed since he'd helped out at the camp a few times. "My team always wins the canoe races," he added for Winnie's benefit, not the girl's.

"Very well. Let's see the pool."

"I had some swimming lessons last summer, and I been on a horse," Teddy added enthusiastically as the group moved along to the pool area.

"Big deal. This pool is bigger than the one at the palazzo, but we had a private beach, too."

"Yeah," Adam agreed. "They could use a beach right beyond the fence where those scrub trees are now. And palms, this place could use some of those. But the banana trees all around the wall make me feel right at home. I'll be staying in one of the cottages for a while,

Winnie."

"Which one?" she asked.

Their eyes locked. Even the Rev saw the sparks this time. He stepped between them. "Nell didn't say yet. Probably right next to Knox and Corazon where they can see everyone coming and going from the camp to keep an eye on the place. Yes, sir, a perfect place for you, Adam."

Adam grinned and shrugged. "Yes, love is best made beneath the palm trees, but no palm trees here."

"And it better stay that way," the Rev admonished. "Come on, the children will be home from school soon. We need to get moving."

Macho raised his head, issued a woof of greeting, and took off in a puff of dust. Anastasia held Titi back with the leash. "You'll get run over, silly dog." Hanging back in their shadows, she let the adults take the lead for a change, even allowing Teddy to go before her. The twelve-person van that Macho greeted unloaded a short, plump Mexican woman first, then a long string of children hauling book bags from the backseats. The more the group increased, the slower Anastasia walked, but Teddy whizzed ahead in his chair.

"Hi, I'm your new brother," he greeted the whole bunch with as much eagerness as Macho who bumped against them and licked faces.

Dean Billodeaux, on the threshold of adolescence and already showing a darkening of hair above his upper lip, practiced his nonchalance. "That so?"

"Mom and Dad could be adopting again," Tommy, freckled and lanky, said.

"Nope, I'm your real brother. My mama said so."

"You don't look like us," Jude, the more aggressive of the petite, curly-headed twin girls, claimed.

Annie and the kindergartner triplets simply stared at the boy in the red wheelchair before looking to Dean for direction. He'd had "the talk" with his dad, already knew about sex and condoms even if he'd never used one. Coolly, he said, "Could be. It's possible." Seven pairs of eyes rounded and seven mouths dropped open.

"Yes, could be," adopted, brown-skinned Xochi said. She always seemed to know more than the others about the ways of the world, whether she actually did or not.

Corazon, the housekeeper, already standing at the kitchen door while her husband took the van around the back of the house, called out, "You go inside now. Get your snacks. Bring the guests. Reverend Rev, Mister Adam, you coming with your lady friend?"

"Uh, no, thank you," the Rev replied when the other two adults showed no inclination to move and in fact swayed closer to each other.

With uneasy glances at Teddy and the little girl with the tiny white dog who hung behind the great bastions of the Rev and Adam, the children filed inside, slung their backpacks into a pile, and took a seat at the long table. Corazon doled out glasses of milk and fig bars made with a whole wheat crust. "One each because we got visitors and only a dozen of these."

"I don't care for any." Anastasia scooped up her puppy and took a seat on a stool away from the others.

Teddy, who found a space in the crowd, accepted his with a "Thank you, ma'am."

Corazon nodded her approval. "Good boy. What

are you called?"

"Teddy Wilkes, and that there is the Princess Anastasia and her dog, Titi."

Dean smirked. "Did you say Titty?" His audience of brothers and sisters snickered.

In all innocence, Teddy answered, "No, Titi, like some people say for peepee."

"Is not! It means tiny in French," Anastasia answered, her blue eyes brimming with tears.

"Can we hold it?" Annie asked. "What kind of dog is it?"

"She's a Bichon Frise, and no, you can't touch her." Anastasia crushed Titi to her chest so hard the pup squeaked.

"She's not a very nice girl," Lorena, the only female among the triplets, said.

"Did you say bitchin' freeze?" Dean smirked again and earned more giggles.

All the young Billodeauxs looked up when they saw their father filling the doorway. "Nice or not, she is your cousin. Stop picking at her. Team meeting in the den, five minutes or less. Meet y'all there."

"Uh-oh," Trinity, the smallest of the triplets, murmured. Round, black-framed glasses magnified his already large, dark eyes.

Mack, the middle of triplets, guessed, "I think he heard you say titty and bitchin', Dean. Now we're all in trouble."

"Titty is not a bad word. Cows have titties. Peepee is just a baby word, and bitchin'… Never mind. It's something worse for a team meeting to be called," Dean answered, not making any of them feel better.

Teddy's pale cheeks burned red, and a tear dribbled

down Anastasia's cheek. She buried her face in Titi's curly white fur.

"Go on. You all done. I got to get dinner started." Corazon shooed them away with a flap of her bright yellow apron edged in red rickrack.

Chapter Seven

Solemnly, the Billodeaux children trekked to the den where their mother and father waited, each sitting in one of the big recliners like the king and queen upon their thrones. The triplets automatically sat cross-legged on the area rug while the older kids crowded onto the long sofa. Teddy and Anastasia stayed slightly outside the family circle.

Joe stood to address his family. He paced with his hands behind his back simply to keep them still as he often did when talking to his teammates. "The young lady over there is your cousin, Anastasia Polasky. Her parents died in a car crash a couple of weeks ago, and she'll be living with us now because she has no other family." The words came out grim and unwelcoming though he hadn't intended them to be.

The children turned to stare at the girl still cradling her dog. Anastasia stood tall and announced, "Princess Anastasia Marya Polasky. You may address me as Princess."

"*Cher*, we don't have real princesses in America. You will just be plain Anastasia from now on, and that's a mouthful in itself."

"We could give her a nickname," Annie volunteered. "Except I'm already Annie, so we can't use that."

"How about Nasty?" Dean offered up for laughs until he saw the expression on his mom's face.

Nell got up and stood beside her husband. She stilled his pacing with a hand on his arm. "Dean Joseph Billodeaux, one more ugly remark at this meeting and you will not be allowed to play football in the fall."

"Dad!"

"You heard your mother. We have some new players on our team, and you will make them feel at home. That's part of your job as the oldest and a leader. Understood?"

"Yeah." Dean slouched back into the cushions and stretched his long legs out in a defiant sprawl.

Annie raised her hand as if she sat in the front row of a classroom. "Stacy would be a nice American name for her."

"It's a cool name," her twin, Jude, agreed.

Nell rewarded them with a grateful smile. "Thank you, girls. I like it, too, but does Anastasia?"

"I never had a nickname or brothers and sisters. I guess it's a good name if I can't be a princess anymore." The newly dubbed Stacy held out her pup to Annie. "Here, you can hold her."

"Make sure she doesn't peepee on you, sis," Dean remarked.

Teddy reddened again. Joe pointed a finger at his eldest son and said, "Very close to a foul, son. Don't get yourself thrown out of the game." Aside to Nell, he remarked, "We should wear whistles, I tell you me."

Xochi with her thick, tangled black curls cascading down her back and her big, chocolate-brown eyes that had seen things early in life no child should ever see, offered, "We can still play at being princesses though we are getting a little old for that. We have to include Lorena even if she is still a baby."

"Not!" Lorena cried.

"I think I might like having sisters," Stacy said, showing some shyness for the first time. "I'm not so sure about brothers."

She gave Dean a sidelong glance. At least Tommy, who had snickered with the rest of them, had the grace to hang his head, but not his older brother. Dean opened his mouth again. Everyone in the room held their breath waiting for his words that came out sullen and accusatory.

"Okay, we have *another* sister, and we have to be nice to her. I get that. Her parents died and all. But, what about the kid in the wheelchair? He says he is your son, Dad, your real son."

"About that…" Joe began.

Teddy gave his wheelchair a mighty shove over the edge of the area rug and straight to the coffee table where his mother's letter lay, now dried and wrinkled but still legible. "This is what my mama said, and I'm gonna read it to y'all. Dear Teddy Bear."

Little Trinity held up a hand. "Is that really your name?"

"Yes, Teddy Bear Wilkes because I was cute as a teddy bear when I was born. You shouldn't laugh at people's names, my mama said—not Stacy's, not mine." He stared at Dean who had clapped a hand over his mouth to hold in a comment sure to get him grounded. Teddy started again.

Dear Teddy Bear,

I am so sorry I have to leave you, but it is time you knowed your real daddy is Joe Dean Billodeaux. He is rich and famous and has lots of kids. He will take great care of you and keep you safe. You be a good son to him. I love you and will pray for you every night, but I cannot keep you no more. I don't have enough money and Newt don't have enough patience. I will never forget you.

Your Loving Mama,

Maydell Wilkes

P.S. Show this letter to Miss Nell and she will take you to your new home.

None of the children said a word. They waited while Dean glared at their father. Joe gathered his wits. He did not want to crush Teddy. Yet, he needed to tell his family, especially his eldest son, the result of an affair with a woman other than Nell, the truth.

Finally, small Lorena ventured, "Maybe Daddy gave his man seeds to Teddy's mother so she could have babies like Aunt Emily gave Mommy her eggs so she could have some of us."

Thanks to Nell's belief in total honesty, his children knew far too much about in vitro fertilization and plenty about adoption. Joe cleared his throat and balancing on the balls of his feet, crouched down to Teddy's level, but he answered Lorena first.

"No, *cher* heart, I did not give Teddy's mother my seeds. I never met Maydell Wilkes. I am not his real daddy. I think his mommy wants him to have a good life that maybe she can't provide. Your mom and me think she will change her mind and come back for Teddy. Until that time comes, he will have a home here and be safe with us. We want all of you to treat him as a brother." Joe looked Teddy in the eye now and saw a heartbreak there worse than losing the Super Bowl.

"My mom is not a liar! You don't really know I'm not your son."

Nell put her hand on Teddy's arm. "Do you remember how Dr. Bullock asked you to scrub the inside of your cheek with that swab earlier today?"

The boy nodded. "That brush has your DNA on it—the stuff that can tell us if you are Joe's son. No matter what the results, you will stay with us until your mother returns. The social worker who had your mother's case came and visited. This is all settled. She will have the special bus come here to pick you up tomorrow for school. I understand you are mainstreamed with the other students and get good grades, especially in reading. Everything is going to be fine." Nell stroked his fair hair.

Joe clapped his hands. "Everyone, go do your homework until Corazon calls dinner. Let's go! Let's go!" His younger children scattered.

"Do you have your textbooks, Teddy?" Nell asked.

"Yes, ma'am. I found them in the bottom of my duffel. I need someone to give me my spelling words."

Almost forgotten in the ruckus, Stacy said, "I'll help you. You want to go upstairs?"

"Sure." Dejection showing in his curved shoulders, Teddy wheeled from the room.

Dean got up slowly, insolently. "I know about illegitimate children because I am one, Dad. You weren't married to Mom when I was born, but this kid is only around eight."

"Football players are often a target for this sort of scam. Have some faith in me, son. I did not cheat on your mother. She believes me. Right, Nell?"

Nell nodded. "It's been a tough day for everyone.

Go get your homework done."

Dean brushed by Adam and Winnie coming into the room without so much as an "excuse me." Nell sighed.

Winnie held up Teddy's file. "We should go over this. You need to know what you are getting into with the boy."

Joe raked his black hair with his fingers. "Come in. Sit down. Let's get this over with now."

To his surprise, Adam took a seat next to the nurse. He smiled broadly. "The Rev and Mintay had to go home, but they said they would pray for you."

Chapter Eight

"Adam, you don't need to stay for this," Joe suggested to the big Samoan whose thick arm had come to rest on the back of the sofa in the general vicinity of Winnie's delicate shoulders. He'd perfected that move in middle school but, hell, they were both adults despite the Rev's concern. Let them do as they wanted.

"I'm good," Adam said, stretching out his legs and making himself more at home.

Winnie on the other hand sat erectly and proceeded to give a very professional report. "My sister and I went over Teddy's records and gave him a quick checkup when she came to do the DNA test. The boy had two surgeries right after birth, one to close the opening in the spine where his cord protruded and another to put in a shunt."

"Why a shunt?" Joe asked.

"To drain the fluids off his brain. It had to be replaced due to an infection at seven months. At four, he had major surgery on his brain stem to improve his breathing, at six a bowel and bladder redirection to get him out of diapers. He can use the catheter himself, and a shot of fluid through an opening in the navel brings on his bowel movements."

"Jesus, he's had more surgeries than me." Joe suspected beneath his Cajun tan he'd gone a little pale.

Knowing her husband's aversion to illness, Nell squeezed his arm. "You okay?"

"Fine. I've come a long way since we started Camp Love Letter. Go on, Winnie."

"The real problem is he will need another surgery to crack the scar tissue on his back allowing him to grow more in the near future. We also found that the braces and boots supporting his lower legs need replacement soon as well as his body brace because he has gotten too big for them. Along with all that, he is getting too large for his current wheelchair. These devices will run into the thousands of dollars and might be why his mother chose to turn him over to you at this point."

At the mention of cracking open scar tissue on a child's back, Joe felt a trifle woozy, but he manned up. "Money's no problem for us. He'll get what he needs."

"Unfortunately, there is more. We found plenty of bruises on his body. Teddy says he falls down a lot, but we suspect abuse, most likely the boyfriend."

Nell nodded. "The social worker already had a file on Teddy. Some elderly neighbors at the trailer court where his family lived called in to report they thought Maydell's boyfriend hit the boy when she went off to work. Unfortunately, both the mother and child claimed everything was dandy, but they were keeping an eye on the situation. I could never convince Maydell her problems went deeper than coping with a handicapped child. The caseworker is glad we are going to foster Teddy."

Because Adam sat there like a huge stone moa statue from Easter Island, Joe felt compelled to bring him into the conversation. "What do you think, Adam?"

"If the mother went away in Samoa, someone else would give the boy food and shelter, maybe many people. The *matai*, the chief of the village, would find a way to get the boy what he needed. As for Anastasia, she would be taught not to speak back to her elders."

"It takes a village to raise a child," Nell said.

"Yes. That could be said of Samoa."

"I think it might do the rest of our children good to have Teddy here. Maybe Trinity will stop complaining about being smaller than the rest of them and having to wear his glasses all the time. Winnie, thanks for bringing us up to date. Are you settled in your room?" Nell asked.

"Not yet. I think Rev left my suitcase on the doorstep before they went home. They foisted me off on you so fast I didn't even have time to unpack there."

"Not foisted. You will be a great help to us."

"Yes, keep the pathetic newly divorced woman busy."

"Not pathetic either," Adam interjected. "I'll get that bag for you."

He stretched as if he'd been in one place far too long. The exercise showed off the wall of his chest muscles, the flatness of his belly, the bulge of his biceps and calf muscles. Both Winnie and Nell watched with rapt interest.

Finished with his stretches, Adam said, "So how many are you having over for Super Bowl Sunday in a couple of weeks?"

"My family, and that's a lot of people, the old guard—Connor, the Rev, Calvin Armitage, Asa Dobbs and their kids, Howdy and Cassie and theirs. Why?"

"Two whole roasted pigs should do it. I want to

build an *umu* oven for you."

"And he cooks, too," Winnie murmured.

"I'll just bet he does," Nell agreed.

Joe frowned. "You can use my Cajun microwave. It will do a small pig."

"No, this will be better, a real Samoan feast. Can we get taro root or breadfruit here to bake with the pig? Coconuts, plantains?"

"The last two, yes. Maybe we could wrap yams and baking potatoes in foil to take the place of the first two." Nell jumped in with both feet. "Everyone brings a side dish and a dessert. We won't lack for food."

"Sounds like Cajuns and Samoans have much in common. We will need banana leaves, too, lots of them, and lava rocks."

"Hey, I usually grill." Joe interrupted the island feast plans.

"And so you shall, dear. The children will still want hotdogs and hamburgers. Won't this be fun, Winnie?"

"It sounds spectacular!"

"Let's get your suitcase, and I will tell you how I make my oven." Adam and Winnie left wrapped in plans if not each other's arms.

"Now that's an original pickup line. He's showing off for Winnie, and you did not have to enjoy the display so much, Tink." Joe wrapped a possessive arm around his wife.

"As you often say, I'm married, not dead."

By the coy way Nell smiled, Joe knew she reveled in his mild jealousy. "While the kids do their homework, why don't we go upstairs? I'll show you how I like to cook."

Chapter Nine

Winnie lay awake on the queen-sized bed under a comforter patterned in lilac blossoms. The feminine, lavender bedroom with the lacy border was intended for Lorena when she could be parted from her brothers. Nell figured that day would come quickly now that her youngest daughter had begun school. Soon, she would start seeing herself as a girl rather than a triplet and want her own space, not a single bed across from her brothers' bunks.

In the meantime, Winnie could enjoy the luxurious space so different from the cramped bedroom entirely filled by a king-sized mattress because the newly minted Douglas Hopper, M.D., dermatology, insisted he needed one. By the time she figured out Doug cheated on her, she came to appreciate that big space in the middle of the bed that neither crossed for months before either called it quits.

He'd said she was tired, bony, no fun anymore. She'd retaliated with adjectives describing him as unappreciative, self-centered, and disloyal. Maybe they were both right. Doug found his relief with a buxom, bubbly blonde. She quit working the double shifts that put him through medical training and noticed her energy return, her gauntness transform into slimness again. Taking after her thin mother and grandmother,

Winnie doubted she'd ever put on much weight. Most women envied her because her quick metabolism ate up the calories in every brownie or slice of cheesecake. Cheesecake. Beefcake.

Her thoughts turned to Adam Malala who had been relegated to the cottage next to Corazon and Knox Polk, but not before he'd helped her prepare Teddy for bed. She'd stripped off the boy's blue knit school shirt and wide-legged khakis altered to fit over his braces with Teddy helpfully raising himself up off the seat of the wheelchair to make the job easier. Then, she peeled him out of his supportive gear like removing a raw lobster from its shell. Both she and Adam noticed the bruises on the boy's pale arms, the imprints of the fingers of a large man who'd gripped too hard. His pallid body bloomed with yellow-edged, purple blotches.

A little shy in front of a woman he barely knew and clad only in his tighty-whiteys, Teddy asked if Adam could take him into the prepared bath. The big cornerback hefted him with gentleness and ease and completed the process of getting the boy into the tub. Leaving the bathroom door cracked just a bit in case Teddy needed him, Adam took a chair and talked to Winnie of their upcoming Samoan feast, what foods he would prepare. The only things Doug Hopper ever brought to a meal were a knife and a fork and a complaint if the dinner was not to his liking.

When Teddy called to get out, Adam took the pajamas laid on the bed, helped the boy to dry and dress. He didn't flinch when Winnie administered the shot through the navel to activate the boy's bowels, just simply carried him back into the bathroom to wait for the results. But then, Adam Malala never flinched.

Despite his size, he could cross a football field with amazing speed, send his body flying into a receiver, and pop the ball out of his opponent's grasp almost as an afterthought.

They had the boy settled in bed when a knock sounded on the door. Stacy in a ruffled and beribboned muslin nightgown fit for royalty entered and asked if she could say goodnight to Teddy. Such a nice gesture coming from her astonished the adults, but not so much the words she had to say.

"Look, Teddy. We're the outsiders here. We have to stick together no matter what."

"They have to keep you. You're family. They don't have to let me stay if it turns out Mr. Joe is not my daddy. The guys hardly talked to me at dinner. I make a step, or maybe a wheel, in the wrong direction, and I'm outta here. I have to be on my best behavior." The boy's eyes blinked heavily as if this day had run over him with a pair of cleats and left him exhausted.

"Well, the girls only like me for my dog and my clothes. I just wanted to say I've got your back if you have mine. Deal?"

"Sure, I guess."

She fingered his ratty paperback copy of a Harry Potter novel on the nightstand. "Can I borrow this? Of course, I had a whole set of the hardcovers at the palazzo, but I never read them and couldn't bring them with me on the plane. Can you believe I don't have a television set in my room? Yours neither, I see."

"Just bring it back in the morning."

"Goodnight, then." Stacy marched across the hall to her own room, probably intending to plague Brinsley with her demands until she felt sleepy.

"Nervy brat," Adam said. "Don't let her get you in trouble, Teddy."

"I'll try to be good. I think I should say my prayers now."

Adam dropped to his knees at the bedside and folded his hands. Caught off guard, Winnie simply bowed her head. Sure, Mintay had embraced the Rev's AME church, but her parents could only be described as secular humanists. Neither approach bothered Teddy. He closed his eyes and made a steeple with his hands over his stomach.

"Dear God, thank you for bringing me to this pretty house with a big gate and alarm buttons. I feel safe here. Bless my new family and especially Stacy who really needs it. Also Nurse Winnie and Mr. Adam who are taking good care of me and my mom wherever she is, okay? Please, let me be Mr. Joe's real son so's I can stay here. Amen."

Without whining for a glass of water or a story or a few more minutes before lights out, Teddy worked himself over on his side, tucked his hands under his pillow, and said, "Night."

Winnie turned out his light. "Teddy, I'll be in the next room with the doors to the bathroom open. Call if you need me."

The boy appeared to be asleep already. She walked Adam to the elevator. From Stacy's room they heard Brinsley reading aloud from the Harry Potter book in his wonderfully appropriate British accent. Down the hall, Nell slipped from the triplets' room and began making her rounds to issue goodnights and lights out warnings to the older children.

Winnie leaned against the wall as they waited for

the lift to arrive. "That Tebowing you did by Teddy's bed caught me off balance. I've seen you do your really intimidating war dance before a game, but never a prayer. Somehow, I thought Samoans were all about rough sports and well, love under the palm trees."

"We are all of those things. The London Missionary Society really did a job on us. I hear a 'let us pray,' and I'm on my knees. If you are out in a village at six p.m. and the church bell rings, you'd better head somewhere for Bible reading and prayers and get off the street. The natives are friendly but don't take sacrilege lightly. Church on Sunday, sometimes twice, no other activities on the day of rest. But, we do manage to offset that with an enormous Sunday dinner. It's the Samoan way. I'd like to take you to the islands someday."

Surely he didn't mean it, but Winnie pushed off from the wall closer to his broad, brown face. Adam leaned in, so close she could feel his body heat and the tickle of his soft curls touching her cheek. Nell came trotting down the hall. They moved apart.

"I wanted to see how Teddy managed tonight."

"Already asleep. He had long, hard day," Winnie reported. "I think Anastasia is still up."

"Yes, ready or not, I should check on her, too. Something tells me she isn't going to like our lights out at nine rule. Adam, you'd better get going. Corazon has the cottage ready for you, and Joe wants to set the alarms. Ever since Tommy was kidnapped, he is really careful about locking up every evening."

"I understand, Mrs. Joe. I'll take the stairs and meet him by the front door. Sleep well, Winnie."

Sure, sleep well. No matter how pretty and airy the

room the only thoughts on her mind were of the little boy who needed her help, and the big, strong man who probably only wanted a roll in sand—and she was perfectly fine with that.

Chapter Ten

At breakfast, Winnie marveled at Nell's precision in getting her family of eight off to school. Corazon had a hot breakfast of oatmeal with raisins and brown sugar ready to serve, pitchers of milk and orange juice on the table, and bowls at the ready as each child appeared at the table. The eldest came first while Nell who rousted them stayed upstairs to help the triplets dress. School uniforms made that just so much easier. Compared to this regimen, getting Teddy into the bathroom, strapped into his braces, and dressed seemed almost easy. The boy tried to be as independent as possible and helped in any way he could.

After breakfast, the Billodeaux kids boarded the white van, girls in back, boys in front since they were dropped off first at the parochial school in town, and the girls at the Episcopal country day school farther out of town. Knox Polk made sure each and every one had their backpack and appropriate attire down to belts and the right color of socks. Being a former military man, the task suited him eminently. He added his own son to the load. Away they went.

That left Adam and Joe in peace putting away man-sized portions of oatmeal and a stack of whole wheat toast slathered with strawberry jam. Nell nibbled plain toast and coffee while Stacy played with her food and voiced her preference for croissants in the morning. Brinsley refused to sit down until everyone else had eaten. With some coaxing, Winnie got Teddy to eat a piece of toast and some of his oatmeal before escorting him to the gates to wait for his bus. From social worker to Nell, all agreed for the time being he would be better off with his regular routine and an aide at the public school who knew him.

Winnie warned him in the afternoon, she would meet him with his crutches and expect him to walk at least half way back to the house using them. Noting his worried expression, she brushed the fine, blond hair out of his eyes and gave him some reassurance.

"Never fear. No one is going to kick you out. You have a home here as long as you need it."

She watched him safely board the bus and turned to go back to the house. Joe's farm truck, the one he had reclaimed in Mexico five years ago, pulled up beside her. Adam leaned out from the open window. "You ready to help me find some lava rocks?"

"Sure, if Nell doesn't need me."

"She's taking that Stacy over to the day school for admission testing. The girl had a private tutor, if you can believe that. They don't know exactly what she learned—except whining, complaining, and lording it over everyone else. In Samoa, I was grateful to sleep on my auntie's screened porch in Pago Pago in order to go to school in the city, me and Sammy Tau and four other boys, too."

Winnie climbed into the high cab of the once silver truck. The finish had worn down to gray, but Knox Polk kept it in good running order and used it for the dirty work around the ranch. She knew the harrowing story of its recovery and always had the urge to look for bullet holes in the chassis. The iron gates of Lorena Ranch opened and closed behind them.

"Sounds like a rough way to get an education."

"Not so bad. Only the smartest and most athletic boys got the chance to leave the village. If we did well, we got scholarships to the mainland colleges, guys like me to big universities with football teams, the others to church-run colleges maybe, to become ministers, doctors, teachers, the kind of people who get a lot of respect back home."

"And football players?"

"Not as much as you'd think. Now a nurse, she has some prestige."

"Really? All I've heard for years is that I should have been a doctor."

"What stopped you?"

"My ex, he had to get his training first." Winnie vowed not to mention Doug again in any way if she could help it. Just what a guy wanted to hear, stories about her ex.

"If it weren't for mine, I'd be in Pago right now."

"You have an ex, too?"

"Ex-fiancée. She wanted another man. Now I don't feel like going home so much."

"Hard to believe she'd want anyone else but you."

"You think?" A grin wiped the momentary seriousness from his face.

They entered the small town of Chapelle and immediately left it, making a beeline for the highway and the sprawling Home Depot that sat at the intersection with the country road. Adam drove carelessly, one hand on the wheel, a heavy foot on the gas pedal pushing the old truck ten miles over the limit.

"Um, Adam. You're speeding."

"You see a cop?"

"No, but…"

"Then, no worries, lovely Winnie."

Taking no risks, she always drove slightly under the speed limit. Despite her fears, they did get to Home Depot alive. Adam parked near several chicken wire pens of rocks and started looking them over. "Louisiana has lots of great stuff, but it doesn't have good rocks," he remarked as he held up a specimen. "Imagine having to import rocks. We need a bunch of lava stones the size of a coconut for the *umu* oven."

Despite having dressed in white slacks and an emerald top she thought made her eyes look greener, Winnie joined in the search for the perfect rocks until they created a small volcano-shaped mound. Adam paid for the stones and heaved them one by one into the truck. She didn't mind watching him one bit as his muscles bunched and his buttocks strained tight in a pair of jeans. Back in the truck, they stopped at the light preventing people from leaving the lot to carelessly stray onto the highway. Adam glanced left, then right.

"Palm trees," he said and tore out onto the highway the second the light changed instead of heading toward Chapelle.

Winnie braced herself. "What?"

"Palm trees. Lorena Ranch needs some palm trees and a beach. Right over there, a nursery with palm trees, good-sized ones, too."

"Are you sure Joe wants a beach and palm trees?"

"Doesn't everyone? I'll pay for them as my gift to Camp Love Letter—and to you."

"I've been to the beach before. You shouldn't do it for me."

Winnie denied the grand gesture though her words were not entirely true. Her parents preferred learning vacations to big cities with streets full of museums and cultural opportunities on every corner. The couple of times she'd gone to north Florida with her college friends, a call from Nana preceded the trip. "Stay out of the sun. Mind you don't make your complexion darker." That advice sucked a great deal of fun out of the experience.

Adam took his hand off the wheel and made an expansive gesture. "Louisiana beaches are nothing. I do it for everyone who comes to the camp."

He appeared to do everything with enthusiasm, whether running down a receiver or in this case cutting recklessly across traffic to reach the nursery. The rocks in the truck bed rolled and banged against its sides as they came to a crossover and turned sharply to gain access to a gravel lot rimmed with towering palm trees, their bulbous bases wrapped in burlap.

Winnie followed Adam in awe as he told an ecstatic nurseryman exactly what he wanted: all the palm trees, large and small, sand fine as sugar to cover an acre of land, maybe some plantings of hibiscus for tropical color. Could the man draw up a landscaping plan and a cost estimate by Friday and have the whole project completed by Super Bowl Sunday? The owner nodded like a bobblehead doll that should have had little dollar signs for eyes and scribbled down all of Adam's directions.

Back in the truck, Winnie sat dazed by Adam's impulsiveness. She doubted she'd ever done anything without thinking it through first, even marrying the white college boy who told her she was smart as well as beautiful and the hardest worker he knew. That had turned out very well for Douglas Hopper, not so well for her, so why not throw all caution to the trade winds and have a fling with the big, happy, uncomplicated Samoan? She still pondered that question when Adam swung the truck into a burger place by the highway.

"You interested in an early lunch? That oatmeal really didn't stay with me," Adam said.

"I guess I could eat a salad with an iced tea, unsweetened."

He sent her to get a seat while he ordered for both of them. Minutes later, he returned bearing a tray crowded with two premium burgers, a super-sized sleeve of French fries, a sweet drink as big as a quart of milk, and of course, her salad and tea.

He attacked a half-pound burger and after swallowing a mouthful, remarked, "Did I tell you Samoans love their junk food?"

"No, but I think I could have guessed."

Adam shoved the fries her way. "Here, share. My mother would say you are too skinny. Can't I afford to feed you?"

"I've heard that remark before." From Doug, but she accepted a few of the fries and fell silent.

"I think you are as lovely as a petal on a pale yellow plumeria blossom. Just saying what *tin'a* would think."

"Thank you," she said, flustered by the lavish compliment, and hastened to change to subject. "Teena, is that your mother's name?"

"No, it is the word for mother or any older woman

deserving of respect."

"Interesting," but she'd lost some of her joy in their outing.

Winnie looked down at her white slacks now soiled with dark marks from selecting lava stones. Not that her attire mattered here. An obese man downing a fried pie and a large orange drink in a corner booth wore a T-shirt that exposed an inch of flab between its hem and his belt buckle. A woman with a small child on her hip stood in line clad in a tank top, pajama bottoms, and slippers. Maybe the fat man and the slovenly mother wondered how a scrawny woman like her held the attention of a handsome hunk like Adam Malala.

"Nearly done?" Adam asked as she picked a cherry tomato from her salad with her fingers and bit into it. "We have an *umu* to build."

A few pulpy seeds from the tomato squirted out and landed on her emerald top. Great, try to be ladylike and a little sexy and a girl ended up with stains on her chest that drew the eye to her small breasts. But not Adam's eyes. Strange, he'd seemed interested in her only yesterday. He polished off the fries, and she pushed the rest of her salad aside. "I'm ready to make an oven."

With Adam behind the wheel, they returned to Lorena Ranch in record time terrorizing only a few moms in minivans along the way. He drove the truck across the sparse grass under the oaks straight to the side of Joe's barbecue pavilion. A quick trip to the barn and back yielded a shovel. Winnie sat on the open tailgate of the truck and dangled her long legs as Adam attacked the dirt packed down by lots of traffic for crawfish boils and weenie roasts in the screened building. She felt very much like a teenager watching her boyfriend show off in a feat of strength as the big Samoan cut through the hard earth and a tangled net of roots to carve out a shallow pit. His arm muscles bunched beneath bronze skin as he strained in the effort.

She liked the feeling. Her parents had frowned on high school dating except for one awkward night at the prom. Study hard. Be a credit to your race. Don't even think about getting pregnant before you turn eighteen. No wonder she fell prey to a user like Doug Hopper when she had no experience at all to sift the phonies from the genuine men.

Whether genuine or not, Adam Malala was all man. The first week in February, albeit in Louisiana, and he'd worked up a sweat. He stripped off the knit shirt clinging to his pecs and tossed it into the truck bed. Winnie restrained herself from picking up the shirt and burying her face to inhale the pheromones.

"I thought a South Sea Islander would have tattoos," she said almost to herself as she eyed his smooth, hairless chest.

Adam glanced up as he leveled the pit. "I have tattoos. If I wore my lava-lava, you would notice, but I think Mrs. Joe might not like it if I took off my jeans. Someday I will show you. Someday soon." The broad smile, the twinkle in the depths of his dark brown eyes returned.

He had to be interested in her. He just had to be. Her eyes strayed to a dark band inked into his brown skin just above his belt buckle. "I'd like that." Saliva gathered in her mouth, and she swallowed hard.

"We both would. Hand me the stones."

Winnie got into the truck bed and tossed the lava rocks to him one by one. He placed each carefully until satisfied with the results. Dusting off his hands, Adam said, "All we need now is a bunch of firewood, a couple of pigs, and lots of banana leaves."

"Good thing we had a mild winter, and the banana plants didn't die back." Winnie took his hand and hopped down from the back of the truck.

"There are many good things about this winter, especially meeting a beautiful woman. I could use a second lunch. You?"

Adam held her hand longer than necessary and seemed reluctant to let it go. She wouldn't have minded if they'd remained united all the way back to the house, but with a final squeeze, he released her fingers. "Corazon probably has something for us."

That assumption proved wrong. They entered into kitchen chaos. Nothing simmered except Corazon's temper as she berated her employers. Not saying a word, Brinsley stood at martial attention near the hallway door.

"What, you no like my cooking anymore? My cousins don't clean good enough? You go out and get a butler to watch me. Do I steal the silver?" Corazon's plump arms wobbled in the air.

"Now, Corazon, after all we have been through together, you know you are like family," Nell soothed.

"He opened the gate and let the delivery man in." The housekeeper's chubby finger wagged at Brinsley. "He answered the phone! This is what I do."

"You do much more than that. You cook and care for a family of ten and all the extra guests we have in the house. You are a marvel!" Joe leaned toward her from his seat at the table, but stayed out of the way of flailing arms and pointing fingers. He tried one of his most appealing smiles to no great effect.

Brinsley took a cautious step forward. "Mrs. Polk, my intention was not to supersede you, but to relieve your day of petty interruptions while you are making meals and overseeing the staff. My stay here will be brief, only until Anastasia is settled. I merely sought to help."

Corazon snorted through her nose so forcefully, she might have been shooting flames in the butler's direction.

Adam spoke up. "What we need is a beach."

All eyes and the perplexed expressions that went with them turned toward the big cornerback. "A beach, that's your solution," Joe said as if he questioned a play at a team meeting.

"Sure. Corazon must feel the stress of caring for so many and her own family, too. If Brinsley would take the calls and such, she might be able to leave the house for a while and stroll beneath the palm trees, feel the sand beneath her feet, listen to the wind sing through the fronds."

Corazon's round, brown face turned dreamy. "My village in Mexico had a beach. The children played there all day long." She began filling mugs from the perpetually ready coffeepot on the counter. "Everyone sit. We talk about this beach. You, too, big-time butler. You not too good to drink coffee with us like you acted this morning."

"Generally, I do not sit in the presence of my employers."

"They are not your employers. They are mine. Sit!"

Brinsley folded into a chair like a piece of stiff cardboard. Corazon plunked down creamer, a bowl of sugar, and a caddy of artificial sweetener. She urged the others to join Joe and Nell at the table. Adam and Winnie took their seats. The only one who didn't was Corazon who moved to the industrial-sized refrigerator and began filling a platter with various cold cuts, three types of cheese, and bowls of sweet and dill pickles. She opened a bread drawer, took out a long French loaf, severed it into pieces along its length, and placed it into a basket. A heap of pumpernickel rolls topped the French bread, and a variety of condiments made their way to the table. Corazon passed out plates and cutlery, finally settled, and said, "The beach, tell me."

Adam smiled broadly at her. The housekeeper beamed back as if only the two of them knew the true value of a beach.

"Today, when I went to get my lava rocks with the very lovely Winnie, I noticed some palm trees for sale. Lorena Ranch has no palm trees, which is a great pity. I bought all the trees, but now we need a beach to place them. Joe, you have an area full of scrub trees near the swimming pool."

Joe nodded. "An old pasture leftover from the ranch's dairy farm days."

"We clear it and cover the dirt with sand. We put in the palm trees and maybe some other pretty plants."

"Who is we?" Joe asked.

"Me and the landscaper I spoke to this morning. The beach will be my gift to Camp Love Letter, no cost to you. All children should be able to play in the sand."

Always practical, Nell said, "Won't the kids bring sand into the pool and clog the filters?"

Getting with the program, Joe answered. "We could put in sprinklers to wash their feet. The children would love to run through them anyhow. I can see it. Yes, I can, me."

"Major plumbing installation," Nell mentioned.

"We could have it done before the camp opens."

"The path through the grove should be cement so the children in wheelchairs can enjoy it, too," Winnie added, mindful of her patient.

"Sure, all that can be done in time, but for now we put in the sand and trees," Adam urged.

Corazon, her face planted between her two hands over a steaming mug of coffee, had a faraway look in her round, brown eyes. "I would like a beach where I could sit in my spare time—if I had spare time."

"While I am here, I can give you that, Mrs. Polk." Brinsley took a small sip of coffee as if he committed some dire breach of etiquette. The others built sandwiches, but his plate remained empty.

Corazon snapped back to reality. "Your offer is good. I get a beach. You can be butler while you are here. Eat! You are too skinny like Miss Winnie," Corazon rolled on, not noticing the other woman's small wince. "Call me Corazon and I call you?"

"I am called Brinsley."

"You got no first name. You born being Brinsley?"

The butler capitulated. "Clive, Clive Leopold Brinsley."

"Ha! No wonder you no say. Clive is okay with me." The phone rang. "Clive, you get that while I eat, no?" Corazon raised a multilayered ham, roast beef, three cheese, and smoked turkey sandwich to her mouth.

Clive, his plate still empty, went to the cordless phone in the kitchen. "Billodeaux residence. This is Brinsley. To whom am I speaking? Yes, certainly. Thank you." He disconnected. "Miss Anastasia is finished with her testing and is in need of a ride home. I would be delighted to retrieve her if you will entrust me with a vehicle and directions."

Nell, in the midst of eating a sandwich much more modest in size than Corazon's masterpiece, forked over her keys and paused in her lunch to write directions to the Episcopal day school. Brinsley, seeming very relieved, left to run the errand.

Winnie's hand hovered over the dill pickles. She made a snap decision and scooped up two sweet gherkins instead. Adam eyed her empty plate, then considered his own holding a half-eaten slab of French bread brimming over with fillings and a twin sandwich beside it. He considered the nearly empty platter. "Here take one of mine, Winnie."

"Oh, I had that salad and some fries earlier."

"You've been lugging rocks."

"Well, you dug a pit."

Nell and Joe exchanged glances. Corazon snatched the extra sandwich. "If you not gonna eat that, I take it to my husband." She stood and patted Adam on the back. "This man knows how to eat, not like Clive Brinsley." She found Knox Polk's favorite beverage in the fridge and made up a plate to deliver. No sooner had her broad behind passed out the door than Adam leaned close to Winnie.

"See, all she needed to be happy was a beach. And so do you."

Chapter Eleven

Winnie waited for the arrival of the special school bus hauling the handicapped students as she had all week long. She carried Teddy's armband crutches. He hated them, but needed to exert himself to learn walking. The minibus with the wheelchair lift swung to a stop as she opened the gate. A round-faced, short-chinned Down's Syndrome girl waved happily from one of its windows. The head of a boy with severe muscular dystrophy lolled against a headrest, but could not turn her way. Most likely, Teddy did not feel lucky about his condition, but thanks to early intervention, he had a good mind that could take him all the way through college. An aide helped Teddy from the bus and left him in her care.

Winnie held out the crutches. "Up we go, half way down the drive before you get to ride."

"Do I have to?"

"Absolutely. Someday you'll want to walk across a stage at graduation, so let's practice now."

"Maybe I won't finish high school like my mom."

"Nell and Joe will make certain you do."

"Only if I'm Daddy Joe's real son."

"Up. You're stalling."

Winnie made sure he had a good grip on the stick crutches before they started along the paved drive. The boy complained about so very little, almost as if he feared making any sort of trouble would get him thrown out of Lorena Ranch. He only griped about the crutches to her. As Teddy toiled slowly along, her mind wandered to yesterday's physical therapy session and to Adam Malala.

Joe had done her a big favor by visiting the home gym when she guided the child through his upper body strengthening exercises after Teddy completed his homework. He squeezed the boy's biceps and assured him he noticed an increase in size. Teddy's face lit with the praise. Of course, the triplets, who had little homework, tagged along and somewhat ruined the moment by showing their daddy what they could do. Even Lorena wanted her arm muscles approved, and Mack made everyone count his pushups. Still, Teddy's glow over his purported father's compliment did not fade. Just those few words made her job easier.

Adam Malala did not, though the fault didn't rest with him. He helped her get Teddy ready for bed every night. Usually they stood by the elevator talking softly while Nell visited briefly with the children at the end of the hall. He stood so close his body heat made sweat trickle between her shoulder blades, but never came as close to kissing her as he had that single time on the first night she arrived.

Instead, he lavished her with flowery compliments. Her eyes were like the green of sea waves sparkling in the sunlight. Her hair, and he twined a curl around his index finger, as soft as the down on an ocean bird's breast. She would have liked to sink her hands into his curly mane and initiate a kiss, but somehow she never had the nerve. Why did he move so slowly, so cautiously with her, a divorced woman who needed and wanted a demonstration of her attractiveness?

Adam always came to the gym while she worked with Teddy. He wore long sweatpants and a hoodie as he ran on the treadmill. Sometimes, he stripped off his top when Joe spotted him in weightlifting. As the perspiration beaded on his chest, she felt the desire to lick it off, laving the valley between his pecs and rounding his dark nipples with her tongue. Joe flashed a wicked smile her way as if he could read every decadent word of the novel in her mind. Teddy, noticing her distraction, began to fudge on his reps. "Ten, twelve, fifteen." She'd gotten her attention back where it should be and made him start over with his count.

Today, Teddy poked along setting his feet firmly each time. He had feeling in his thighs, but not his lower legs. Still with exercise and massage, he might stimulate his nerves to grow. He stopped so suddenly Winnie nearly bumped into him with the wheelchair. "What's that noise?"

"That racket? Bulldozers. They've been getting the lot ready for the beach all day. Frankly, I was enjoying the silence when they took a break."

Teddy's pace quickened. He moved so fast his feet flopped carelessly, and Winnie feared he would fall. The boy turned on the side path toward the pool and kept chugging along as eager to see the big machines in action as he would have been to meet the ice cream truck. The other boys, large and small, were already lined up along the chain-link fence around the pool: Joe and Adam, Dean and Tommy, Mack and Trinity. They watched in rapt attention as the big shovel of the bulldozer pushed small, uprooted trees toward a far corner of the lot. Teddy leaned up against the fence at the end of the line.

Joe greeted him cordially. "Have a good day at school, Teddy?"

"Same as always." He shrugged his small shoulders.

"You sound like all the rest of the kids. See that pile of brush the bulldozer is making? I'm thinking we should have a bonfire."

"That would be cool."

"You bet it would."

Failing to find the big machinery fascinating, Winnie joined the girls at a poolside table where Brinsley stood at rigid attention seeming very out of place in his dark suit and tie. He served the after school snacks as formally as a British high tea.

Winnie took a seat under the striped umbrella. "What do we have here?"

"Scones," said Stacy. "Brinsley got them for us. We have currant, cranberry, and lemon. Would you care for one?"

"I'd love it."

As Winnie seated herself, Dean shouted over the noise of the machinery, "Sissy food!"

Stacy shot back, "Civilized food, you big lout."

The girl not only passed her entrance exams for the Episcopal day school but excelled to the point that the administrator suggested she be placed a grade ahead with her cousins. The twins and Xochi had not been thrilled by this development, but since the puppy had broken the ice on their relationship, they tolerated it. Now, they giggled over her calling their sometimes-overbearing big brother a lout. Clearly, they were enjoying their tea party and Stacy's in-your-face reply to Dean.

Xochi's brown countenance warmed with a wide smile. "I'm beginning to like you, Stace."

Stacy leaned over and patted Titi curled at her feet. She coached the dog conversationally. "If Macho tries to roll you in the dirt again, you just bite his ankle." Macho, locked out of the pool compound for putting his feet on the table, whined at the gate at the mention of his name. Stacy broke off a corner of a scone, fed it to Titi, and lobbed the rest over the fence to Macho who caught the treat in midair.

The girl had bribery and dominance all figured out, Winnie thought, and wished she'd had half that much confidence at the age of nine. Maybe she would be a doctor by now instead of a divorced nurse.

"More milk, anyone?" Brinsley asked. "Would you care for some iced tea, Nurse Green?"

Winnie nodded. He filled one of the tall plastic glasses in tones of melon, green, and yellow that matched the umbrella for her first, then poured more milk into upraised cups. Taking a silver tray of scones to the men, he offered them around. Adam grabbed one of each flavor. Dean refused the offer, but the others picked up one each. Rather than nibble like the girls, they finished theirs in a few big bites.

Trinity, on the end of the line next to Teddy, said, "Your wheelchair looks like fun."

"It can be, not always. I wish I could run."

"Can I try it out?"

Although a twinge of anxiety crossed Teddy's face, he said, "Go ahead."

Trin carefully wheeled himself around the perimeter of the pool. Getting out he said, "Harder than it looks. You must have strong arms."

"I sure do. I can race my wheelchair."

Mack, the biggest of the triplets, asked for a turn and took the chair for a spin. While he would not confess to needing any special strength to maneuver, he did admit racing the wheelchair would be fun. "Camp Love Letter has wheelchair races. I bet you could win."

Joe gave both his little boys a smile of approval that quickly turned into a frown when Dean forced his overgrown twelve-year old frame into the small chair without asking permission. The oldest Billodeaux boy, his chin nearly resting on his knees, pushed off with a mighty shove. Whether by accident or intention, the wheelchair sailed over the lip of the pool and sank into the deep end.

Dean kicked free of it and sputtered to the surface. "Cold in here!" He stroked toward the edge and pulled himself out. The girls burst into laughter as he straggled from the water.

"That was a dumb thing to do," Stacy remarked without sympathy. She earned a small chorus of "yeahs" from the rest of the females.

"For sure a dumb thing to do in February. Go into the pool house and get a towel," his father directed.

Teddy wobbled on his crutches and sat down hard on the ground. "My chair! I can't go to school without my chair. What if it doesn't work anymore? What if Dean broke it?"

Dean stopped in the doorway of the pool house. "Oh, shut up, you wimp. Dad, my dad, will buy you a new one that isn't all beat up."

Joe covered the space between the fallen Teddy and Dean with the same quickness he displayed on the football field. He grasped his oldest son by the shoulders. "You march over there and apologize. Help the boy up."

"Why, because he really is your son, because you cheated on Mom?"

"No, because I'm trying to raise you as a decent human being. For the last time, I am saying Teddy is not my son. Now do as I told you." He gave Dean a shove in the right direction.

"Sorry, I guess."

Using a strength most boys his age did not possess, Dean heaved Teddy to his feet. The crippled boy hung his head to hide the tears streaming down his face. Reassure one child, hurt another. Joe shook his head in frustration as Dean stomped past on his way to get a towel. Tommy, ever Dean's best pal, moved closer to Teddy, who cringed against the fence.

"Dean isn't really mean. It's hormones Mama Nell says." Then, he trotted off after his buddy.

A huge splash drew everyone's attention back to the pool. Two oversized athletic shoes sat on the rim. Adam Malala surfaced, dragging the chair with him into the shallow end. He wheeled it up the ramp installed for the Camp Love Letter kids.

"Still working fine, but we should dry it off. Maybe Knox can check the gears for you, Teddy. Want me to carry you back to the house until we are sure?"

Teddy made his way to his beloved and yet hated wheelchair. "No, Miss Winnie, could you get me a towel to put on the seat? I want to take my own self back to the house."

Winnie did this small service, opening the gate for him, and walking behind as he went along. Carrying the boy's sticks, Adam escorted them. She could have sworn steam rose off of his big body, his long, bedraggled hair already beginning to curl again. A family in crisis, a patient to care for, and her mind took her straight to bed with a Samoan lover. She had sunk lower than the wheelchair in the deep end of the pool.

Chapter Twelve

Spurred on by a cash money incentive, the landscaper worked like the devil in debt to complete the beach and palm grove before Super Bowl Sunday. He plugged the tall, graceful-necked trees into the earth, shoring them up with ropes and stakes until they rooted. Not very attractive for the moment, but he screened the stakes with a border of short, bushier palms bearing sharp, pointed leaves along the fence surrounding the pool and set groupings of dwarf banana trees, hibiscus, and cannas into the gentle curves of the walkway that wove through the garden.

On the Friday before the deadline, dump trucks filled to the brim with pearly white sand arrived, and the mostly Mexican work crew began hauling and dumping wheelbarrows full on top of the bare, scraped earth until a beach evolved. The process drew the Billodeaux children after school, blithely skipping out on homework that could and would be done on Saturday before the big party the following day.

Brinsley served them a less than elegant snack of peanut butter and jelly sandwiches on whole wheat bread cut into triangles, but still placed on a silver tray poolside. Corazon was getting used to having a butler in the house. At the moment, she relaxed in the kitchen with her coffee in hand and enjoyed the company of her own son, a big baby and now a husky little boy. Even the maids who came in the mornings to clean and do laundry performed better under the butler's cold eye. They might have been Corazon's livelier, prettier cousins, a seemingly endless procession of young women on their way to better jobs, education, or marriage, but they completed their tasks more efficiently with Brinsley double-checking their work. Once, the maids had been housed on the grounds, but Nell long ago decided to pay them better and get them rooms in Chapelle after more than one of their boyfriends set off the alarms by climbing over the fences after dark and a few flashed their dark eyes at Joe. Knox picked up the maids daily during the week after dropping the children at school, and now delivered them into Brinsley's competent hands. Knox Polk never talked much, but all assumed he enjoyed having a less fatigued wife, too.

The Billodeaux kids had already put their mark on the concrete path by scraping their initials in the wet cement. Titi and Macho contributed by running along the path before it cured, and Teddy, dared to do it, wheeled across one damp section. The landscaper offered to repair the damage, but Joe and Nell told him to leave it be. Still, Winnie and Adam offered to keep an eye on the brood as the final touch fell into place, a line of low solar-powered lights snaking along the walkway. Before the contractor wiped his hands and held them out to receive Adam's substantial check, the children shucked off their shoes and socks and charged into the palm grove with two barking dogs at their heels.

"See, everyone loves a beach and the feel of sand

between their toes," Adam said to Winnie as he paid the landscaper at one of the poolside tables where she sat with Teddy.

Putting aside his sulky pre-teen act, Dean chased his sisters and Stacy around the trees in an impromptu game of tag. He made an extra effort to catch Stacy and dump her into a mound of sand with a heavy-duty touch of the hands.

"You got sand in my hair and made my uniform dirty. I'm coming for you, Dean Billodeaux."

"We'll help!" The girls reversed the chase. They had little luck as Dean weaved among palms and easily outran all the younger children until Tommy intentionally slowed enough to be caught and then ran down his elder brother for them. Teddy glumly wheeled his chair to the edge of the new walkway.

"Want your sticks to walk in there?" Winnie asked.

"No. I can't feel the sand between my toes even if I didn't have these stupid boots and braces on. I'll only sink and keel over, then Dean will laugh at me."

Adam had the boy out of his chair and seated under a palm before Winnie could protest. "You can sift the sand through your fingers and enjoy the sigh of the breeze in the palms, not a bad way for any man to spend some time."

Two winded dogs soon joined Teddy, then the triplets, who began mounding sand into what they claimed were castles. Teddy moved his legs wide apart and started to dig out a moat for them. Adam leaned one muscular arm lightly against an anchored tree and spoke softly to Winnie. "Today the children enjoy the beach, but tonight it belongs to us."

She shook her head. "I can't go out at night and

leave Teddy alone. He might need me."

"Then tomorrow night, lovely Winnie, whose skin is as soft as moonlight through the palms."

He drew one finger down the side of her face, and she shivered as if he'd disrobed her. "I don't see how one day will make any difference. My routine with Teddy will be the same."

"I've stayed here before. Saturday is movie night, popcorn and a family flick, maybe something more adult after the kids are in bed. Easier than taking ten children to the movies and buying them refreshments, Mrs. Joe says. We slip out and have two whole hours together. You know, Winnie, love is best made beneath the palm trees."

"I'm not certain. I—"

"I built this place for you. In Samoa when we court a woman, we bring gifts to the family. This is my gift. When we are finished with it, the campers will enjoy it, but first, it belongs to us."

Understanding dawned. "So that's what you have been doing, courting me. But why? I'm a divorced woman, not some shy little virgin."

"The Rev made it very clear that if I desired you I must court you properly."

"Well, thank you, Revelation Bullock, for that! All this time, I wasn't sure you were really interested or simply flirting with your fancy words and gestures."

"Samoans enjoy flowery speeches, the longer the better. Tomorrow night?"

Now that the words were said, the offer made, Winnie hesitated. "You do know one cold winter could kill these trees and a hurricane might come along and blow away the sand."

"But not before tomorrow night, the only thing that truly matters, my lovely Winnie."

All her life, she'd planned ahead, years ahead, and once she married Doug, she'd planned for both of them. When he would finish his medical training, where they would open his office, and what year to start their family—last year.

"Yes, tomorrow night."

****

Anticipation built as Adam, Winnie, and Nell scoured the grocery stores of Chapelle for tropical fruits, denuding the entire display of exotic offerings at the Winn-Dixie. Adam wheeled a cart entirely filled with coconuts and topped with a few bags of spinach and some plantains. Bless her heart, Winnie could not hold back thoughts of great big hairy balls as she watched him gather what he could for a traditional Samoan feast. All the while, he grumbled about a complete lack of taro and breadfruit, two of the few starchy foods Cajuns ignored. Winnie smiled at him with a foolish grin she saw reflected over and over in the mirrors above the produce. By the time they got back to the ranch with their bulging bags—bulging being another word that brought prurient thoughts to her mind—Joe and Knox had returned with a truckload of banana leaves and two slaughtered and cleaned pigs for Adam's inspection. Approved, the swine went into the coolers, and the children helped unload the heap of banana leaves by the barbecue pavilion and *umu* pit. The men stacked split pecan logs from the woodpile over the lava rocks and covered them with a tarp to keep the mound dry and ready for the firing of the oven in the early morning.

Even with all the preparations for the party, time ticked by slowly for Winnie. Adam on the other hand seemed entirely relaxed. When Nell suggested an easy dinner of salad and pizza, he happily chipped in for four fully loaded while the children clamored for their favorites. In the end, the deliveryman hauled fifteen pies to the Billodeaux residence. Adam devoured two with everything on it by himself while Winnie pecked at the slice on her plate and sipped a diet soft drink. She wasn't good at spontaneity while Adam appeared to live no other way. Her joyous anticipation slowly turned to dread way down in the pit of her stomach.

With movie time set for seven p.m., Joe cranked up the popcorn machine in the home theater while Nell herded the kids into their seats. Teddy sat on the end of the first row in a special indent made for wheelchairs, and Stacy took the seat next to him as merry popping and a buttery aroma filled the air. Dean and Tommy slipped into the second row directly behind them. Nell began handing out red and white-striped boxes of popcorn and finally settled herself at the far end of the row near the triplets. Joe joined her, slinging an arm around Nell's shoulders as if he planned to make out with her during the entire film. Winnie and Adam lingered near Teddy and close to one of the exit doors.

"You two want popcorn before we get started?" Nell asked.

"Ah, no. Adam and I are going for a walk. It's a nice night for—walking."

"In the palm grove," Adam added, not so helpfully.

Teddy stared at his nurse with a look of desertion in his eyes. "How come? It's a real good movie about a dolphin that lost its tail and learns to swim again with a fake one. Don't you want to see it, Miss Winnie?"

Winnie recognized Nell's subtle psychology in film choice. Maybe she should stay and support her patient. She hesitated while Adam took her hand and prepared to lead her out the door.

Dean leaned forward and said loud enough for Teddy and Winnie to hear but too low for his parents to catch on the other end of the row. "They want to be alone to do what grownups do when they lock the bedroom door and tell you not to knock unless there is blood on the floor or the house is on fire."

"And what's that?" Stacy piped up as the theater darkened and the opening credits of the move started to roll.

"You and Teddy are too little to know."

"I know," Teddy insisted, his cheeks flushing pink in the light from the screen. He turned his wide blue eyes away from Winnie, who blushed herself.

"Stop whispering, Dean," Jude demanded. "The movie is starting."

"Teddy, I'll be back in time to help you get to bed. I promise." Her patient did not answer.

Across the dark room, Joe's voice said, "Go on. Enjoy yourselves. I mean that."

With that blessing, Adam took possession of her narrow shoulders with one big arm and guided her into the night.

Chapter Thirteen

Winnie and Adam moved through the grove of oaks into shadows made deeper by the bright security lighting around the house. With a minimum of toes stubbed on gnarled roots, they arrived at the pool with its underwater lights shining brightly beneath the clear water.

"We should get some beach blankets," Winnie suggested.

"Sand makes a great bed, but okay."

She found a couple of thick covers and also snatched a flashlight from a utility shelf while Adam waited patiently. He did not seem to know the meaning of the word "rush" unless it applied to football. As for her, she'd checked the weather report twice during the day, cool but clear tonight. They would be happy for the blankets in the end.

"You know, our eyes will adjust to the darkness, and the moon is up, but sure, bring the flashlight if it makes you feel better."

He divested her of the roll of bedding and let her lead the way to the solar-lit walk into the palm grove. Halfway to the back of the beach, he steered Winnie from the path and guided her to where two palms crossed, artistically backlit by the moon. "Here."

Fussing with its corners and wrinkles in the cloth,

Winnie laid down one of the blankets and made a pillow of the other. She lay down and stared directly into the eye of the man in the moon far above them. Adam stretched out by her side and rested his head on his crooked arm. He ran a finger over her lips.

"Soft as moonlight, pretty as a plumeria blossom." The finger roved down the length of her neck and over the slope of her upturned breasts. "Like a wave coming to a crest." He kissed her in no hurry at all, his lips broad and bold on hers.

Involuntarily, her hands rose to keep him there, and tangled in the long, soft mane of his curls. He edged closer, and she felt his other hand moving under the clingy pale yellow top she wore, neither low-cut nor particularly sexy, but easy to remove along with the zipperless brown stretch pants and sling-back shoes she'd chosen that morning for the same practical reason. Adam paused to divest her of shoes, slacks, and shirt, revealing a second layer. The demi-bra flattered her small breasts, she knew. The panties weren't lacy, but sheer and low-cut in that same light yellow color. She'd looked up the plumeria blossoms he kept comparing her to and chosen accordingly.

He gazed at her long enough for her doubts to return. She should have gotten a wax down below, not that she was very hairy, and she'd always considered that process embarrassing and unnecessary for a married woman and a nurse with no time to primp. Certainly, he'd seen better breasts. All football players had, she was certain. He opened the front catch of her bra and exposed what she had to offer.

"These have beckoned to me from the first time I saw you. They offer themselves to me." He crouched

93

between her legs, lowered his mouth to an uplifted light brown nipple, and sucked. It puckered with the strokes of his tongue. He paid the same tribute to the other, and she felt his adoration clear to the tips of her toes and in the very center of her being.

He removed the panties and stroked her with one large finger. "Not ready yet, my Winnie. I can tell. You are thinking too much." He raised that finger carrying her scent to a small crease between her eyes and rubbed it away. "You need a distraction. Want to see my tattoos?"

No, she did not. He probably had a Sinners devil on one hind cheek and his college mascot on the other. She wanted him to plunge into her and make her stop thinking. Winnie delved her hand into his jeans and found no briefs underneath. He'd come prepared, too. She pulled off his black Sinners T-shirt and attacked the zipper of his jeans, parting easily from the strain of his erection against the fabric. She pushed the jeans down. Oh my god! Now she was distracted, completely distracted, and not only by the length and breadth of what he offered.

From an inch above the waist to tops of the knees, Adam's tattoos covered him thickly like another piece of cloth. Patterns accented by heavy dark patches ran around his hips and thighs, but all the lines converged on his erect penis. She groped for the flashlight and turned the beam on his body as he rose to step out of his pants. The length of his erection and even his scrotum possessed designs. Patterns of leaves, swirls like waves and water, and small animal figures emerged against the dark background. As he turned his back, modeling, she swore she saw a chain of oblong figures that resembled tiny footballs. "Incredible," she breathed.

He gave her full frontal nudity again. "That's good, right?"

"Yes, very distracting. That had to be incredibly painful." She gestured to the main attraction.

"Believe it or not, the area around the navel hurt more." He lay down beside her, arms in back of his head. "Go on, you can touch it. The color won't come off."

She traced the designs along his hips and back to his penis over and over. It gave a small nod each time she did. "But why, when no one sees this?"

"A very painful rite of manhood. Sammy Tau and the rest of the guys I lived with in Pago, all except the one headed for the ministry, we went together to get our tats before leaving for mainland colleges. Took a month to complete them in the traditional way. The ink is put in this comb-like device and pounded under the skin with a mallet."

"Dear God!" Winnie's hand moved protectively over his scrotum.

"They can do more delicate work, too, but for the dark areas, that is the way to get the best effect. Our group vowed we would never forget our roots in Samoa. I let my hair grow out for the same reason. Of course, Sammy never left the islands."

Winnie noticed a slight droop in his erection. Feeling daring and free of inhibitions for the first time in her life, she stoked his shaft and knelt to place her lips on its bulbous head. She took him in and swirled her tongue around its tip just as he had done with her nipples. They tightened again at the thought. The throb of him against her palate was answered by a thrum between her legs.

"Winnie." Adam tugged gently at her shoulders. "Are you ready—because I sure am."

"More than."

His large hands cinched around her waist, raised her up, and settled her right where he wanted her to be. His hips pumped from below, and repressed Winnie Green threw back her head and let the breeze in the palms fan the soft waves of her hair out behind her. Her knees sank into the sand beneath the blanket as she pushed against him. She absorbed the moonlight shining on his bronzed skin and the song the fronds made above her. Gradually, she allowed her eyes to close as that feeling low in her body built and built and built. Adam at the last moment flipped her over into the sand and dominated her with the last few strokes that brought them both to fruition. Slowly he withdrew, keeping his weight off her delicate figure and drawing her to his side in an embrace beneath one arm.

"See, love beneath the palms is the best—as long as we don't get hit by coconuts." He gently rubbed the sand from her shoulders and hips.

She nodded, sifting some of the granules in her hair onto his chest. "We should go back soon, but I admit, I could lie here all night long."

"You sure? Because I brought three condoms. And they are still in my jeans. Sorry. You weren't the only one who got distracted."

"No worries, as you like to say. My sister, the doctor, handed me birth control pill samples the day she brought me here. The Rev might be the moral conscience of that family and his whole congregation, but Mintay is practical down to her toenails. I think she hoped we'd get together from the very start. I put them into use during that courtship period when I wasn't sure if this would ever happen or not."

"Very glad it did, my lovely Winnie. No worries about STDs either. Too much London Missionary Society upbringing for me to be a devil with the ladies, like Joe in his day. Besides, I was keeping myself clean for my *taupou,* that virgin princess I was supposed to marry."

Winnie experienced that same sinking feeling she'd had when Doug told her about big-busted, blonde Talia. "Now I understand the first words you said to me. Must be hell settling for second best." She rolled away from him even though she ended up in the sand.

A muscular arm gathered her in again. "After tonight, I'm pretty sure I'm over her. I want to be with you. When can we do this again?"

"Your cottage anytime the children are at school. I'm fairly certain our walk in the grove did not fool Joe and Nell one bit, and not even Dean, judging by his ugly remark to Stacy."

"Dean's opinion doesn't count. None does but ours. Too bad coming here in daylight would be a bad idea."

Winnie got to her knees and brushed off the sand again. She found her clothes and put on a show for him as she dressed in the moonlight, a reverse striptease. He could have used a condom again when she finished, but they really had to get back and put Teddy to bed. Adam covered his tattoos, and she lit their way to the house before the movie and the popcorn ran out.

Chapter Fourteen

Winnie slept soundly once she washed the sand out
of her hair and off her body, but the household awoke
early on Super Bowl Sunday. She and Teddy were the
last to arrive at the breakfast table that held only a
pitcher of orange juice, a container of milk, and a
variety of fairly healthy breakfast cereals. She supplied
Teddy with his choice and a cup of juice before pouring
some coffee and making toast for herself. Beyond the
kitchen door, she recognized Adam's voice organizing
some event that started the children chattering. Eager to
join them, Teddy bolted his food. The sound of a solid
whack and a chorus of "ahs" prompted him to scoot
outside and join in the commotion.

Winnie admitted watching Adam splitting coconuts
with a single blow of a machete went right up there
with seeing him tackle an opponent on the football
field. Putting all his considerable strength into his
swing, he raised the heavy-bladed knife again and
dispatched another. Coconut milk splashed. The dogs
lapped it up. Joe and Knox Polk got into the act and
showed off for their ladies. Nell allowed Dean and
Tommy to take a turn, but held the others back as bits
of shell went flying. Once all the coconuts had been
slaughtered, interest diminished considerably when the
meat inside the husks had to be pried out with a

screwdriver or knife, a more difficult and less masculine task.

"Why do we need so much coconut?" Winnie asked.

"To make *palusami*. You can't eat roast pig without *palusami*, lovely Winnie," Adam answered. "Next, we grate it and squeeze out the coconut cream."

"I remember grating coconut for my Nana's custard pies when I was a child."

"Good, then you have experience. All of this must be grated and squeezed dry. You be in charge. I must start the wood to heat the rocks for the cooking."

"I have experience in getting my fingertips and knuckles grated, that's all."

"You will do great! Call me when all the coconut meat is shredded."

The children wanted to join in the grating, and as Winnie predicted, adhesive bandages and antibiotic ointment soon came in handy. They lost interest with injuries and shot outside when the rented rock climbing wall and party bouncer shaped like a castle at the girls' request arrived. However, Nell called them back to task once both were erected to entertain the children expected to arrive in a few hours. She set the youngest to wrapping white and sweet potatoes plus plantains in aluminum foil and insisted the older girls continue shredding. "Slave labor," Stacy muttered. Dean and Tommy begged off saying they had to groom and saddle the ponies for rides and ducked out for the barn. Teddy, working a grater, gazed wistfully after them.

Nell and Corazon fixed large platters of tropical fruits: wedges of papaya and mango, slices of star fruit, kiwi, and pineapple. "I can count on Mintay to bring a large green salad every time, but unless one of Joe's sisters does a pot of green beans fixed with salt pork, fruit will be about the only non-starchy side dish," Nell claimed.

Winnie sucked a scraped knuckle. "Want to switch jobs for a while?"

"No way. He's your Samoan, not mine. I don't have to learn to make *palusami*."

"He's not mine exactly." Winnie ducked her head and even looking down, still managed to knick herself on the grater.

"Ha! All that sand you dragged in last night is a dead giveaway."

"Don't say anything to my brother-in-law, okay?"

"Now why would I? You can make your own decisions."

Nell abandoned the topic of conversation as soon as her mother-in-law arrived with a roasting pan full of rice dressing and a large bread pudding topped with six inches of meringue to be shoved into the refrigerator and warmed later. Mawmaw Nadine, a robust woman with a head of thick iron gray hair, pointed at her cheek. "Which of my grandkids is gonna give me some sugar?" She bent down to receive kisses from the triplets, Xochi, and the twins.

Stacy held back. "You, too, *cher* heart. You my honorary grandbaby." Because it was hard not to comply with anything the forceful mawmaw wanted, she offered up a rather dry kiss. Teddy remained where he sat studiously working his grater, but Nadine came to him. "You my son's foster child. Come on now, a big smacker right here." She offered a cheek, and Teddy did his best to make his kiss the biggest of all.

Then with her usual energy, Mawmaw Nadine grabbed a grater and pitched in, all the while talking about cooking and her family, two favorite topics. "Now, Lizzie will bring the French bread like usual and a red velvet cake from Pommier's Bakery. I think Izzy is doing white beans with ham and the Watergate salad. Eenie said she might make a potato salad and a pecan pie. Allie usually does baked beans and a coconut cake. We gonna have lots of coconut, looks like."

"For a special Samoan dish Adam is making," Winnie told her.

"Oooh, he's cookin' for you, *cher*. That's a good sign. Too bad you divorced and won't be able to marry in the church."

"Actually, neither Adam nor I are Catholic."

Nadine shrugged her shoulders. "Well, we ain't all lucky enough to be Cajun. Guess it works for you." Sturdy arms pumping, she made huge inroads into the heaps of coconut.

By the time Adam poked his curly head into the kitchen, they'd completed the first part of the preparation. "Now we ring out the cream."

Lacking anything better, they used cheesecloth to do this task. He tossed aside the dry shreds, added salt, pepper, and sliced onion to the cream, then laid out his spinach, making it into leafy cups on top of a swath of banana leaves. He poured the mixture into the cups and sealed up the packets of banana leaves.

Mawmaw Nadine at his elbow, remarked, "So, not a dessert then?"

"Nope. Savory. We could have made it with canned coconut milk, but this is much better."

Nadine, the queen of making food from scratch,

101

nodded approval, but Winnie rolled her green eyes. "Now he tells me—after I spent half my day making the world's most laborious starch."

"You'll love it. I have to go tend my rocks. I need to prove I can feed you well. A Samoan man who cannot cook in an *umu* is no catch at all." Adam returned to his pit oven.

"A great big hunky catch who can cook a whole pig," Nell remarked with a sigh.

Mawmaw Nadine shook a finger at her daughter-in-law. "You got my son already. He can cook a pig, too, but not in a hole in the ground, and don't you forget it."

"Only joking. Joe and Nell forever."

Winnie stared at the packets of *palusami*. "What if I don't want to catch him? What if I only want to have some fun for a while?"

Nadine turned the shaking finger on her. "You don't throw away a catch that big, *cher*. You don't want to keep him, you shouldn't mess wit' him."

Car doors began to slam, frightening the mockingbirds already staking out breeding territory in the bushes. Bringing side dishes, desserts, and numerous children from college age down to grade school size, the extended Billodeaux clan arrived. Right behind them, the New Orleans contingent made up of former and current Sinners and their families came bearing pots of jambalaya, red beans and rice, and a tower of King Cake boxes from the best bakery in the city. Once every guest had a cold drink in hand, the crowd gathered around the *umu* to watch Adam poke hot stones inside the pig carcasses and lay the meat out just so on the glowing lava rocks. He piled on more steaming rocks, threw in the potatoes and plantains and lastly placed the packets of palusami, all to be smothered in a thick layer of banana leaves that left a long, lumpy green hump in the earth.

"How long before we eat?" Nell asked.

"Two pigs—an hour or so."

"That quickly!"

Immediately, a chain of women transferred dishes that needed to be heated to the top of Joe's vast grill inside the barbecue pavilion. They covered the length of two picnic tables with cold foods and set up the desserts in the formal dining room inside the house to be available when darkness fell and the game began. When this frenzy of culinary arrangement ended, Nell and her favorite guests gathered in a ring of folding chairs under the oaks to take a breather before the meal. Winnie declined a rest despite her long efforts in making *palusami*. She and Adam took Teddy to the riding ring for a promised turn on the horses. Stacy bobbed by Teddy's side on the white mare giving him instruction he did not need and confusing the western-trained horse with her posting and commands.

"Winnie says Teddy should do more riding to strengthen his core and thighs," Dr. Mintay Bullock observed.

"She's a good nurse. Thanks for bringing her over to fill the gap until Nurse Wickersham is free," Nell answered.

"You know I had ulterior motives for that."

"What?" asked Precious Armitage, wife of the nose guard. Big, black and bodacious, she wore the red, white and blue jersey of the team she favored tonight. It spanned across her enormous breasts.

"No, don't tell me. I see it all now. Adam just snaked his arm around yo' sister's waist. They got it going on. Too bad. I hoped Adam might stay single until one of my girls finished college. Whatever happened to the blacker the berry, the sweeter the juice, as my Calvin likes to put it when we in bed? Hate to say it, but your sis is the most bourgy girl I ever seen. Look at that hair, and it ain't even extensions. Why she's hardly black at all. Now if I was light-skinned I'd want to be the tawny kind like Sharlette."

Sharlette Dobbs, wife of Ace, preened a little. "Why thank you, sister," she said to her best friend. Elegant and always well-dressed, she stretched out long legs clad in skintight leggings and topped with a belted leopard print tunic that extended to her knees. She crossed her gold-sandaled feet and called out to her two teenage daughters who stood at the base of the rock climbing wall. "You keep an eye on Prince now." Her son, around the same age as the twins and Tommy, scrambled up the outcrops with Mintay's athletic daughter not far behind.

Sharlette got an eye roll and a sassy remark in return. "We're tired of taking care of the royalty. When is dinner?"

"Soon. You watch him until then."

The two other mothers in the circle sat quietly because both had worn-out sleeping toddlers in their laps. The leggy, blonde sports photographer, Stevie Riley, wife of the retired Connor Riley, supported her tow-headed daughter, Josee, on a shoulder. Her son, Jack, equally white-haired and blue-eyed, bounced in the jumper along with a redheaded little terror named Maureen Mariah McCoy, the daughter of Cassie and

Howdy, the Sinners' kicker. The triplets tumbled around with them.

"I never knew motherhood would be so—so engrossing. I might have had kids sooner if I'd known." Stevie patted her daughter's back.

"I never knew it could be so daunting," Cassie McCoy said, careful not to disturb little Wayne, the image of his father, curled in her lap. "Wayne has been easy compared to Maureen. I guess my mother got her wish—that I'd have a child exactly as troublesome as myself someday."

Nell squeezed Cassie's hand. "You turned out fine in the end."

"Because of Howdy. He's steady. I needed slow and steady and didn't even realize it."

"You think this thang with your sister and Adam is going anywhere, or is she just keeping him warm until my daughter graduates college?" Precious said, not giving up on the topic.

Mintay shook her head. "I only wanted her to let loose a little after that shipwreck of a divorce."

"I think Adam is taking this a little more seriously after what the Rev said to him about courting Winnie. He isn't a player when it comes to women, you know. His fiancée jilted him for his best friend. I'm afraid he's on the rebound, and Winnie seems unsure where all this is going." Nell expressed her concern.

"What kind of crazy woman would dump a man like Adam?" Precious asked. "Just look at him, he can rock one of those aloha shirts. Not many men can pull that off!"

"Evidently he was dumped by a Samoan virgin princess."

"Oh, not good," Mintay said. "Our entire lives, Winnie felt she had to compete with someone better and failed. She is far prettier than I am, and I guess that made people take her more lightly. Nothing wrong with being a nurse and not a doctor, I keep telling her—but she should go to med school now. I did get the better prize when it came to husbands."

A murmur of agreements went around the circle. "Now if only I could prevent the sisters of the church from stopping by with their fried chicken and mac and cheese. I'd like him to live past fifty." Their eyes swiveled toward the Rev standing near the pig pit and wearing one of his old team jerseys stretched tight across the belly.

"Doesn't look like Winnie is giving up Adam anytime soon. She's about glued to his side and has her fingers in all that nice curly hair down his back," Sharlette observed. "I wouldn't mind taking a turn with that."

Brinsley approached to ask if any of the ladies would like another drink of any kind. Sharlette and Precious placed their orders. "Now that is a man who does *not* rock an aloha shirt. I don't think I ever seen whiter arms sticking out of one of them," Precious commented. "A shirt like that should be topped with a lei and a big, brown smiling face, not the kisser of doom."

"Adam talked him into the shirt. Brinsley is very uncomfortable in beachwear," Nell said, defending the butler.

"I never thought you'd be the one to get a butler. Why, you don't even cater parties like these," Stevie remarked.

"We will never have a catered party as long as Mawmaw Nadine lives. She firmly believes home-cooked is better. As for the butler, he is only temporary until Stacy gets used to living here. Brinsley is her only link to my sister and her former life."

Brinsley walked up and presented Sharlette and Precious with two uncapped light beers sweating from the cooler on a silver tray. They nodded their thanks, and he moved off to accost others about their desires. Precious watched him go, so straight and so out of place. "Still a person could get used to having a butler pretty quick."

Over by the riding ring, Adam looked at the sun rather than his watch and beckoned Teddy and Stacy to bring their horses to the gate. He helped the boy down and into his wheelchair. Stacy dismounted with ease and flipped the reins to Dean as if he were merely a stable boy attending to the stock. Even from a distance, Nell knew her son's jaw clenched. Winnie pushed Teddy across the uneven ground between the ring and the pavilion. Along the way, they spread the word that the pigs should be ready. Mothers hailed children, grungy from climbing, jumping, and riding, to go wash their hands.

Releasing a cloud of steam, Adam raked the wilted banana leaves from the top of the *umu*. Joe used his barbecue tools to remove the packets of *palusami*, the baked potatoes and plantains to a tin tub. Howdy McCoy and Connor Riley carted it off to the table set aside for the pigs and already covered in oilcloth and banana leaves. It paid to have half a football team to transfer two heavy, roasted pigs onto a plank and into the pavilion. Nell quietly requested that the black-eyed heads of the animals be removed from sight. Precious offered to take them home to a relative who made hogshead cheese and always bemoaned the difficulty of finding a good fresh head, though she wasn't sure a roasted head would do.

After that, everyone got down to the business of eating, filling plates to heaping and gamely trying the *palusami* which they declared tasty, okay, or never again depending on the person. Winnie fell into the "okay for all that work" category, disappointing Adam just a little. The two of them sat cross-legged on a blanket with a selection of foods laid out on fresh banana leaves as he wanted to give her a Samoan experience.

Adam gestured to the crowd perched wherever they could find a space. "This is very Samoan, a big feast for the whole village."

"The Sinners are a village?" Winnie questioned.

"Yes, my village when I am away from home. Too bad I could not find any taro. We like to eat with our hands, and pieces of taro make a good scoop. Potatoes crumble." Still, he popped a piece of yam into his mouth and offered a bit to Winnie.

Winnie ate it off his fingertips, slick and greasy from the roast pork. If they hadn't been surrounded by an audience, she would have sucked them clean, he was that tasty. She offered him a slice of mango the same way.

"You must come with me to visit Samoa."

She nearly choked on a succulent piece of roast pork. "It's a little soon to be meeting your family, Adam."

"For a vacation, just a vacation."

Somehow, she didn't think so. "Are you sure this isn't about the princess who got away?"

"Pala is her name, and I have another princess now. Winnie, I never held her close to my heart as I have you. Last year, I remarked to my mother that Pala had turned into a beauty and filled her role as *taupou* very well. My mother told my father. He spoke to her father and uncle, the *matai*, the village chief. Pala must have agreed to a courtship because before I knew it, I was taking gifts to her family and eating with them regularly. When Pala and I walked out together, half the village followed. She remained reserved as would be expected of the *taupou*."

"This was an arranged marriage?"

"A very traditional one. My family has been accumulating fine mats and other gifts for most of a year in expectation of the wedding. Such a bride would bring prestige to my family. Pala is all a Samoan woman should be and so I ought to be happy with her, right?"

"I suppose." Winnie studied the abundance of food she had little appetite for anymore and crushed a blackened bit of pigskin into the banana leaves with her thumb.

"Only now, I don't think I want a Samoan wife anymore."

Her eyes moved from the feast to Adam. "Is that so?"

"Winnie, come to the islands with me as soon as you can."

"I'd have to wait until Nurse Wickersham arrives to care for Teddy. I'm not sure. Samoa is very far away, and I should be looking for a new job. I don't want to be a burden to Mintay and Rev any longer than I must."

Nell clapped her hands to get everyone's attention. "Finish eating. The pre-game show is on and dessert is in the house. Every one of you take home some of this pork and anything else you want. I know y'all brought coolers."

"That, too, is very Samoan. Every person takes home part of the feast. I have no interest in seeing the pre-game show and want only one kind of dessert. I think we have time for a trip to the palm grove before anyone will miss us."

"I can't. Teddy."

Teddy sat nearby, a sturdy plastic plate almost empty in his lap. Stacy had taken a seat beside the wheelchair and handed him his drink whenever he wanted it. She fed Titi a morsel of pork. Macho gnawed a crunchy pig tail and a couple of the ears with great contentment. The girl gave the couple a genial smile, far from her usual sullen expression when she failed to be the center of attention. She'd been listening in on the adult conversation of course.

"If you want to go for a walk, I'll take Teddy inside for dessert and get him a good spot in the theater to watch the game."

Winnie considered the offer. Stacy, though bossy, did pay attention to Teddy and helped when she could. Their little nightly tête-à-tête continued before both went to bed. Within the large Billodeaux family, they had formed their own group of two.

"Teddy, do you need to relieve yourself or anything else?" she asked.

Embarrassed in front of Stacy, he wrinkled his nose. "No! I'm okay. Go for your walk. I don't need a babysitter all the time."

"If you are sure…"

"Jeez, go walk with Adam. I can get inside by myself." He pushed his chair in the direction of the house.

Adam threw the meat scraps to Macho and gathered the banana leaves with the rest of the remnants to fling into a trashcan. "Sounds like he means it to me." He neatly folded the blanket and tucked it under his arm.

"Teddy," Winnie called after the disgusted child. "We won't be gone more than an hour. If you need me, have someone call from the gate to the grove."

"Yeah, sure." The boy made steady progress toward his dessert with Stacy tagging after him and giving the wheelchair a shove whenever it hung up in heavy leaves or a small hole.

Winnie conceded to Adam, "To the palm grove then."

Chapter Fifteen

Stacy took possession of wheeling the chair. She leaned over and whispered in Teddy's ear. "They are going to do grownup stuff, sex things, aren't they?"

"Probably. Let go of my chair. I can do this myself."

Instead, Stacy flashed a sweet smile when Sharlette Dobbs complimented her on being so kind. "I wish my daughters were half as helpful."

Stacy tipped the chair slightly to gain the concrete path. "Let go," Teddy growled. Titi yipped at their heels.

"Wait here. I'm going to put Titi inside. I don't want her barking and giving us away."

"Giving what away?"

"I want to watch the sex stuff. That Dean thinks he knows everything. I bet he never actually watched anyone having sex."

"You don't want to, either. It ain't nice."

"How would you know?"

Teddy snorted. "I lived in a trailer, not a wing of the palace, Stace. The walls are pretty thin. Ours had a crack between the two bedrooms. Once, I watched Newt and my mother go at it. Mama called that 'doing the nasty', and it was. Lots of moaning and grunting and bumping against the wall. She said she had to let

Newt or he'd put us both out on the road with no way to get back to Tennessee."

"It's Newt that sounds nasty. I bet it would be nicer between Winnie and Adam. Come on. When will we get another chance this good? It's you and me against the rest of them, remember?"

"You can't brag about it to anyone, or we will be in big, big trouble."

"This is for my own information," Stacy sniffed in her most superior manner. "Be right back."

She grabbed Titi and caught up with the triplets filing into the house. "Lorena, would you watch my puppy for a while? I need to help Teddy do something."

"Sure. I love your doggie." Innocently, the little girl held out her arms to accept the fuzzy bundle.

"Thanks, Lori." Stacy dashed back to Teddy who had wheeled farther down the path and around a bend to avoid people stopping to ask if he needed help.

"It's getting dark. You won't be able to see much," he said, still trying to talk her out of it.

"The pool and the pathway have lights, but we'd better wait here a little and let them get good and started."

****

Deep in the grove beneath the same crossed palms, Adam flicked open their blanket and spread it out. Judging by the many small footprints in the sand, the visiting children had enjoyed his gift, but now the place belonged to them. As soon as he stood again, Winnie unbuttoned his aloha shirt and ran her hands over the smooth contours of his chest. Adam shoved down his jeans and stepped out of them, athletic shoes and all. He immediately went to work unknotting the flowered blouse Winnie had tied at her small waist. With his erection pressing hard between them, he divested her of the top and bra. Sliding her slacks and panties down to her ankles, he held them while she kicked free of the rest of her clothes. On the way up, he licked the inside of her thigh and tested her response with the tip of his tongue. She leaned back against one of the palms as if her legs could no longer support her.

"Ready so soon?" he asked.

"Oh, yes."

They sank onto the blanket, but he kissed her lips and teased her nipples before going any farther. Winnie dug her nails into his back and flexed her hips against his erection. He sank into her depths. She raked her fingers through his hair with abandon. Adam began moving over her, but suddenly Winnie put a staying hand on his chest.

"Am I hurting you?" He leaned close to ask his question.

"No, I heard something in the bushes," she whispered.

"Probably a raccoon or one of those crazy mockingbirds. They never sleep. I have one near my cottage that sings all night."

"I doubt even a mockingbird can simulate whispers and giggles."

With his lips against her ear, he said quietly, "Probably that damned Dean and maybe Tommy spying on us. Give me a second. I'm going to scare the hell right out of them."

Slowly, he withdrew from her, but remained lying down. Then with one sudden spring, he jumped to his feet and flexed his muscles. His erection pressed against the maze of his dark tattoos. The rising moon backlit the fury of his wild hair. He crossed his eyes and stuck out his tongue before uttering a war cry that did flush a mockingbird from a nearby tree and at least one child from the closest thicket of short palms and red-leafed bananas. Running footsteps beat against the sand.

Adam whipped on his jeans. Winnie huddled under the blanket she'd drawn over her nakedness. "I'm going to catch that snotty brat while you get dressed."

He dug in with his toes as if starting a sprint, but went no farther than the clump of concealing plants. "Looks like we have a bird in the bush after all."

Putting on her clothes under the cover, Winnie asked, "Who?"

"You won't believe it."

With his hands over his eyes as if covering them would make him disappear, Teddy sat in his red wheelchair mired in the sand. Obviously, he'd tried to escape and only gotten himself in deeper. In the distance, the sharp slap of footsteps fleeing on the concrete path sounded clearly through the grove.

Winnie rounded the bushes and stared at the culprit. "Teddy! How could you? Did Dean talk you into this?"

"No," the boy mumbled, still shielding his eyes. "I didn't watch. I swear I didn't."

"Well, you certainly didn't get out here on your own, so who *was* watching?"

Adam squatted down by the wheelchair where the moonlight made shadows of two deep indents in the sand. Unlike the flat patterns made by other children's sneakers, these betrayed the unmistakable sign of the heels on a pair of small party shoes. Only Stacy had worn dressy footwear with her designer jeans and frilly blouse to the pig roast. He answered Winnie's question. "The Princess Anastasia, right?"

"I can't tell you. I promise I didn't look until you yelled, Mr. Adam. You were like the Incredible Hulk out there, really scary." His small shoulders trembled under the weight of Adam's hand.

"Sorry, I was trying to frighten the older boys. But, we're both dudes, right? You've seen naked guys before, so no big deal."

"Yeah, Newt, my mama's boyfriend, liked to lay nekkid on the sofa when she wasn't around to complain. He never shut the bathroom door either."

"Sounds like a great fellow. I'm glad you didn't peek on Miss Winnie, but still you should apologize to her."

"I didn't want to do it, Miss Winnie. Stacy pushed me over here. Please, please forgive me and don't tell Daddy Joe or Mama Nell. They'll put me out on the side of the road."

Winnie knelt by Teddy's side and took his hands. "They will do no such thing. You have a home here for as long as you need it. Still, what you did was a very naughty deal, and they need to know. I blame myself, too, for letting Stacy take my place. I should have watched over you. We'll both accept our punishments. I might have to leave."

"No!"

"It's up to your foster parents. I don't want to wreck the party, so until it is over, I won't say a word. Let's get you back to the house. We'll watch the game and forget for a while."

****

Nell did a child count as anyone with ten children would do. Joe sat in one oversized recliner, sleepy Mack and Trin tucked in beside him. Her eyes skimmed over Precious and Calvin Armitage and the Rev overwhelming the large sofa with Mintay squeezed into one corner. Sharlette and Asa Dobbs claimed the loveseat with their son, Prince, between them. Connor Riley had possession of the other recliner. He held his two blond children while Stevie lounged on the floor between his legs and rested her neck against the seat. Nell spotted the twins' curly heads next to Xochi's braids in the swarm of girl cousins and guests of all ages sitting on cushions in front of the big screen TV. Lorena was with them petting Stacy's dog.

That accounted for six. Nell made her way to the theater. Dean and Tommy sat in the last row with their feet up on the seats in front of them and a large bowl of popcorn on an adjacent seat. Eight. She searched for two blond heads among the dark Billodeauxs filling the rest of the space. Cassie was removing her tiny fury of a daughter in the midst of a hissy fit from the theater. Her husband attempted to rock Wayne to sleep despite the uproar. Near him in a very dark corner, she picked out Stacy by her white, ruffled blouse in the dim theater. Nine.

Retracing her steps, she went to the elevator and rode it up to Teddy's room. No sign of him. She tried the kitchen where Corazon and Knox Polk attempted to explain American football to Brinsley as they watched on the set the housekeeper used for her Spanish language soap operas. Chubby Junior Polk worked on a mound of desserts at the table. "Have you seen Teddy?"

she asked.

Four heads shook and showed immediate concern. "Should we start a search?" Knox asked as head of security among other duties at the ranch.

"Let me get Joe, then we'll go looking."

In the overcrowded den, Joe was up on his feet and shouting, "You call that a block?" The instant replay showed the quarterback suffering a tremendous sack. "My mother could do better than that!"

Mawmaw Nadine probably could if riled enough, Nell reflected. She tugged Joe's arm. "Teddy is missing," she told him over the angry roar of the crowd in the distant stadium.

"Save my seat for me, guys," he said to Mack and Trin before following his wife to the kitchen.

They caught Knox strapping on a very official utility belt holding a weapon and a flashlight heavy enough to be used as a club. Brinsley, still in his absurd tropical shirt, offered to help. "Could he be with Miss Stacy?" he asked. "I noticed them together shortly before we came inside."

"No, she's in the theater. Must have come in the front door without him. Do we have any more flashlights?" Nell started searching drawers until Corazon handed her the one she kept handy for power outages. "Let's go!"

Joe pushed her into a kitchen chair. "You stay here. I'll get the camp lanterns in the barn. No sense in all of us tripping over tree roots." He turned the doorknob only to find Teddy, Winnie, and Adam on the other side.

"Thank God!" Nell raced over to the wheelchair bound boy. "We were so worried about you."

"He went with us for a walk in the palm grove," Winnie claimed.

Nell and Joe exchanged another of those married people, mind-reading glances. "Really?" they said simultaneously.

"Hey, we're missing the game. How about some dessert, Teddy? I have my eye on the coconut cake. What do you like?" Adam said cheerfully.

"I guess dessert would be good. I like red velvet."

Adam steered the boy away. Winnie faced her employers, her friends. "I'll tell you everything tomorrow. I promise."

Chapter Sixteen

By the time the chaos involved with getting ten children off to school and waiting with Teddy at the gate passed, Winnie missed her chance to confess. On her walk back to the house, Nell whizzed by in her small, red car on her way to provide free psychological services at Dr. Bullock's clinic. She thought to find Joe in the barn, but he'd already ridden out on Lazy Boy to check his small herd of Charolais cattle and take an extended morning ride. Adam policed the picnic area, picking up stray trash and shoving the party debris into a black plastic garbage bag, probably already doing community service for their sin.

By his grin and his greeting, he had sinning more on his mind than punishment. "Hey, lovely lady, help me to finish here, then we can go over to my cabin and complete what we started last night."

"Why am I the only one deeply concerned about this?"

Adam heaved his big shoulders. "Strict upbringing, overdeveloped conscience? They were worried about Teddy. He's fine. Kids get curious about sex. No big deal."

"Egged on by Stacy, he spied on us doing something we shouldn't when he needed my attention."

"In Samoa we have lots of children running around

the village and not so much privacy. So they learn by hiding in the bushes and watching. Normal curiosity, that's all. They just better not get caught. That's how I learned. I mean they weren't going to teach me in Sunday school, though come to think of it, the first woman who took me to her bed did teach catechism at the church."

Shocked, Winnie squeezed an abandoned cup of beer too hard before dumping the contents on the ground. Watery amber liquid oozed through her fingers. "How old were you?"

"Fourteen, closer to fifteen, but big for my age. Miss Lola was a widow who enjoyed turning boys into men. Kept us from getting the village girls pregnant."

"That's child abuse!"

"The guys she took in didn't think so. I mean she wasn't one of those sad, sicko forty-year-old teachers who want to marry a teenage boy and have his babies. When she finished with us, we got a pat on the behind and her blessing. She moved on to someone else."

"No one stopped her?"

"When a place has little privacy, people pretend not to see and hear. Works for everyone. Speaking of privacy, my cottage door locks."

"We should finish here first." Winnie looked around desperately for more garbage to collect.

"We're pretty much done. The guests were a tidy bunch and used the trash barrels."

"As they should."

The family van came down the lane bearing the household maids. Brinsley met them at the kitchen door. "Dulcita to the theater to sweep up the popcorn and mop. Isabella, vacuum and wax in the den. The dining room also needs attention." They went to work promptly without stopping in the kitchen for coffee and a chat, as had been their habit.

Knox Polk parked the van and sauntered over to the couple. "Good work. Help me get a burn pile together, Adam, then you two have the rest of the day off."

Adam lugged trash bags four at a time to an open area bald of grass and dry leaves. Winnie watched as Knox set the pile afire. "Are you sure we can't help with anything else?" she asked.

"Definitely. Got it all under control." Knox gave them a half-smile, his equivalent of an ear-to-ear grin in anyone else. "The rental folks will be here soon to take down the bouncer and the rock wall. We about got it licked. You two go on and enjoy the beach. No security cameras installed out there yet."

"Cameras?" Winnie's eyes widened.

"Sure, all over the place to protect the kids. But, we haven't gotten around to wiring the beach yet." Knox prodded the fire with a poker to encourage the flames.

"Not in the daylight!" Winnie whispered to Adam.

"My place," he answered, hardly lowering his voice. He took her hand and pulled her along. Behind them, Winnie swore Knox chuckled—or maybe the noise was merely the dry crackling of the flames.

At the cottage, Adam locked the door and drew the blinds. He took Winnie into his arms beside his unmade bed and ran his hands soothingly up and down her ribs. His lips nuzzled the corner of her neck beneath the soft curl of her hair. He paused when she failed to respond.

"Beautiful Winnie, are you always so tense with your lovers? I thought we passed this point the other night on our beach."

She stiffened like the rib of a palm leaf beneath his hands. "Other lovers? I've only been with you and my ex-husband. He did say I'm a lot of work in bed."

"Not work, pleasure. Sorry. *Palagi* women have a reputation for being loose like in the movies. That does not apply to you, I know."

"*Palagi?*"

"Not from the islands, a foreigner."

"We aren't on the island now, so you are the foreigner."

"Please, lovely Winnie. Let's not argue. Lie down, and we will—"

"I can't. Not when last night is still on my mind."

"Wait! Will you come with me to Samoa when all this is sorted out?"

"I don't know. I really don't know."

She turned the lock and retreated to her own room in the big house far from the allure of Adam and the chattering of the maids downstairs.

****

Corazon called Winnie for lunch. "Barbecued pork sandwiches and white or baked beans to go with them."

"Sounds good. I'll be right down." She'd washed her hair, painted her nails with clear polish, and started reading the Harry Potter books, all to pass the time when she truly yearned to return to Adam's cottage. Nell would probably label it self-inflicted punishment.

Everyone sat around the table doctoring their sandwiches in any way they chose with a choice of sauces, *Joe Dean's Hot and Spicy* or *Connor's Mild and Sweet,* the products that supported Camp Love Letter, and toppings ranging from sliced onions and green peppers to leftover coleslaw.

Corazon passed the bean pots. "So much *puerco* to use up. Tonight we have shredded pork enchiladas with rice and tropical fruit salad."

"Sounds good to me." Joe, not a picky eater, added a few extra drops of hot sauce to his sandwich since his *Joe Dean's Hot and Spicy Barbecue Sauce* had been toned down for the commercial market.

"One pig would have been enough. I guess I was showing off." Adam slapped together two sandwiches and piled beans onto his plate. "On the other hand, you can never have too much pork."

"You paid for them. We'll freeze a bunch of it. Now, about last night, Adam says the two of you went to the palm grove for a little together time and Stacy and Teddy spied on you."

Winnie's face heated, and not only from choosing Joe's special sauce. "I let my own desires get in the way of my duty. I should not have allowed Stacy to take Teddy into the house, which she lied about. Nothing would have happened if I'd stayed with the boy as I am paid to do. If you feel you need to fire me, I understand."

"I keep telling her it was no big deal. Kids get curious. Teddy is fine being alone sometimes. He even said he didn't want a babysitter. Sorry I flashed Stacy, but she sort of had it coming. I thought we only had boys in those bushes." Adam bit into his overstuffed bun and bits of pork dropped back onto his plate.

Nell set down a much smaller version of his sandwich topped with coleslaw. "I never intended that you spend every second with Teddy when other adults are around to watch him. Heaven knows his mother left him alone with that boyfriend of hers, no prize, that one. I should be learning about his care, and I've put it off. I didn't want to get too attached if Maydell came back to claim him."

"You are being far too understanding. I failed you because I wanted to be with Adam."

"Hell, Nell and me used to sneak off all kinds of places. Once we did it in the cab of my daddy's cane tractor during the lunch break." Joe got an elbow in the ribs from his wife.

"Before we had children," Nell corrected. "Winnie, you came to help us at a moment's notice. I hope you will stay on another week. Nurse Wickersham called me at the clinic today and said her patient passed away during the Super Bowl. Too much excitement for him. She wants to stay with the family until the funeral but can be here by the weekend. Does that work for you?"

"Yes, I'd be happy to stay, and I promise I won't neglect Teddy again. He is a dear child."

"Hardly neglect. We have bigger issues such as lying, spying, and leaving Teddy to take the rap. I thought Stacy showed some adjustment when she shared Titi and befriended Teddy. Much to her disgust, Xochi tells me all the boys at the day school are in love with the girl just because of her blue eyes and blonde hair. Her teachers say she is very bright, yet still we have this situation. Joe, we need to make both children feel more a part of the family, especially since we got the DNA results back this morning. Teddy is not Joe's son, but we knew that all along, didn't we?"

"*C'est vrai!* It pays to keep your DNA on file. The tests get done faster. But, you're letting your sister's spawn off the hook?" Joe shook his head vigorously.

"No, we will administer the usual punishment to Stacy and think of something Teddy can do to make amends. Adam, can you help Joe move a heavy box from storage after lunch?"

"Sure. Pass the beans, please."

"Team meeting after school?" Joe asked his wife.

"You betcha. Winnie, any idea what is next for you? We wish you only the best."

"I believe I'm going to Samoa. I need to get away for a while." If Nell told Mintay what happened and her sister squealed to the Rev, she truly wanted to be on the other side of the world by the time he knew the story of the interlude in the palm grove.

"Our kids driving you to a foreign country?" Nell asked.

"There are just so many of them. You never know when one will interrupt—something."

"Gotta be fast," Joe said.

Adam's hand covered hers. "Good, we go to Samoa. Eat. My mother will say I don't feed you after I just roasted two pigs."

****

"Finish your snacks. Your papi says team meeting today as soon as you are done," Corazon announced.

Dean groaned. "What now? Last time we got these two." He pointed a cheese-stuffed celery stick at Teddy and Stacy seated at the far end of the table. "Tom, you think Mom is having more babies?" His eyes flicked toward the triplets.

Trinity answered. "Nope, she's all out of the people eggs Aunt Emily gave her."

"That's why the three of us, Jude and Emily are half-related to Stacy. We are all from Aunt Emily's eggs," Lorena schooled Dean.

"Don't you think I know that? This family is so embarrassing."

Tommy thumped his oldest brother on the back. "And complicated, very complicated."

"Finish, I tell you." Corazon removed the fruit and vegetable plate in case any of them thought to delay by having seconds. "Teddy, you don't eat nothing?"

The boy shifted in his chair. "No, ma'am. I'm feeling kinda sick."

Stacy, eyes down, continued to nibble on an apple wedge as the rest of the Billodeaux children began to file from the kitchen to the den where their parents waited. Teddy sighed deeply and moved his wheelchair away from the table.

"Come on, Stace. You have nothing to worry about. You're half-related." Still, she let him go first as if his chair were an armored vehicle she could hide behind in case of emergency.

Adam, Winnie, and Nell already occupied the sofa. The triplets, free of any guilt, snuggled in alongside them. Xochi and the twins claimed the loveseat while the oldest boys folded their gangling legs and sank to places on the floor. That left Stacy and Teddy exposed in the center of the room. Before they could move, Joe placed his hands on their shoulders.

"Don't go anywhere. We understand the two of you violated the privacy of Winnie and Adam last night. Team, what is our rule about that?"

Xochi helpfully repeated, "No interruptions unless there is blood or fire."

"Right! And no spying, which is worse. Maybe you two didn't know these rules because you are new here.

Now you do. This won't happen again. Apologize to Adam and Winnie."

Beneath Joe's hand, Teddy began to tremble, but Stacy offered a rather defiant reply. "Okay, I'm sorry— but I only wanted to know what Dean knows."

"Then, you come to me," Nell said sternly.

"Yes, go to the expert at explaining these kinds of things, not me. You also went off without telling anyone where you were going," Joe continued enumerating their transgressions.

"Well, if we did that you would have stopped us," Stacy replied with irrefutable logic.

"Tommy, tell Stacy what happened the time you went off on your own," Joe demanded of his second son.

Turning a shade only a redhead could produce, Tommy answered, "I got kidnapped and taken to Mexico. I had to be rescued and put a lot of people in danger."

"So, we don't do that ever," Joe continued. "One more problem—the one that galls me the most. Stacy, you deserted your teammate when he needed you. You ran away, and let him take the hit for both of you. For all this, you will muck out the stalls every day on your own for a month."

"Shit patrol!" Dean said with glee.

Nell leaned forward and popped him lightly on the head. "What did you say, son?"

"I meant manure duty. It's your favorite punishment. I knew it was coming."

"Dirty work for dirty deeds. I've always found it appropriate." Nell sat back again.

"*Merde*," said Stacy, but her elders let it pass.

"Teddy, you will help Corazon in the kitchen. You are perfectly capable of taking out the trash, cleaning and setting the table, and whatever else she wants you to do. We haven't heard your apology yet," Joe prompted.

"I'm really, really, really sorry, Miss Winnie and Mr. Adam. I swear I didn't peek."

"Apology accepted," Winnie said with her face as agonized as his.

The twins started to rise from the loveseat, but Joe waved them back. "We have another matter to discuss. The DNA test results came back. Teddy is not my biological son."

Dean let out a breath like he'd been holding it since Teddy arrived, but the boy in the wheelchair went into a panic. "Please, please don't put me out. My mama might have lied, but she told me I needed to go to a safe place. Newt said I was too much trouble to take care of and if she didn't get shut of me, he'd chop off my head and leave my body in the road like that other man who had a handicapped child."

Winnie rushed to his side and took his wrist. "Listen to me, Teddy. Don't let your blood pressure shoot up. You are safe here."

Dean's pre-adolescent shell cracked open and exposed the nice boy inside. "Who would say that to a little kid? Don't you worry, Tommy and me will be around to protect you."

"We have locks and alarms and cameras and Mr. Polk to protect us from bad men," Xochi, who still suffered from occasional nightmares about her parents' deaths, offered.

"Macho will bite his leg off!" Trinity said.

"And Titi will pee on his feet," Dean added, breaking the tension whether he intended to or not. Teddy gave them a wan smile, and the others laughed in the way of people trying to deflect terrible thoughts.

"Look, son." Joe ruffled Teddy's fine blond hair. "Today, we are making you an official member of the family. You, too, Stacy. See that big chest in front of the fireplace?"

The girl trio on the loveseat let loose with an "Ooooh!" full of the reverent superstition their mother tried so hard to quell.

"It's just a big wooden box with some blankets in it. Nothing to be afraid of," Nell hastened to say.

But, Joe's voice lowered the way it did when he told ghost stories around the fire at Camp Love Letter. "The blankets were made by an old *traiteur,* a woman who not only healed but had the sight. She could foretell the future. When Mama Nell and me married in the Church, she sent us this box with a blanket she made for each one of our children. Madame Leleux said we'd have twelve, this way, that way, all ways. We think you and Stacy are the next two members of our family. Go pick out your blanket."

Before Teddy could turn his chair, Stacy shouted, "Me, first!" She bolted across the room and threw open the lid of the scarred old chest with the reddish finish. Fishing inside, she raised a fluffy, white bundle and shook it out. "It's beautiful!"

She held up an afghan large enough to envelop her, done in a popcorn stitch with a lacy edging. Each square of the blanket centered around a crocheted pink rose.

"Ours were all pink," Jude said, talking for Annie

as usual.

"Mine had the colors of Mexico," Xochi shared.

"Want me to bring one to you?" Stacy asked Teddy.

"No, I want to pick it by myself." He wheeled close to the chest, delved as far as his arm could reach, and drew out a green blanket with a brown border decoration somewhat abstract, but on very close inspection, resembling a ring of teddy bears subtle enough not to embarrass a boy of his age. "That old lady knew I was coming."

Nell shivered as she always did when the chest came out of storage. "Joe, Adam, you can take it away now."

"Still two more in there," Joe said as he closed the lid.

"At least these two came potty-trained," his wife answered.

Chapter Seventeen

The following morning, Nell sat quietly savoring a second cup of coffee when Winnie returned from the bus stop. Winnie glanced around but no sign of the big, handsome Samoan remained in the room, not even his breakfast platter. Too bad. With the Teddy situation resolved, she thought she might take him up on yesterday's offer now that she could keep her mind on what they wanted to do.

"If you are looking for Adam, he went out with Joe and Knox to survey that big heap of trash trees they removed to make the beach. Joe wants to see if any of the wood might be useful, then they will burn the rest. He thinks snakes could get established in there if he leaves it too long. I'm all for the big burn in that case."

Winnie poured a deep mug of coffee for herself as well. "A wood pile like that would be attractive to children, especially your children. No sense in inviting broken legs either."

Nell did not disagree. "They will be at their manly stuff with chainsaws all morning. I have no appointments. Want to go to the mall?"

"Why?"

"Because you are going to Samoa, girl. This is Louisiana and the new swimwear will be on the racks by now. Wait until the end of March and you won't find a thing. Believe me, by the time I start thinking of supervising the pool at Camp Love Letter, all the good stuff is gone. You have the perfect shape for a bikini."

"Skinny, you mean."

"Lithe and sexy."

"I'd need to get a wax."

"You're on! Maybe I'll do something special to surprise Joe."

"The two of you are still so bad!"

"I hope so. You'll need sandals and backless sundresses in wild colors, too."

Winnie shook her head. "Actually, Adam told me to bring a modest white dress and a hat for church. Never expected that."

"Me neither, but we can put a modest white dress on the list. Drink up and let's go."

Within the hour, they left Lorena Ranch and the sound of chainsaws behind and headed for the city. First stop, the bikini waxing place, not all that busy on a Tuesday morning well before spring break. They hobbled out, genitals stinging, an hour later.

"Haven't done this since college. I forgot how much it hurts." Winnie slid cautiously into Nell's small car.

"Like childbirth but over much faster. Next time I skip the landing strip idea and leave more fur. Is it noon yet because I could certainly use a mojito to ease the pain."

"Not for two more hours."

"Then on to bikini shopping—for you, not me. I might have gotten my nip and tuck but nothing quite erases the signs of multiple pregnancies."

For a moment, Winnie lost the joy of the day. "I

thought I'd have a baby by now."

"You have plenty of time for that. Right now, you have a piece of Samoan beefcake to enjoy. Live for today!" Taking some of her pubic discomfort out on the other drivers by laying on the horn, Nell wove in and out of traffic hastening their arrival at the mall.

Putting aside the always terrifying prospect of searching for a bathing suit, they hit the big department stores in search of the modest white dress and found one at Macy's. The sleeves were sheer but the neckline high, and the slim skirt fell below the knees. Its fit complemented Winnie's figure without clinging. Nell brought her a wide-brimmed straw hat with a jaunty sunflower in the brim to top it off.

Winnie regarded herself in the three-way mirror. "I look like my nana heading for all day services at the Baptist church."

"Then I would say your nana is an attractive and well-turned out woman. Shoes, you need white shoes."

"Adam says they have a rainy season and a not-so-rainy season, but it is hot pretty much year round that close to the equator." Nell led the charge to the shoe department where they decided on strappy sandals considering the climate in Samoa.

Coming out of Macy's they both decided it prudent to try on bathing suits before getting any lunch. "I always have the best luck with the specialty shop that carries swimwear and ballet gear. Yeah, I know. Odd combination, but they are still in business."

Nell led Winnie to the small store where very reluctantly the divorced nurse tried on the extremely skimpy garments Nell kept thrusting into the dressing room. "You have to get the strapless one in the wild, tropical print and maybe the aqua with the tie around the neck in case you do intend to go swimming. Here's a cover-up that matches both."

Still stunned by the whirlwind that was Nell when she wanted to get something done, Winnie checked out her purchases while her volunteer shopping advisor tried on a retro red and white polka-dotted one-piece perfect for family fun that suited her small, perky figure. Nell joined her shortly with the new suit draped over her arm.

"Really didn't need a wax for this one, but I will think of you and Adam together on a tropical beach every time my crotch itches as it grows out."

"Please don't!"

Nell simply laughed and gathered their many bags. "Food court! I am starved."

Gabbing and giggling about their day, they careened around the corner where the maternity shop sat. "That's where I got some of my tent-sized clothes when I carried the triplets," Nell pointed out. She slowed just enough to misjudge the exit of a shopper from the store and plowed right into the pregnant woman.

"Oh, I'm so sorry! Did I hurt you? Maydell?"

Teddy's mother clutched a large, stuffed bag over her stomach. She wore one of the shapeless flowered dresses that always reminded Nell of Depression-era flour sack garb, but Maydell did have her running shoes on and run she did.

"Winnie, can you stop her?"

Winnie tossed her packages to the ground. Longer-legged than either of the other women she did manage to grab the woman's arm and bring Maydell to a stop before she managed to flee into the crowded maze of the food court. "I think we both want to talk to you about abandoning Teddy."

"Please let me go. I did what was best for my son, I swear. Newt's coming back for me in the truck in half an hour. I gotta be outside waiting." Maydell's stringy blonde hair lashed around her thin face as she tried to escape again.

Nell, awash in the morning's shopping finds, loosened a finger and pointed to an empty table with three chairs. "Then we have half an hour to talk. Sit."

Winnie escorted her to the chair, knowing Maydell would bolt if she let go. They hemmed her in on either side. As she sat, Teddy's mom continued to hold her maternity wear sack over her belly as if it were a life preserver.

Nell eyed her suspiciously. "Are you expecting, Maydell? Is that why you deserted Teddy?"

Maydell hung her head and like Teddy, her long bangs fell across her blue eyes. "Yes'm. Only this one is Newt's, and it ain't got nothing wrong with it. I had the tests done at the University Medical Center to be sure. Newt has a job offer in North Dakota. He says he will take care of his own kid, but not Teddy. He said if I didn't dump my son, he'd kill him. We been staying in Lafayette ever since I left my boy with you, Miss Nell. I knew you and your husband would be good to him because of that camp you run."

"You lied about Joe being his dad."

"I couldn't think of no other way to get you to take him. A child like Teddy is a fearsome responsibility. I thought it would give you some time to get to know my boy, what a sweet child he is, while you checked. I can't take him back."

"He is sweet," Winnie felt compelled to say. "How could you? Leave that jerk and take your son back."

"With another 'un on the way and no means to support either kid?" Maydell shook her head. "No, Newt is being real good to me now, careful how he treats me. He give me a debit card to get nice clothes for when I really start showing."

Nell took Maydell's very cold hand. "We want to keep Teddy, but the process would be easier if you relinquish him for a formal adoption. I can give you the name of our lawyer here in Lafayette. If you go to him and have him draw up papers giving up your rights to the child, we can proceed from there. As soon as you leave here, I'll call him and say to expect you."

"I won't have to see Teddy, will I? 'Cause I can't look into his pretty blue eyes and leave him again." Maydell sniveled into a paper napkin left on the table.

"No." Nell took another napkin and wrote out the name and address of the lawyer. "Ask Newt to take you over there this afternoon. He should agree since he wants to be rid of Teddy. And if he doesn't, tell him we'll hunt him down and have him arrested for child abuse."

"Newt didn't mean to hurt him. All that about killing my boy is just talk—most likely."

"I saw the bruises. We know what he said about harming Teddy. You believed it enough to want your son in a safe place." Winnie twisted a third napkin in her hands. "I will testify against this man if I must."

"All right. I'll get him to take me to the lawyer. Let me go now, please, before he comes."

At Nell's nod, Winnie removed her hand from

Maydell's arm and pushed aside some of the shopping bags to make an escape route. The woman took off like a squirrel with Macho on its tail. She went out the door of the food court and frantically waved the paper napkin holding the lawyer's address. An old, dark blue pickup truck with deep scratches on its side stopped and enveloped her like a dumpster accepting trash.

"You let her go just like that," Winnie marveled.

"I've seen cases like this before. No education, little income, far from any family, she'll stay with her abuser. You save the ones you can, Winnie, and in this case, that is Teddy. I could really use a drink now. One mojito and some lunch, then we'll both go back and meet Teddy when he comes home from school." Nell contacted the lawyer and asked him as a special favor to Joe Dean Billodeaux to draw up the proper papers immediately. She promised some game tickets for next season as an added incentive.

"Sorry to ruin our shopping trip, Winnie."

"Teddy is worth ten shopping trips, and compared to my ex and this Newt, Adam is worth that and a painful bikini wax."

Chapter Eighteen

Neither woman told Teddy of their meeting with his mother. In private, Nell discussed the adoption with Joe. Winnie refused to run off to a tropical island with Adam until she met and briefed Nurse Wickersham on her patient, but by Saturday she'd packed her bags and stowed them in his SUV. She waited with all the Billodeaux family for the arrival of her replacement who came within minutes of her stated time.

A former nun, Nurse Wickersham descended with great dignity from the airport limo. Very old school, she wore a starched white uniform, cap, stockings, and shoes—no friendly, fluffy kitty and cute puppy scrubs for her. Her short gray hair combed back severely, her thin lips and stern eyes did nothing to comfort Teddy who clung to Winnie's hand. "Please don't go, Miss Winnie. She scares me."

Trinity, who had knocked his round black glasses askew waving frantically at the new arrival, said, "Don't be afraid. Nurse Shammy loves little kids. She kept us three alive after we got born."

Nell gave them a nod, and the triplets raced over to the limo to hug Shammy's legs before the driver could unload her baggage. She crouched to take them into a strong-armed embrace and kissed each small head. Looking up at the rest of the family, her face changed entirely with the addition of a rather horse-toothed smile. "So glad you are all well. This must be my new patient. I can see you have outgrown your wheelchair young man and need a new one. That will be our first concern."

"This one is fine, ma'am," Teddy murmured, wheeling back a little and very nearly crushing Winnie's toes.

"Nonsense! The next will be even better."

Nell hugged the woman who had stood by her in childbirth and afterwards when they brought the triplets home. "I kept telling you that you didn't need to leave when the children started kindergarten. Good to have you back again."

"I would not have you pay for an unneeded service, but I believe Teddy and Camp Love Letter might keep me busy until retirement." Her sharp eyes scanned the rest of the group and stopped on Brinsley. "Another new addition to the family besides your niece and Teddy?"

"Yes, Clive Brinsley, our butler, at least temporarily."

"Indeed, a person should not stay when his presence is of no use. Shall I carry your bags to your room, Nurse Wickersham?" Without waiting for her permission, Brinsley moved forward to grasp the single black suitcase and small carry-on so vastly different from Stacy's luggage. Striding briskly, he disappeared into the house, bag and baggage.

"He is staying across the hall from you, but I don't think that will be any problem," Nell informed the nurse.

"I should say not!" Nurse Wickersham exclaimed

as if she and Brinsley might be accused of trysting.

"He and Corazon have prepared a lovely tea to welcome you back."

"A tea?"

"We will have coffee, too. Let's go inside, everyone."

Only Stacy in a yellow and lace party dress and T-strapped shoes appeared entirely comfortable at the tea party. At least clean and tidy if not particularly mannerly, the rest of the children dug into the crustless cream cheese sandwiches, currant scones, and Pommier's petit fours. Adam, joining Winnie on the loveseat, overwhelmed the delicate teacup from the rarely used set of good china. Joe looked as if he wished he held a beer. Teddy stayed right beside Winnie like he'd never agree to let her go no matter how hard Nurse Shammy tried to coax him to talk to her from her seat in one of the recliners.

In the end, Adam broke up the party. "We should get going soon if we want to make to New Orleans before too late."

"I need to review Teddy's file with Nurse Wickersham first. Perhaps, we could look over it in the dining room."

Nurse Wickersham and Winnie adjourned to the room holding a lengthy mahogany table that seated fourteen and was rarely used. They covered only a tiny part of its shining surface to lay out Teddy's records and study his routine and exercise schedule. Seeing the younger woman's concern, Shammy patted her hand. "I will give him the best of care."

"I know. It's just that his mother abandoned him, and now I am going, too."

"Visit when you can. Write and do that Skype thing on the computer. However, I believe you and Adam have a future to explore. I could feel the vibes." The comment seemed so strange coming from the narrow lips of the ex-nun that Winnie smiled.

"Yes, you may smile, but living with Mr. and Mrs. Billodeaux came as a great revelation in sexual matters. I am now more attuned to such things."

"All I ask is that you stay attuned to Teddy. He needs stability."

"That I can provide."

Adam knocked. Jingling his car keys, he said, "Ready?"

"As I will ever be." Winnie said good-bye to the family and especially Teddy, promising him postcards and souvenirs from Samoa.

"But who is going to put me in the tub if Adam goes with you?" he asked, breaking her heart a little.

Brinsley stepped up. "I would be happy to provide that service and assist with any of your other needs, Master Teddy."

"See, you have plenty of people to help, and a new family. Don't be afraid anymore, Teddy. I'm going to a foreign place, and I need to be brave, too. When I get back, we'll have a long visit."

Adam edged her toward his car as if she might try to escape. She waved all the way down the drive until they turned out of the gate and hit the road to New Orleans to catch their flight to the tropics.

"You want to stop by your sister's place before we leave?" he asked as they approached the highway.

"No, we talked last night, and I'd just as soon not get a lecture from my brother-in-law."

"Me, neither. Samoa, here we come."

****

Their first stop was neither the airport nor a tropical isle, but Adam's city condo where he wanted to pick up a few things for the trip. Intending only to stay at Lorena Ranch long enough to get Joe's advice and delay going home for a while until his anger abated, he'd remained to court Winnie. That had gone both better and worse than he'd wanted. With all those kids around, he might as well be back in his home village. While he admired her devotion to Teddy, he'd definitely taken second place to the likeable boy. They needed to be alone—but that wouldn't happen tonight.

Adam turned the key only to find the door unlocked, and he should have expected that. Burdened with their bags, he nodded for Winnie to enter. A greeting of *talofa* came from came from three huge men who occupied the sofa and a good part of the floor. Browner than Adam, they blended with the décor of cocoa and cream accented by wallpaper patterned in palm leaves. A large, glass-topped coffee table supported by thick bamboo legs held giant buckets of Popeye's Fried Chicken, one mostly down to the bones. One visitor scooped into a container of dirty rice dressing with his fingers and raised the glob to his mouth. All of them barely took their eyes from a soccer match playing on the immense TV.

"The fridge is empty, cousin. We had to go get some food. You eat yet?"

"I had British high tea earlier."

This brought an outburst of uproarious laughter from the gigantic trio and a number of comments in Samoan. They offered him a box of biscuits and a chicken leg.

"Later, maybe. Guys, this is Winnie Green. She'll be staying in my room tonight. Tomorrow, we leave for Tutuila. Winnie, my cousin, Tapu, and his friends who are visiting from the islands."

After much elbowing and cordial smiles, they offered her a beer. Winnie passed on that. Tapu paused in his meal and asked, "You leaving your car in the garage?"

"No, taking it to the airport." Tapu's broad face showed its disappointment at Adam's statement.

"Come on, Winnie. Let's get you settled for the night. Here, for groceries." He left Tapu with a wad of money from his wallet that erased some of his cousin's unhappiness.

They passed three disheveled bedrooms before coming to Adam's. Tasteful *saipo* cloth hangings decorated walls that echoed their rich earth tones and repeated again in the spread on the vast king-sized bed. Other than a dresser, a chair, and a wall-mounted flat screen TV, the room had little other furniture. A large closet stood open revealing gaps in its orderly collection of clothing. Adam withdrew a large suitcase from the back of it and started transferring his belongings from the smaller bag he'd taken to Joe's ranch.

"You stay in here tonight. I'll sleep on the sofa. No one will bother you."

"But, it's your place. You shouldn't have to do that. Stay with me," Winnie said from her perch on the single chair.

"No, it is better we stay apart for now. Word gets around. I am sure Tapu will tell everyone I am too cheap to let him use my car, but he knows nothing about driving in a city and will wreck it or kill all three of them." He regarded his wardrobe choices. "At least, they didn't take my white suit." Carefully, he folded this item, still in its dry cleaning bag into his suitcase.

"Tapu steals from you?"

"No, he is my cousin, so he cannot steal from me. He just takes what he needs or tickles his fancy. He would give me the shirt off his back, too, only I have lots more shirts." Adam added several of these in tropical prints to his suitcase along with some khaki shorts and tossed in a large pair of leather sandals. "What the hell, I'll buy whatever else I need when we get to Pago. I don't need much in the village but a couple of lava-lavas." He snapped the case closed and removed it from the bed.

"How long has Tapu been staying here?"

"About a month. He is looking for work. His friends showed up around the time I left for Joe's place."

"How long will they stay?"

"No telling. Probably until they run out of food again. It is expected I will offer hospitality to anyone who comes to my door from the village."

"Different strokes for different folks, I guess."

"Ah, lovely Winnie. You don't know the half of it. Sleep well and prepare for some culture shock."

****

By the time Winnie woke and showered in a stall with so many nozzles it gave a therapeutic massage as well as a bath, the aroma of coffee brewing drew her from her room to the kitchen. Someone had gone out already and brought back a grocery bag full of warm beignets pillowed in powdered sugar. Eating two with her java, she tried not to keep count of how many Tapu and his buddies put away. She placed two more on her plate to save them for Adam after he bathed. He gave her a thankful grin as he downed them and a cup of coffee.

"We can get more at the airport. Here we go."

They left New Orleans just as the bells tolled for Mass at St. Louis Cathedral and arrived for their flight out of Louis Armstrong International Airport to Los Angeles in plenty of time. After descending through the smog layer in California, they switched to a night flight bound for Hawaii and a layover for a few days to see the sights.

Adam appreciated her bikinis on the beach and the presence of Winnie in his bed. With his lovemaking always relaxed and unhurried, she unfurled like the plumeria blossoms at night.

"Did we stop here to get me acclimated to the tropics?" she asked as she lay in his arms and traced a finger around tattoo circling his navel.

"Hawaii will not prepare you for Samoa, lovely Winnie."

"You make your homeland sound like the ends of the earth."

"Pretty close to it."

Another lengthy night flight finally brought them to Pago Pago, island of Tutuila, American Samoa.

Chapter Nineteen

"Not quite what I expected," Winnie said as they traveled from the airport to their hotel. "Pago Pago seems to be smaller than Chapelle with twice the number of fast food joints and even more litter."

"Actually, a bunch of separate villages strung out around the harbor make up the place, but you'll like where we are staying. First though, you should see our most famous landmark." Adam whispered a direction to their driver who gave a short laugh.

Instead of turning toward some picturesque destination, they skimmed the edge of the deep blue harbor and passed a grim row of gray warehouses. The atmosphere grew increasingly thick with fishy odor until even Winnie, trying to be polite by ignoring the stench, wrinkled her nose. "What is that?"

"Tuna cannery. If you don't work for the government, you probably work here. And there he is, Charlie the Tuna in person." The large, blue statue complete with natty red beret and hipster glasses rose up in front of the packing plant and offered them a smiling welcome.

"Really, this is the best you can do?"

"Joking. To Le Falepule, driver."

Their taxi swung around and outraced the stink to enter a steep, secluded drive outside the town but not all that far from the airport. Greeted by genial hosts, they were shown to a room decorated very similarly to Adam's in New Orleans. Within a half hour, they sat on the terrace and sipped drinks from the honor bar while taking in a breathtaking view of the sea.

"More what I expected," Winnie confessed. "Somehow though, I did think your family would meet us at the airport. Shouldn't you call them, and let them know we are here?"

"They know. Coconut radio. The second we set foot in the airport, some cousin or auntie who works there contacted the village you can be certain. Before we left Louisiana, I let my parents know I wanted to show you some of the island before they gave you the full treatment."

Winnie took a sip from a tall, cool glass whose contents offset some of the heat and humidity playing havoc with her hair. Louisiana in overdrive, she thought. "Exactly what is the full treatment?"

"Oh, you know, the *'Ava* ceremony, a feast, and a *fiafia*. The last is an evening of singing, dancing, and entertainment. I understand we are expected to participate fully." He recognized her immediate anxiety by the crease forming between her brows. "No worries, lovely Winnie. Be gracious, have fun. No one will laugh at you."

"This *'Ava* ceremony—what is that all about?"

"In the States, they call the stuff kava. You've heard of it? Anyhow, you accept a ceremonial drink of this mildly narcotic beverage, no worse than what you have in your hand right now, but it doesn't taste as good. Just choke it all down and be a good sport. It's an honor, okay. I'll coach you about what to say and do.

Now forget about it until the time arrives."

"When will that be?"

"When we get there and when they are ready."

Pure Adam, nothing seemed to bother him deeply. She envied him with his easygoing style and laidback ways. After they finished their drinks, he summoned transportation again and directed the driver to a car dealership where he wrote a check for a bright yellow, open-sided Jeep just like that with no holdups for a credit background search. Judging by all the cheerful greetings and hearty handshakes, everyone on this rather small island recognized Adam and knew he was good for whatever costs he incurred. He accepted the keys and drove them directly to one of the strip malls where lava-lava shops flourished like tropical flowers.

Adam held up lengths of cloth in solid colors, stripes, or floral-patterned for her approval and added those she gave the nod to a steadily growing pile on the counter. "You need something to wear in the village and to cover up those bikinis of yours. That semi-transparent thing you had on in Hawaii won't work here."

Puzzled, Winnie asked, "Why?"

"Not modest enough."

"But a wraparound piece of cloth is?"

"Can't see through it, right? You need some *puletasi,* too, for dressing up a little more. It is the Samoan missionary answer to the muumuu and a helluva lot more attractive."

"Not buying anything for yourself?"

He glanced at the heap of cloth strips. "I did."

Their overjoyed clerk showed them to a room lined with the traditional Samoan dresses and began pulling out samples of the two-piece outfits with long skirts and full bodices possessing short sleeves and high necklines. This time Adam gave her little choice. He selected one in gleaming gold with black, brown, and orange designs on the top and bordering the skirt, another of deep green festooned with blue flowers, and the last pure white scattered with red blossoms.

Winnie was about to announce she could pick her own clothing when Adam cut her off by saying, "Golden like your skin, green as your eyes—and I just like the last one."

Making one final stand for female independence, she dug out her credit card and prayed the dresses wouldn't put her over the limit. Adam handed it back. "These are gifts, and to refuse a gift is a grave insult."

"Well, I wouldn't want to insult you."

He urged her to wear one of the outfits to dinner. She rather foolishly chose the white garment because the others seemed too formal. Pleased, Adam robbed the shrubbery at their hotel of a matching red flower for her hair and tucked it in beside an ear. If she'd known he would guide her to a Korean restaurant on a backstreet where the spicy food made her nose run, and she'd dribble red pepper sauce down the front of her beautiful new gown, she would have insisted on wearing one of her sundresses. The tears she produced weren't only because of the fiery kim-chi.

Adam wiped them away with the edge of his thumbs. "The hotel will launder the dress. All is well."

She spent the night proving to him that she was not as clumsy in bed, a gift from her he did not refuse as she lowered herself over him, long legs astraddle, and rocked him to completion as he fondled her upturned breasts.

****

At breakfast, Winnie devoured half a papaya and several of the sinful buns dripping in coconut cream while Adam put away corned beef hash with eggs and a side of Spam. "You never worry about cholesterol?"

"Nope. Today we tour the western side of the island. Bring a bathing suit and a lava-lava, but wear a dress so we can go into the cathedral without upsetting anyone."

He, evidently, was ready to go in a bright red shirt, a mid-calf length lava-lava sprayed with crimson flowers, and his heavy leather sandals. She followed his directions and soon they tooled along in the Jeep through the suburbs and out into the wilder part of the island. Adam stopped before a statue of the Virgin Mary. She expected to see the church sitting beyond it, but instead a mound with star-like projections rose nearby. Adam led her to a platform overlooking its levels.

"The *Tia Seu Lupe* where they say the ancient chiefs competed in pigeon catching contests. Maybe so, but I feel the power of old Polynesia here, the *mana* of its first gods, defeated but not entirely gone. When you do the *'Ava* ceremony, it is important that you spill some of your drink on the ground for the spirits that still linger here and say, '*Manuia lava*' before swallowing it down in one long gulp. Got that?"

Winnie nodded and repeated the words with great solemnity. "What am I saying, a prayer to the old ones?"

"No, basically 'bottoms up' would be a good translation."

"Oh, you!" She playfully slapped his arm.

"Doesn't matter. You still have to say the words."

They moved on to the cathedral with its impressive dome and bell tower. Winnie found herself charmed by the stained-glass portrait of the Madonna wearing a *puletasi* and a Christ over the altar offering two devoted Samoan worshipers an *'Ava* bowl. "See, even Jesus drinks *'ava*, Winnie," Adam quipped. Indeed, the baby Jesus in the cathedral's crèche scene lay in an *'ava* bowl instead of a manger. Winnie stocked up on postcards she knew the Rev would love.

Next up, another ancient site atop a cliff. Adam narrated the story. "In a time of great hunger, a village cast out an old woman because they did not want to feed her. Her granddaughter led her to this place and together, they threw themselves into the sea. When the family realized their fate, they came here greatly ashamed and cried out for the women. A turtle and a shark were summoned by their calls. They believed their kin had been transformed and saved in that way."

Winnie waited for a punch line. None came from Adam. She gazed down at the rugged lava walls. A rough surf forced its way into a blow hole and sent up a spray of salt water. "It is a sacred spot," he finally said.

"We believe what we must to live with ourselves," she answered.

"And now a special place where we can have a picnic and swim."

The special place appeared a little doubtful as they stopped at a cluster of convenience stores to get bottled drinks and snacks before turning down a side road that eventually led past a pig farm. Adam parked the Jeep at the start of a vague trail. "Ignore the smell," he ordered.

"Change into your swimming suit and lava-lava here."

"Right here with a little, pink house sitting over there?"

"No one is around. Go to the other side of the Jeep if you want."

She did want. Getting into the bikini in a hurry, no problem. Knotting a lava-lava with no practice, a big one. Adam came around the vehicle and wrapped her like a precious gift all tied up with a pretty knot of cloth. He grabbed the picnic basket.

They started down a narrow trail, very rough underfoot, and eventually veered toward a stream. Wading that, they continued up a steep slope and came to the head of a waterfall plunging through the rainforest to a pool below. "*Nu'uuli* Falls," Adam said, spreading his arms as if giving her the place for herself alone.

Like a picture postcard of a tropical paradise, the water tumbled over lava rocks to its destination. They made their way to the basin of cool water and ate a lunch of juicy mangoes and little skewers of chicken and vegetables the hotel prepared for them. Winnie sipped her water, and Adam chugged a large orange drink. He offered her some of his potato chips purchased at the convenience store, but she shook her head. Chips had no place in her idea of paradise, but Adam did.

"Let's swim!" She unknotted her lava-lava and turned to the pool. Before she could dive, Adam hooked a thumb in the back of the strapless bikini and released the catch. Her breasts tumbled out and the tips puckered under the fine spray of mist from the falls. She turned toward him. "Adam! What if someone sees?"

He threw furtive glances right and left. "No missionaries, no tourists. We are alone." Without hesitation, he peeled off his shirt and untied his lava-lava. As she might have expected, he wore nothing beneath. "Step out of that bottom and get in the water, Winnie."

She raced to obey. He followed, plunging in with a great splash. They swam and splashed and cavorted in refreshing water. Winnie convinced him to spread his legs to allow her to dive through the tunnel he made with his great thighs. She tickled his genitals as she passed and surfaced directly in front of him.

"See what you've done, Miss Winnie Green." Adam pointed to a burgeoning erection.

"I plan to do more!"

She scissored her legs around his waist and laid back, exposing her breasts to his touch and letting the water support her. Slowly Adam spun her in a circle. The rush of the falls flashed by, its sound muffled by the walls of greenery. Curious colorful birds in the bush cocked their heads, viewing the performance. Far above, the smallest patch of sky watched them like single blue eye. Look at me, Winnie Green, living a scene from a romance novel, she wanted to shout.

Adam drew her up against his chest. She locked her arms around his thick neck and lowered herself onto him with her legs still grasping his waist. He supported her hips with his broad hands as they made love slowly at first. Then, he moved her hard and fast against him, getting just the right angle that sent her over the edge into her private paradise where he joined her very shortly.

Cradling Winnie against him, Adam knelt in the

warm water still joined to her. She ran her fingers though his wild hair and rested her head on his shoulder. "I think you could easily pass for one of the old gods with your fine brown body and excellent tattoos," she murmured.

"Maybe Fatu and 'Ele'ele, our Adam and Eve. Their names mean heart and earth."

She placed one hand over the expanse of his chest. "Yes, I can feel yours beating beneath my hand. If I never lived another day, this one moment would be enough."

He kissed her lips. "You will have many more like this."

She gathered him close and shook her head against his flesh. "Fantasies never last."

"Who said this is a fantasy?" With that, he brought his hands to her waist and propelled her through the air, dunking her deep. She came up sputtering with her soaked hair curling over her face. She raked it back and said, "Well, not anymore."

Adam looked up to where the sky's blue eye had closed a gray lid. "We have to move. The rain is coming in, and we don't want to get caught before we cross the creek again."

He shoved his shirt and her bikini into the picnic basket and wrapped them both in their lava-lavas for the trek out. They were within sight of the Jeep when the sky began to weep its own waterfall of tears. The drive to Pago Pago with the road made treacherous by the downpour, wandering pigs, and village dogs who did not mind the rain, became part of her adventure. Back in the city, they parked haphazardly near a building proclaiming itself the Pago Pago Yacht Club.

"Let's go in and get a drink before dinner," Adam suggested.

Winnie disagreed vehemently. "Not with my hair all curly and damp and not a hot comb in sight, not to mention wearing a wet lava-lava."

"You look great." He retrieved his wrinkled red shirt from the picnic basket, put it on, tucked it in. "But if it bothers you, take your dress inside and change in the ladies room."

She did that, managing to finger-comb her hair into some semblance of order. By the time she joined Adam on the covered deck, he offered her a mai tai topped with a cocky paper umbrella to sip. They had the place to themselves, but Winnie glanced around cautiously. "You sure we aren't going to be thrown out of here—because back in the States these kinds of places are members only."

"I'm a member."

"Call me impressed. You own a yacht?"

"Nope, but my father is a fisherman, and I paddle a mean war canoe. I only come here to have a drink and watch the clouds pile up against Rainmaker Mountain, wettest harbor in the world." He took a pull on his bottle of Vailima, the local brew, and watched the rain pock the surface of the bay.

"You haven't said much about your family." Winnie removed the paper umbrella from her drink and twirled it between her fingers. "Your dad is a commercial fisherman?"

"Nothing much to say about them. My father fishes to feed the village, but doesn't sell much of his catch. Commercial ambition is not highly thought of in our culture. My mother is big in the women's society. I am their only child. She said having a ten-pound baby broke her in two. She didn't want any more kids. Sometimes, I wonder if I was conceived under the palms and my parents were forced to marry."

"I begin to understand. This love under the palms is illicit sex?"

Adam grinned. "The very best kind of sex. My mother says my father is a good and simple man who never raises his hand against her. They are happy. They live the *fa'a Samoa*, the traditional ways. When I am done playing football, they want me to come back here and live as they do. Maybe become a *matai*, a chief, the big man in the village. My parents found the gifts and the money to offer the *tufuga* for doing my tattoos because a true *matai* should have them. The tattoos remind me I am Samoan." Much of the joy drained from Adam's face.

"Is this what you want?"

"I feel I will disappoint my entire *'aiga*, my extended family, if I don't."

Winnie took a long swallow of her sweet drink and let it slide down her throat before she said, "Been there, done that. Two college professor parents saying study hard, make something of yourself, marry a man with a future, don't fail your race. So I marry Douglas Hopper, doctor to be, when I am only nineteen. I put his future ahead of mine and become a nurse rather than a doctor. A bunch of years later, my nursing degree is all I have to show for my time. And you know what? I like being a nurse, especially when I can help children like Teddy. Maybe I don't want to be a doctor."

She made a fist and pounded it on the small table that held their beverages. "Now it's Winnie Green time, and I will do what I want. Coming here with you finally made me realize I'm taking a great big step just for myself."

"A very *palagi* attitude, Winnie Green. Foreign ways don't go over so well here—unless it is fast food and big cars. Speaking of which, I could go for some Mexican food tonight. How about you?"

She knew he had turned their first really serious conversation into a dinner invitation, but didn't press. "Sure, Mexican is fine with me."

Chapter Twenty

After an evening spent in a cantina right in the middle of Pago Pago where the burritos arrived Samoan-sized, putting American super-sized to shame, and far too many Vailimas were consumed, Winnie did not particularly want to get up for another road trip in the morning. The place had offered music and dancing as well, and man after man approached Adam and quaintly asked for a turn with his lady. Always feeling awkward and inhibited, she wasn't fond of dancing, but she stayed out on the floor all night. None of her escorts were Adam. He held court at the bar and paid for as many rounds as were bought for him.

Winnie learned flowery speech from her partners came with the whole package. Maybe they intended to set her up like some latter day Sadie Thompson ditched on a foreign shore and earning a living on her back. None became obnoxious, just rather persistent, until Adam claimed her at the end of the evening. Since he could have thrown most of them into the street with ease, her admirers gave way easily and cheerfully.

How Adam faced his usual huge, greasy breakfast, she could not fathom. She stuck to pineapple juice, tried to down a poached egg on toast and lots and lots of the hotel's rather weak coffee. Despite her queasy stomach, he took the Jeep up the side the Rainmaker Mountain and through the pass into the National Park of American Samoa, acres and acres of unspoiled tropical rainforest teeming with birds, island wildlife, and dramatic vistas. Almost offhand, Adam pointed out a directional sign partly obscured by vines and marking a rutted dirt road that ran down the mountain to the coast. "The way to my village."

"Shouldn't we stop there?"

"Not today. I know a spot where we can meet the guardians of the forest."

"You going to tell me who they are?"

"I'd rather surprise you."

In deference to the heat and water-laden air, Winnie wore one of the lava-lavas and her sandals. Giving up on retaining her usual smooth curls, she drew her hair back with a band. When Adam parked and led her down an ill-defined path into the forest, she traipsed along enchanted by the flitting, colorful birds and huge trees draped with orchids. They came to a clearing with a dead tree in its middle. The atmosphere changed from steamy and dew-laden to slightly foul. Adam pointed to the strange brown fruit hanging from the branches.

"Quiet now. There they are—the guardians of the forest, our flying foxes."

Winnie raised her green eyes and peered more closely at the lumpish sacks. Suddenly, she understood what she saw. "Bats! Great big, blood-sucking bats. Oh, God! Oh, God!"

Covering her hair with her hands, she turned heel and charged back into the rainforest. Unfortunately, her shrieks disturbed the flying foxes. They spread leathery wings and crashed into the foliage after her. She ran faster. Adam called, "No, no! They eat fruit. They pollinate flowers and hurt no one."

She thought the path lay straight ahead, that the road and the safety of the Jeep would appear at any second, but she did not remember passing such a large banyan tree or the clump of spiky scarlet flowers. In the distance, she heard Adam shouting for her, but no miraculous path opened at her feet to show her the way back to the glade. Only trees and more trees, ropy vines and thickets of tall ferns no matter which way she turned.

Something landed in the wide canopy of the banyan with its many branched roots digging into the jungle soil. One of the horrid, fox-faced bats stared at her. Not wanting it to attack, Winnie stood perfectly still. Another landed nearby. Both flopped upside down and toed their way among foliage probably searching for the banyan's fig-like fruit. Adam's words finally registered. They eat fruit and hurt no one. Not finding a meal and having been disturbed from their rest earlier, the bats dropped from the limb and began a leisurely flight back to their roost, she guessed. Adam called again from the direction the bats took. She followed and broke into the clearing on its opposite side. Somehow, she'd circled round dodging trees instead of running straight.

More bats returned to the dead tree slicked white with their droppings. Adam gestured to her to cross the glade. She did so quietly, giving the roost a wide berth. He folded her carefully in his arms and kissed her gently on the forehead. She whispered, "Can we go to the Jeep now?"

He nodded and found the faint path to the road. Once back at the car, he said, "The guardians of the forest are said to help the lost. Now I know that is true. They brought you back to me. I thought I'd have to organize a search party."

"Sorry for being so silly. Bats freak me out."

"I guess they do most people, but here they are revered. I think you've had enough of the rainforest for today. How about some beach time? We can swing over to Alega and get some swimming in before the afternoon storms arrive. Wear the suit that covers you a little more and bring a fresh lava-lava. This one is done for." He ran a finger up a long rent in the side of her garment and tickled her thigh.

She had no memory of having ripped it in her panicked flight. "Open space, sunlight, and sea sound great to me about now. I'm with you."

"You certainly are."

****

Crowded among Samoans enjoying a day at the beach, Winnie earned the compliments of many men eyeballing her attire. Most of the sea bathers went into the water wearing long shorts or lava-lavas. Adam rolled his up into a sort of loincloth that suited him well, though he glared at two rare rainy-season tourists who attempted to take a picture of his tattoos without asking permission. Before he could knock the camera from the man's hand, the fellow recognized him through the viewfinder and asked for an autograph instead.

Holding out a travel guide, the guy said, "Would ya make that out to Charlie and Livy Diggs?" His bleached blonde, highly-tanned wife fished a pen from an overstuffed beach bag.

The fan with the bald head and loud Bermuda

shorts chattered on and on about his life and his luck in finding the famous Samoan Sinner right here on this beach as Adam signed. His wife, whose boob job bulged out of a skimpier top than Winnie's, and whose buxom bottom should never be seen in a bikini, couldn't take her eyes off of Adam's body art or wet loincloth.

The urge rose in Winnie to push Livy into the sand, but she practiced complete restraint when the couple asked her to take a picture of them on either side of the big man, the wife clinging to his bicep and the husband slinging a sun-burned arm over Adam's shoulder. Oh, how she wanted to pitch the camera into the surf when Livy kept her hand on Adam's arm long after she snapped the shot. Jealousy she had no right to surged through her system. Last night she'd danced with a dozen men, and Adam hadn't cared at all. Keep it light, Winnie. Keep it light like Adam did. The fortuitous arrival of the afternoon storm making its way across the bay prevented her from doing anything equally as stupid as fleeing from bats.

The blonde's husband thumbed his travel guide. "Hey, Tisa's Barefoot Bar is right over there. Let me buy you a drink and a burger while we wait out the rain. What do you say?"

To Winnie's dismay, Adam said yes. As the first drops fell, Charlie Diggs of Paramus, New Jersey, covered his bald head with the travel guide and headed for the bar. Livy grabbed the bulging beach bag and rammed a wide straw hat over her bleached extravaganza of hair. She tripped over something invisible in the sand, seized Adam's arm for support, and did not remove her red-polished claws until they reached their destination. Winnie trudged along behind with their beach blankets wrapped around her shoulders and their dry lava-lavas bunched under her arms. She and Adam changed in the restrooms. Livy drew a long, gold patterned caftan from her bag and considered herself dressed. Charlie scooted back to their rental car to put on a shirt and get an umbrella, but at last they were all settled and awaiting beverages and food.

Somehow, Livy managed to make Adam the center of a Diggs' sandwich with Winnie on the outside of the group like the dill pickle no one wanted. Considering last night's overindulgence, Winnie chose the local *koko* over alcohol and indulged in its chocolate deliciousness while the others had beer. That and the sound of the rain soothed her despite Charlie's endless conversation.

"I met my jewel at a casino in Atlantic City. Imagine the luck. I've always been a lucky guy," the tourist said.

"Sometimes, we are meant to be in certain places at certain times to meet someone," Adam remarked. He smiled at Winnie over the top of Livy's big hair.

"Me, I own a bowling alley. Turns out Liv loves to bowl and gamble. So do I. A match made in heaven, I say."

Winnie glanced down to notice Livy's foot as it slipped from her sandal and began to rub Adam's calf. Or a marriage made in hell. She doubted it would last out the year.

"I says to Livy, where you want to go on our honeymoon? You name it, Paris, Hawaii. I got the dough. She says she been to both those places with her first two husbands. She wants me to surprise her. I check out Samoa, two fucking days to get here and it turns out to be the rainy season."

Adam agreed. "Rains here a lot even in the dry season."

"Now I don't mind staying indoors and celebrating our nuptials, but Liv, she wants to see the island. Say, maybe you could show us around tomorrow."

"Sorry," Adam said. "We're flying out tomorrow."

Winnie stopped sipping her *koko*. "We are? Yes, I forgot we are. But, you should drive up and see the rainforest. Be sure to find someone to show you the guardians of the forest."

Livy reluctantly dropped her foot into her sandal again and addressed Winnie. "Come on, tell us what they are."

"No, I want you to be surprised."

Adam winked at Winnie over the blonde bombshell's head. "Thanks for the burger and fries. I hope you enjoy Samoa. We have to get back to our room and pack."

"Maybe Charlie and me will fly down to New Orleans to see you play in the fall," Livy hinted. "Look, write down your address, and we'll send you a copy of that picture of us together."

Adam smiled cordially, but stood and reclaimed Winnie with an arm around her waist. "Just send it in care of the Sinners. I'll get it. Nice meeting you."

They headed back to the Jeep unmindful of the rain. "Thanks for telling them that little white lie about our leaving tomorrow. I couldn't take much more of Liv and Charlie. I don't know how you could stand them," Winnie said.

"My parents raised me to be polite to my elders,

and Livy was certainly that, but I wasn't lying. While you were getting yourself out of bed, I made reservations to fly over to Ofu. It has the best and most deserted beaches in the world. I'll teach you to snorkel."

"A deserted beach, I like the sound of that. Snorkeling, not so sure."

"Nothing to it. The reef sharks and sea snakes won't bother us, but you do have to watch out for the poisonous spines of the stonefish."

"Maybe I'd rather take my chances with the fruit bats again."

Adam laughed his way back to the hotel. At the very least, she amused him.

Chapter Twenty-One

The small plane bumped along on the air currents and finally made a neat landing on Ofu's small airstrip wedged between the mountains and the ocean. That landing alone would have been enough excitement for Winnie to last the entire day. Adam carried their bags directly to the nearby lodge and checked them into a plain, tidy room with a private bath. He rented a truck, borrowed snorkeling gear, and asked that the meal coming with the accommodations be packed as a picnic. Though the shore near the hotel looked perfectly fine to Winnie, he drove them to Ofu Beach, part of the national park, and offered her four totally deserted miles of white sand, swaying palms, crystal clear water, and coral reefs. A volcanic peak, sharp as a shark's tooth, rose behind it. "A perfect paradise," she had to admit.

Adam started her out in the waist-deep shallow water until she got the hang of the ungainly flippers and clearing her facemask and snorkel. If she faltered, his big arms were there to catch her. Gradually, he inched her into deeper water and over to the reef that mushroomed from the sea floor and gave shelter to all manner of small, bright fish. A reef shark chasing down a meal did startle Winnie enough to send her sputtering to the surface, but again Adam was there to steady her.

They ate lunch in the shade and dozed until the wind picked up and the sky darkened in preparation for the daily storm.

Racing for the truck, Winnie got inside and scorched her bottom on the overheated upholstery. "We should have parked in the shade."

"Only if we want dents in the truck." Adam pointed to the coconut-laden palms. "You never know when one of those babies will fall." A storm-tossed tree illustrated his words by releasing a huge, green nut that landed like a bomb nearby. He drove away from the beach. "Not a good idea to stand under them, either. Death by coconut," he said somberly.

She thought he teased her again. "Yet you made love to me under the palms at Joe's ranch. You're joking."

"You have to pick your spot carefully. Besides, Louisiana palms don't get coconuts, not that I noticed. A coconut can give a person as good a concussion as a linebacker, believe me. Only an idiot hangs around under them."

"So all this stuff about making love under the palms isn't true?"

He gave her that grin of his, so blazing white against his dark skin. "It's a metaphor for fooling around sexually, Winnie. I thought you'd figured that out."

"Oh, I see." They weren't making love; they were fooling around sexually. Exactly what she wanted and needed, all she had planned on when she met Adam. No longer an easily flattered nineteen-year-old college student, she knew people did not fall in love in such a short period of time. Of course not. That would be ridiculous, especially when Adam, handsome, rich, generous, and good-natured could have anyone except this Princess Pala.

Back at the lodge, they had more than enough for dinner and hiked it off climbing to Maga Point to watch the sunset over the Pacific once the rains passed, another picture postcard moment in Winnie Green's life. They might have been on a secluded honeymoon, only they were not. When the rain returned in the morning and the small airplane did not, they cozied up in the lodge watching old movies on the DVD player and trying to beat each other at board games and cards. A third day doing the same bothered Adam not at all.

"Won't your family be worried?"

"No, people get stuck on these islands all the time, especially during the rainy season."

"Maybe we shouldn't have come if they are waiting for us."

"Not a problem, like I said," Adam replied a little tersely.

Winnie slapped down a winning hand in gin rummy. "Is it me—the reason you don't want to go home—because I'm black. I can stay in Pago Pago or fly home if my presence is difficult for you."

Adam laughed so hard the cards in his hand sprayed across the table. "You are lighter than most of the people in my village. You have golden brown hair and green eyes. They will see you as a white foreigner, a *palagi*, and treat you that way. Race is not much of an issue here as we are all mixed in some way or another. You are not the problem, lovely Winnie. The village will welcome you, I keep saying. Me, I am the problem."

"I can't see how. You are famous, wealthy, very generous—and yes, extremely handsome. Don't let that go to your head. Any village would be proud to claim you. Explain this to me."

Adam, damn him, gave her another one of his big shrugs. "You would have to be Samoan to understand." He shuffled the cards. "Best of three?"

The skies cleared overnight. In the morning, the light plane skittered to a stop on the soaked runway, picked up its passengers, both willing and reluctant, and sailed into the perfect blue sky back to Pago Pago.

****

The next day, Adam lingered over his breakfast and generally delayed their start toward his home village, but eventually he could not put it off any longer. With Winnie at his side, Adam took the Jeep over Rainmaker Mountain again and this time turned off on the rutted road past its peak. Halfway down to the sea, only half-glimpsed where the forest gave way now and again, a small tree uprooted by the rains blocked their path. Adam got out and shoved it to the side. Winnie gave him a round of applause.

"Don't. This just means they aren't keeping up the road the way the village should, but that is pretty hard to do during the rainy season. I guess the *matai,* our chiefs, will have it graded when the weather gets a little dryer."

She remained quiet as they churned along over teeth-rattling ruts and potholes. They came around a final curve and the village lay before them stretched out picturesquely along the beach and a small stream that flowed from the mountaintop. Two identical white churches anchored each end of the town. A tiny elementary school, a clinic, and a large traditional open-sided *fale* with a palm-thatched roof held the center. Simple homes of cement block painted various colors and shuttered with louvers filled in most of the gaps. Only three houses rose to two stories and these hugged close to the *fale* and the churches. Adam parked in front of an exceptional rambling white frame, single story home with a wide verandah, red tile roof, and slender turquoise columns. A couple of inviting rockers sat on its porch.

Unfortunately, the village dogs arrived to cancel that invitation to linger with their snarls and barks. Unlike Macho, they meant business. Winnie drew her legs up on the seat. Adam got out, picked up a few stones and shouted, *"Alu!"* as he chucked them at the beasts. The mongrels slinked away and were replaced by an imposing woman nearly as scary. She dominated the porch with her height and breadth wrapped around by a queen-sized lava-lava of purple and orange. Her wide bare feet slapped on the wooden steps as she came toward the car. Much lighter in complexion than Adam, her skin tone hinted at an ancestry containing white sailors very taken with Samoan girls. She wore her thick black hair parted in the middle, drawn back and turned under at her neck.

"My mother, Ela Malala."

"Son, you have been gone so long the village dogs have forgotten you." With that statement Ela's stern expression cracked into a smile. She kissed both of Adam's cheeks, and after he helped Winnie from the Jeep, she applied the same greeting to her guest.

"Talofa, Winnie Green. *Afio Mai!* Come in, come in and see where you will stay!"

Following his mother's impressive backside, Adam trailed behind with their bags. He cleared his throat loudly at the threshold, and Winnie remembered to slip her feet out of the pair of inexpensive slides he'd recommended for the trip. She half expected to find nothing but a sleeping mat in the bedroom, but it held a modern four-poster bed enveloped in a ring of mosquito netting and accompanied by a simple dresser and a single chair. Mats did cover the floor. Once Winnie assured her hostess that she would be very comfortable, they moved on to Ela Malala's pride and joy—the bathroom with a sparkling white porcelain commode, a sink and a shower. A water-filled bucket and a roll of toilet paper sat prominently on the back of the toilet.

"After you flush, you must refill the tank and get another bucket ready for the next person, "Adam advised.

"From where?"

Adam gestured toward the creek and the sea. "Plenty of water all around."

"But no need to use the beach for your business," his mother pointed out.

As they returned to the porch passing through other sparely furnished rooms, Adam asked after his father. Ela answered, "Helping with the feast to honor you and Winnie. We used some of the wedding goods since there will now be no wedding—and the gifts the Tau family owed us for the insult."

"They did a formal reparation because of Pala?"

"Yes, we let the Taus sit in the sun all day before we invited them in and accepted their presents, a good traditional way to end the matter. Now if you want nothing to eat or drink, you must go to the *fale* for the

'Ava ceremony, and I need to help with the cooking."

Adam answered for them. "Nothing for us if we are feasting later. Winnie, you must try all the foods prepared so as not to offend anyone, but only a mouthful or two, or you won't last to the end."

She nodded and tried to take Adam's hand for reassurance. He drew it away. "No PDA's in the village. Public affection between a man and a woman is immodest."

"Okay. I understand." She understood she was on her own and had to watch her every move. All the way up the mountain and back down to the beach, the usually laidback Adam had coached her in Samoan customs. Winnie wished he'd started this the second they left the mainland instead of leaving it until the last minute. Pago Pago, so Americanized, had given her no hint of what was to come.

Ela Malala walked with them as far as the ceremonial building, then slipped away to the cookhouse behind it. Before they could run the gauntlet of older men with imposing bellies waiting for them, another fellow came around from the rear and wrung Adam's hand.

"My father, Noa."

While Adam got his size from his mother, he certainly inherited his charm from his father. Under a bush of curly black hair and beneath two large dark eyes sparkling with mischief lay Adam's broad smile welcoming her to the village. Noa Malala had a spare brown body made even darker by the sun and deep lines in his face grooved by the same source. His muscles were hard knots from hauling in the nets, and at the moment, though his hands were clean, he smelled vaguely of fresh fish.

He shook Winnie's hand. "I think you are prettier than Pala, but I must not say that too loud or the Taus will want their presents back."

Winnie mustered a nervous smile for him and a faint, "Thank you."

"Now, I must go finish preparing the fish for the *umu* and you must drink *'ava* with the chiefs." With a wink, Noa Malala returned to his more humble duties.

Adam steered her to the assembly of elders who shook her hand and preceded them into the *fale*. Each of the *matai* settled cross-legged before a particular post in the building and beckoned Adam and Winnie to a place of honor. The men continued to chat, slapping their thighs and shaking hands with new arrivals while Winnie studied the inside of the *fale*. Far above, the interlacing of the branches holding the thatch made a pattern like the most delicate of fretwork. Flowers and garlands of leaves adorned the rafters and twined up the posts.

They sat on comfortable mats. She mentally thanked both her Pilates and yoga instructors that she could sit like a tailor for long periods of time since Adam had told her pointing one's feet at a person was the height of rudeness. Shoes left outside again and wearing only the flowered lava-lava Adam insisted on as the proper attire for *'ava* drinking, she made sure enough of her was modestly covered. Mentally rehearsing the ceremonial words she needed to say when given the *'ava* cup, she barely noticed a sudden cessation in the conversation.

A man younger than most of the *matai* entered and made his greetings to all but Adam. Bending his legs and tucking in his lava-lava to show his tattoos, he slipped into a less honored place in the hall. The beginnings of a prosperous belly lapped over the cloth tied at his waist. Winnie thought how much more attractive Adam's muscular, sculpted thighs displayed the designs compared to this man's meaty legs. She disliked his narrow eyes, flat nose, and heavy lips, even the fat ear lobes displayed by his close-cropped hair. No surprise when Adam whispered, "Sammy Tau." How could any woman want that when she could have Adam?

Another young man, slight of build with short, wavy hair neatly combed back from a high forehead, entered tardily and did pause to shake Adam's hand. He wore a dark lava-lava and shirt, and an incongruous clerical collar. Among all the bare-chested men, he seemed so very out of place yet sat among the most respected of the chiefs.

"My childhood friend, Davita Tomanaga. He is now the Methodist minister," Adam said just before a sharp clap of hands declared the opening of the ceremony.

A young man entered bearing the kava root for inspection by the highest chief. Approved, he delivered it to a four-legged *'ava* bowl, and the village maiden entered. Masculine eyes followed as she progressed to her place behind the bowl. The hand-painted *saipo* cloth she wore clung to her rounded hips as she swayed to her ceremonial position and slid gracefully onto the floor cross-legged. She carefully positioned her skirt and exposed smooth, brown thighs looped with tattoos like ropes of pearls. Another young man rushed to fill the bowl with water. Pala, because it could be no other,

175

began macerating and kneading the root to bring out its narcotic juices.

Winnie wanted to laugh at the absurd headdress the maiden wore, a nest of orange hair or fiber full of shells and tiny mirrors affixed to her flowing black locks with two carved wooden skewers that made the woman look as if she'd sprouted devil horns. However, the face that sat beneath that headdress was so beautiful in its symmetry, its smooth tan skin, its shapely lips, and luminous eyes that ridicule became impossible. If sailors had wet dreams of South Pacific women, they dreamed of the incomparable Pala.

Every movement graceful, the village maiden impassively continued her task. She rung out a muslin cloth straining the liquid and tossed it to one of the young men who discarded the debris and returned it to her. The process repeated as she made the brew while one of the talking chiefs leaned on his staff, droned on in Samoan, and gave his back an occasional swat with his official fly switch. What he said, Winnie had no idea. At last, Pala completed her task and filled half a coconut shell for the inspection of the head *matai*. He in turn indicated that the pastor should drink first, but did accept the next offering. Early in the order of names called, the maiden filled a shell for Adam who drank before Sammy Tau. He performed the offering to the old gods, said his ceremonial words, and tossed out the dregs after gulping down the *'ava*.

Winnie heard her name and accepted the refilled coconut bowl from the young man. She swore it contained double the amount of fluid resembling dirty water that Adam had downed, but she flicked her offering droplets, said her words, and choked the whole mess down. Murmurs and nods of approval followed from her audience. The ceremony continued until all had been served.

Winnie leaned closer to Adam. "My tongue ith numb and I feel dizzy."

"Completely normal," he assured her, but he did not slur *his* words.

The village maiden paraded out of the *fale* and the *matai* stood to stretch before the feasting began. Adam rose and followed Pala. Winnie unknotted her legs and, despite a little vertigo, went after him. He called after his former fiancée, and she turned with that fluid movement her limbs did so well to face him. Winnie stayed back and leaned against one of the poles of the *fale* to watch the confrontation.

"Pala, I respect your decision to marry someone else, but I need to know why."

Yes, why would such a beautiful woman throw over Adam for the flabby Sammy? Winnie wondered and waited. She thought Pala's dark eyes flashed at her, then away again. The woman answered in English as if she wanted Winnie to overhear.

"You do not live the *fa'a Samoa* anymore, Sammy said. You are wealthy and do not share enough with the village. You put yourself before the family. Sammy told me what my life would be like if I married you. We would live on the mainland and never come home to Samoa. There, I would be nothing more than another pretty face, your arm candy, and when you tired of me you would sleep with many *palagi* women because that is what American footballers do." Pala stood tall and delivered her accusations like the stones tossed at the village dogs.

"That is not true of all of us. I waited a year for you. Did I not send money for new roofs for both churches? Of course we would visit the islands even if we lived in America, and a beauty such as yours would shine among others like a star compared to a light bulb."

Pala had not finished. "I would have no honor, no status, other than being your wife. Sammy said in the States, a girl like me who did not choose to go to college is regarded lightly. The old ways mean nothing there. Here, I am revered as the village maiden and will marry a future *matai*. As Sammy gains in rank, I will oversee the women's societies and support the church, and always be respected by my people."

Adam nodded. "I see. If that is what you want, I wish you well, but do know you plan to marry a liar who betrayed his best friend."

A heavy-set man pushed by Winnie as she wondered if Adam wanted Pala back, if he expected the maiden to the change her mind this very minute and marry him. Had he totally forgotten she existed faced with so much natural beauty?

Sammy Tau placed a heavy hand on Adam's shoulder. "Is he bothering you, Pala?"

Before the maiden could answer, Adam summoned up the strength and lightning reflexes that made him an outstanding cornerback, spun and drove his fist into Sammy's gelatinous gut. "Liar! Traitor!"

Doubled over, Tau sank to his knees in the sand. His share of the *'ava* spewed from his heavy lips. Pala screamed. Children and dogs gathered drawn to the excitement like sharks to chum. Several of the *matai* rushed past Winnie and called for a stop to the violence.

The preacher grasped Adam's arm as if to forestall another punch, but the cornerback merely loomed over Tau casting a dark shadow upon him.

"Come talk with me," Davita Tomanaga said calmly and led Adam back to the *fale* where Winnie stood. "My good friend, you must know the *matai* decided the Taus should atone for Sammy's actions. Your family accepted their apology. The matter is at an end for the good of the village."

"No one consulted me about it."

"They never would. Their word is law here. As a Christian, I ask you to forgive Sammy in your heart."

"Because you asked me, I will try."

The clergyman dropped out of his expected role as peacemaker for a moment. "Adam, do you remember when we were in high school in Pago? All the girls ran after you, and Sammy ran after those girls and caught a few. He drank too much, he ate too much, he played too much to succeed the way you did. He still does. His spirit is greedy. He will not make a good *matai*, though because of his plans to marry Pala he has been accepted into a junior position by her uncle. She did not choose the better man, but perhaps she selected the life she wanted."

"I understand that. My quarrel is not with Pala."

Sammy Tau, back on his feet again, brushed the sand from his knees and being larger than the men surrounding him, shouted over their heads. "You are jealous because I will marry the village maiden, and you have only that skinny white bitch."

Over the uproar his words caused among the *matai*, Adam roared back, "At least my woman is useful as well as pretty. She is a nurse, not some outdated figurehead."

So, she was Adam's woman and useful. That struck home. She'd been useful to Doug Hopper sending him through med school. Was her use besides caring for the sick helping Adam get over Pala? Did she continue to use Adam for the same reason, to get over a bad marriage? Winnie hoped they'd moved beyond that to true affection, but perhaps not.

The elders opened their circle around Sammy in a direction away from Adam and the *fale* and sent him on his way with some sharp remarks in Samoan. The pastor interpreted their actions for Winnie. "They are upset he insulted a guest. He is not welcome at the feast."

"Maybe we shouldn't go either."

"The feast is given in your honor. You must attend," Davita said. "The fault is not yours, but I'd say Adam is heading for trouble if he can't contain himself."

"I'm fine. Let's eat. And remember, Winnie, try everything," Adam prompted.

Chapter Twenty-Two

The *matai* reassembled in the *fale* and took their accustomed places. Sammy Tau's space remained conspicuously empty. The parade of food began with the head chief and the pastor partaking first, then Winnie and Adam. She soon lost count of the many dishes.

Of course, succulent roasted pig formed the centerpiece of the meal, but moist, flaky fish baked in coconut cream followed. Also, chicken and turkey and a procession of seafood: sweet, fresh lobster, turtle tasting strangely like beef, and chewy octopus. Winnie managed to pinch off a tiny tentacle and get it down. She recognized the *palusami*, only this variety came with real taro leaves and corned beef. Chop suey and rice dishes galore added a little oriental touch, then the surprise of plain old American potato salad, all to be scooped up with the fingers or on a piece of baked taro.

She especially liked the thin, crispy tidbits offered in one bowl and took a second. Leaning toward of Adam, Winnie said, "These are good. What is it?"

"A type of fried worm. Try not to think about it."

Winnie reached for her coconut shell full of a sweet, red beverage and took a large swallow. "Tell me what I'm drinking and that it won't make me drunk."

"You're safe. Cherry Kool-Aid."

A girl offered her a washbasin of sticky stuff turning out to be thickened coconut cream that could be eaten only by immersing the fingers and taking out a chewy glob of the *pisua*. Sweets appeared, enough cakes to compete at a county fair. Winnie, full to bursting, accepted only bites or just a dab of frosting when she could get away with it. At last, the feast ended with a bowl of water passed for washing the hands. The mats before them still overflowed with food.

"Is all this going to go to waste? Do you have enough refrigeration here to preserve all this stuff? I mean that potato salad will turn in the heat," Winnie worried.

"No problem. This will all be gone by morning."

At that moment, the rest of the village came to eat. Old women slid whole cakes into baskets toted by grandsons. The basin of *pisua* vanished along with most everything else in a very short period of time as everyone helped themselves to the feast and carted away what they fancied.

"Efficient, I guess," Winnie said.

"No one goes hungry. You might want to rest before the *fiafia*. It's likely to go on into the night." Adam steered her back to his parents' house.

She lay down beneath the veil of mosquito netting on the comfortable bed and curled around her overstuffed stomach like a python that had swallowed a pig. The drumming of a light rain on the roof lulled her to sleep. Louder drums woke her as well as the giggles of girls passing by her window. The house filled with their chatter as the group entered by the front door. Adam's mother came to seek her.

"You missed evening prayer, but no matter. As

long as you were not out and about, no one noticed. The young women are here to take you to the dancing," Ela told her.

"Give me a minute or two."

Winnie rushed to the bathroom to brush her hair and repair the light makeup she wore. She shed her lava-lava dribbled with food stains and chose her most attractive one of green with yellow flowers for the festivities. Fairly sure it wouldn't fall down, she added a couple of safety pins just in case. As soon as she presented herself to the girls, all much younger than she, they crowned her head with fragrant plumeria blooms, and slipped a floral *ula* around her neck before hauling her off to a circle lit by a bonfire, lanterns strung between the trees, and a large tropical moon nude in the sky now that the rain had passed.

It appeared the entire village had arrived before her. A boy's group similar in age to the girls who escorted her took up a large area. Mothers nestled small, dark-eyed children between their crossed legs. Some nursed chubby infants. The elderly sat near the front in the best seats to view the performances. Winnie searched among the crowd for Adam, the minister, anyone she knew, but found only Adam's parents across the way and the snake-eyed Sammy Tau too close for comfort.

Her escorts deserted her and formed two lines, kneeling to perform an intricate percussive display of sticks snapped together. At the end, they were displaced by the young men who wore their lava-lavas rolled up tight to dance vigorously and sing a song accompanied by a guitar, two ukuleles, a traditional drum, and an oil can bass fiddle with one twanging string. In the next act, three old women related an obviously hilarious story with bawdy overtones even Winnie caught without understanding a word. A pause occurred to allow everyone a leg stretch.

Sammy Tau approached her. "I ask you to forgive my earlier words spoken so rashly. Though thin, you are very lovely like the plumeria blossoms you wear in your hair tonight."

"Thank you. I've heard that before."

"From Adam, naturally. He will be very busy proving he has not abandoned the *fa'a Samoa* in the coming days. I would be happy to show you around in his absence."

"I appreciate that, but have plans of my own."

"What plans?" he pressed.

"While I'm here I will offer to help at the clinic."

"Very noble, but not much fun. I know *palagi* women seek fun when they come to the islands. I can show you a good time better than Adam. He's always been like that stick in the mud Americans talk about."

"Not that I've noticed."

Though he did not touch her, Sammy sat very close blocking her view of the performance area. A male figure entered silhouetted against the fire. The drum rolled. "Please, you are in my way."

Sammy did not budge. Winnie sifted through her tiny Samoan vocabulary and came up with the word Adam used to chase the dogs. "*Alu!*" That got Sammy Tau to move his oleaginous bulk, a look of pure hatred glinting in his narrow black eyes. If this was paradise, surely that man personified the snake that inhabited it.

As Sammy shifted away, Winnie recognized the male dancer who stood before her—Adam, every taut, muscular inch of him gleaming with coconut oil. The same combed through his hair made black ringlets fall down his back and across his chest, and tucked behind one ear, a red hibiscus flower. Two slashes of black much like the shading he used on the football field lay under his eyes. Anklets of brown nuts rattled as he began to dance. He wore nothing else but his tattoos and a thick skirt of shredded leaves tied round his waist.

The drumbeat matched the thud of Winnie's heart as his feet kept time. His wrists turned in subtle motions, and his eyes glanced sidelong at her. The pounding accelerated, but he never lost control of the undulations of his legs, the smooth gestures of his arms. The tattoos on his thighs seemed to do a mesmerizing dance all their own.

The girls' group had reformed around her and watched avidly. The one who sat closest, the single young lady of the group who had overdone both her makeup and the amount of her perfume, whispered, "You are one lucky lady." A chubby one sitting behind prodded Winnie's back. "You must dance with him!"

Totally untrue that people with any amount of black blood possessed a natural sense of rhythm. Winnie got slowly to her feet. The girl who loved blue eye shadow nudged her into the circle. Winnie dug deep and came up with some of the graceful moves from her brief flirtation with ballet in middle school. Adam smiled. In that second, she wished he'd take her hand and run away with her into the jungle to do this dance in a prone position. The music stopped.

The audience slapped their hands and thighs in approval, maybe not of her dancing but for being a good sport. Adam excused himself because, "I'm not going to wear leaves all night." He returned shortly in his lava-lava minus the nut anklets, but with his skin still glistening in the moonlight and the hibiscus flower behind one ear. He stayed beside Winnie for the remainder of the performances with the strongly perfumed girl pressed near him a little too closely.

The last act began—a solo performance by the village maiden to end the evening. Pala wore a less absurd headdress, a simple crown of ti leaves. Like Adam, her every motion was exquisite, but graceful and feminine compared to his totally masculinity. Had they danced together, they would have been the perfect couple, Winnie admitted to herself. Pala and Sammy, the only two bad experiences in an otherwise beautiful and enchanting evening.

She knew she could not take Adam's hand on the way back to the house or put her arm around him without offending her hosts, though some of the girls from her group held hands with each other, and in fact some of the boys did, too. Instead, she settled for murmuring, "Your dance was the sexiest thing I have ever seen my life, Adam Malala."

"You think?"

"I do think. If it were allowed, I'd take you under the palms right now."

His grin showed whitely in the moonlight. "Not a good idea, but I know of a banyan tree where we'll never be found." He veered from their path, and she followed him into the dense growth at the base of the mountain. Another handy thing about lava-lavas—easy to take off even when held together by safety pins and a great ground cover for two people who wanted to make love.

Winnie lay beside Adam and stroked her hands over his slick body all the way to the root of his awakening penis. She ran her fingers up and down its oiled length until he became fully rigid. Take that perfect Pala who knew nothing about men. A thought occurred. "It's not part of the village maiden's job to anoint the male dancers, is it?"

"Absolutely not. I greased myself. Makes great lubrication for more than dancing, lovely Winnie." He sniffed her crown of pale yellow plumeria flowers. "Now you smell like the beautiful blossom you are." He removed it from her hair, leaving her clothed only in the *ula* of brilliant red flowers like the single hibiscus he wore behind his ear.

He rolled over, parted her legs, and slid inside so well-oiled he soon built up a rhythm faster than his dance. Winnie grasped his ringlets, shredding the petals from the hibiscus, and held on for the explosion within. It came upon her gradually, building and building until she convulsed with its force. Moments later, Adam allowed his release. They lay side by side with hearts beating like the village drum, eyes staring up at the brilliant light of the moon that filtered through the banyan's leaves as they caught their breath. A giggle came from the other side of the tree so wide around it could have housed a small family.

"We aren't alone," Winnie whispered, frantically trying to rip her lava-lava from beneath Adam and put it on. He sat up and covered himself with his own loincloth. Groans and sighs made their way through the many branches to their ears. The voices, high and adolescent, urged each other to completion, which judging by the boy's great gasp and the girl's angry response arrived far too quickly.

Adam stood. "Let me handle this. Stay here."

Not trying for quiet, he rounded the huge trunk. Winnie caught a glimpse of bare, narrow brown buttocks as the boy flashed her way trailing his lava-lava and crashing into the bushes as he made his frantic escape. She moved soundlessly to the curve of the trunk where she could see and hear the rest of the drama. The overly made up girl from the *fiafia* lounged against one of the tree's many roots and let the moonbeams play over firm, young breasts and a small, round belly flaunting the dark indent of her navel and shadowing the cleft between her legs. The teenager made no move to cover herself, as lacking in modesty as Eve before the apple.

"Get dressed, Lita, and go home. Shame on you for being out here with a boy who thinks so little of you he runs away and lets you take the blame," Adam pronounced.

"He believes you will thrash him."

"I probably would."

"Doesn't matter. He did not satisfy me. I think you could." The girl stood and advanced on Adam like a famished mongoose after a tasty snake.

"You are a child. I am your elder. Go back to your parents' house."

"I am only two years younger than Pala, and you would have married my sister. Let me tell you, I will always be better at this than her." Lita advanced close enough to tug on the knot of Adam's lava-lava. Winnie gasped at her audacity, and the girl heard.

"Oh, I see. Adam Malala is out here with his *palagi* woman and has nothing left to give me." She shrugged her delicate shoulders. "I won't tell on you if you don't tell on me. The *matai* will not like the example you are setting." Casually, she wound her lava-lava around her ripe body and sashayed off toward the village.

Winnie moved around the tree to stand beside Adam. "So that skanky piece of work is Pala's baby sister."

"Yes, you could call her the anti-Pala. I heard she goes under the palms with all the village boys."

"I understand sibling rivalry, but with me and Mintay it came down to good grades and who would marry first. I won that last part, unfortunately. What will happen to this girl?"

"One day she'll get pregnant, and the ministers and *matai* will ask her to name the boy and force a marriage. Unlikely they will stay together. Her family will raise the child."

"Are we really in trouble for being out here?"

Adam heaved his big shoulders in that way of his. "We need to be more discreet while you visit here. We must cool it a little, okay? This place is more conservative than Texas, only we have palms instead of cactus, jungle instead of desert, and far fewer guns. I don't want you to get a reputation like Lita has."

Winnie nodded and sighed. Just another evening in paradise gone wrong.

Chapter Twenty-Three

By the time she rose the next morning, Winnie found Adam had gone fishing with his father. Ela made tea and pointed to a bowl of tropical fruit salad as well as several leftover cakes from the previous day's feast.

"Eat when you are hungry. Take what pleases you. Tonight we will have fresh fish. Oh, you are invited to Reverend Tomanaga's house this afternoon."

Winnie helped herself to the fruit salad and a slice of one of the plainer cakes. "What time?"

"Whenever you want to go. We do not hurry here. I have choir practice, but feel free to walk around the village. If the dogs bother you, shout and throw a rock."

Winnie wrapped herself in a lava-lava, saving her *puletasi* for the visit with the pastor. When she went outside, she discovered her shoes missing from the porch. Fortunately, Ela had not left and offered to find them for her. She returned a bit later with the slides in hand.

"One of the girls took a liking to them, but said they pinched. I explained your feet are too tender to walk without them, and she gave them back. No problem."

Winnie slipped her feet into the shoes, which felt a little looser than before and headed out for a walk on the beach. Having used the bathroom that morning, she brought along the water bucket for refilling. She made an abrupt U-turn after she'd gone a ways when she came across an old man relieving himself on the sand, all the while gazing out at the beautiful scenery.

Hastily returning through the village, she scooped water from the stream and avoided Sammy Tau who sat unmoving in the shade, brooding like an ancient god displaced. He did not speak to her. Other villagers greeted her cordially in passing as they made their way to vegetable plots on the mountainside. They carried hoes and other gardening implements to work the communal gardens as they had for hundreds of years, beating back parts of the jungle but never taking more space than they needed to sustain the village.

Back at the Malala home, Winnie stowed her shoes under one of the porch chairs for safety and delivered her bucket to the bathroom. Ela still remained in the house.

"Won't you be late for practice? You needn't stay on my account."

"I will go at the right time. We are fined for being late. That way we make sure everyone gets there when they should. Otherwise, who knows?"

"Noa and Adam are fishing, and I saw some of the men and women head off with gardening tools, but Sammy Tau just sits in the shade. What's up with that?" she asked her hostess.

"He is *musu* today, doesn't feel like doing anything. I suspect he will be *musu* as long as Adam is here."

"And that is all right? He sits around while others work."

"Sure. Next week he will work, and someone else

will be *musu*. It balances out."

"Whatever you say. I think I'll go to the clinic and offer to help while I'm here."

"Good idea."

She would have gone immediately if her shoes hadn't disappeared again. Winnie found them on the feet of a child playing nearby and politely requested their return. The little girl kicked them off and ran away laughing with her friends. Shod again, Winnie made her way to the clinic where two nurses on contract worked to provide basic medical services. She soon learned one was being courted by a village boy and the other could not wait for her contract to expire so she could get back to Pago Pago and the wider world. Winnie offered to substitute, giving them both valued hours of free time, enough to go into the city or visit with the young man's family. Delighted, they showed her around the small, clean building and accepted her promise to sub on Monday.

Returning, she placed her shoes under the porch steps before going inside. Adam and his father had returned smelling of the salt sea and their catch. Ela sat with them. Choir practice must be in the afternoon, Winnie figured. Noa gave her his fine smile. "My son is very strong. We caught many fish, too many for the village to use."

"Now my husband must go up to the main road and sell the seafood before it spoils," Ela replied with a hint of censure in her voice.

"Sorry. I will drive him up there in the Jeep and stay with him," Adam offered, looking shame-faced.

"No, no. You and our guest are invited for tea with Pastor Tomanaga this afternoon. *Tam'a* will sit in the sun alone and sell his fish."

Noa helped himself to a piece of cake. "I have more sense than to sit in the sun. I will find a shady spot and sell out my catch in no time, Ela. We will give the money to the church."

"Here take the Jeep to get you up there and back, *tam'a*." Showing more faith in his father than he had in his Samoan cousin's driving ability, Adam handed over the keys.

Mollified, Adam's mother cut a large chunk from the sweetest cake and ate it with her tea. Adam went off to shower away his sweat and the fish stink from his body and Winnie to put on her *puletasi* and try to conquer what the humidity was doing to her hair. When they met again, she wore the blue and green outfit and Adam a formal dark lava-lava and a somber shirt. As he strapped on his sandals on the porch, Winnie searched for her shoes. Gone again!

"Stealing seems to be a problem in the village. My shoes keep disappearing."

"Not stealing, but taking something that tweaks the person's fancy. Your shoes are more interesting than the rubber flip-flops most of them have. I told you about this in New Orleans. If you went to their house and decided you liked something there very much, they would give it to you willingly. It evens out."

"Except I don't have feet impervious to hot sand and sharp little chunks of lava rock."

"Not yet. I'll go look for them."

Adam hadn't gone out of sight when he paused to speak to one of the wrinkled grannies so quick to grab part of yesterday's feast. Winnie's eyes trailed down the old woman's worn lava-lava to her spindly ankles.

She wore the plain black slides that looked big as orthopedic shoes on her aged feet. Adam shouted a few phrases in Samoan. The granny nodded and stepped out of the shoes. As she hobbled Winnie's way, she spoke a few courteous words and moved on as steadily as one of the sand-scuttling crabs.

Adam played Prince Charming and placed the slides on Winnie's feet. "So beautifully narrow and high-arched, Cinderella," he said with his winning smile as he ran a tickling finger along that same arch.

Winnie curled her toes. "Save the lavish compliments on my feet. I really need a pedicure. What did the old woman say to me?"

"She's sorry your feet hurt. Word is getting around that you need your shoes, but this one is hard of hearing."

"I am not exactly sure I like having communal shoes, but I'm beginning to understand why your parents have very little furniture. Anything not too heavy to lift simply walks off."

"You are getting the idea. I told you to leave everything at the hotel except your lava-lava, *puletasi,* and church clothes. Now you know why."

They set off for the pastor's fine, two-story home next to the church. The temperature climbed and clouds bearing the afternoon rain as reliably as an UPS delivery swept in across the sea. People who spent the morning in the communal garden or banana plantation returned from their labors with baskets of taro roots and fingers of fruit. Sammy Tau still sat glaring in his protected space. No one paused to try to jolly him out of his mood and certainly not Adam and Winnie.

They arrived on the airy verandah of the pastor's

mansion right before the torrents fell. A pretty woman whose pregnant belly strained the loose top of her *puletasi* greeted them and escorted the guests to a high-ceilinged room possessing an impressively carved dining room table already set for tea and six massive chairs capable of holding a Samoan of any bulk. Small dishes of nuts and plates of quartered, crustless sandwiches surrounded three pre-sliced cakes prettily decorated with fresh flowers. As if awaiting the second of their arrival, a girl darted in with a steaming kettle of hot water and filled a silver teapot.

The pregnant woman beckoned them to sit. "I will get my husband."

She had no need to leave the room as the door across the hall opened and Davita Tomanaga left his study to join them. Adam shook the hand of the much slighter minister vigorously. "Not doing bad for the runt of our group of boys."

The pastor shook his head ruefully and said mostly for Winnie's benefit, "The furniture is compliments of one of our late Victorian missionaries. All the rest—well, our people love to make gifts to the church and the minister. If I go elsewhere, all of this will remain behind. You've met my wife, Lila. We expect our first child any day now. She attended boarding school with Pala, came to visit, and was foolish enough to stay and marry me."

Lila smiled shyly and gazed on her husband with large, soulful dark eyes brimming with admiration and love for her man. Her lovely face lacked the strong bone structure of many Samoans and sat small and delicate above her swollen breasts and huge belly. "Please sit and I will pour the tea. We had an English headmistress at our school and she taught us how to do it properly. We thought Winnie would be more comfortable at a table than on a mat, but I understand she did very well at the feast and impressed the *matai*."

"They stopped eating exactly at the point when I couldn't hold another bite, thank heaven."

"We do, and often."

Following a brief blessing, they worked their way through nuts, sandwiches, and small talk. Lila insisted Winnie take a thin slice of each of the cakes that she had made fresh that morning. Thinking of bending over a hot oven at nine months pregnant in this heat and humidity, she could hardly refuse to taste each one. Before Lila could urge her to eat a second helping, the serving girl appeared to deliver a message.

Lila stood with the help of the stout arms of her chair. "You must excuse me, but the women have gathered for a Ladies Aid Society meeting in the church hall. So nice having you here, Winnie. Adam, do take some of this food home for Ela and Noa. Please, both of you come to worship with us tomorrow."

"I would like that, but I believe Adam told me his family is London Missionary Society."

"Only because they love to stay late at a *fiafia*. The Methodists want everyone home for prayers and tucked in after six," Adam interjected. "Most of the villagers go to both services since the times are staggered for exactly that reason. Not much else to do here on a Sunday but worship and eat."

The reverend nodded. "Sad but true about the dancing. I make myself scarce early so I don't have to chastise any of my congregation who want to stay late for the festivities. Earlier preachers felt dancing after dark led to sin."

"Imagine that," Winnie said, keeping a very straight face.

"Pala does her job well shutting down the events by midnight," Lila mentioned in praise of her friend.

"Yes, she is practically perfect," Winnie agreed without a hint of sarcasm.

Lila took a black umbrella worthy of a London businessman from an ancient elephant foot stand by the study door and went out into the rain. They watched her progress through the downpour from the dining room window. Others oblivious to the weather covered their heads with large banana leaves and scuttled through deep puddles in bare feet to their destinations.

The conversation indoors turned to old times. Adam asked after their mutual friends. They recalled the antics of the boys who slept on Auntie's porch in Pago, those selected for more specialized schooling in the city.

"I know how you and Sammy turned out, but what about Losi, Pisa, and Pati, the old gang? I admit I lost touch with them in college since we each went to different schools, or not, in Sammy's case," Adam asked.

"Pati and Pisa send contributions to the *matai* and the church, but we never see Pisa. He did not finish med school but got a doctorate in philosophy instead. Not much use in the islands. He married a *palagi* woman and has a couple of children." The minister's eyes turned briefly toward Winnie, then fixed on Adam again. "He teaches at Berkeley."

"Did Pati get his degree in accounting? The village teacher said he had a brilliant mathematical mind,

Winnie."

"Oh, yes. He works in Pago, has a city wife, and four children. As expected, he provides free financial advice to the *matai* who rarely take it. Many in the village give away so much to attain status their families live in poverty. Pati tried to teach them differently, to earn and save, but that is like the trying to contain the sea with a dike of sand. Pati drinks too much, I am afraid." Somber, Davita turned to Winnie. "It is not easy balancing the *fa'a Samoa*—the traditional Samoan way of life—with the modern world."

Before she could reply, Adam cut in as if trying to lighten the mood. "What about Losi, always our joker, our trickster, but a talented artist, too?"

The reverend bowed his head and murmured a few words. "God bless his soul. Even when we were young, I suspected he might become a *fa'afafine*." He explained to Winnie, "That is a man who lives as a woman, who might even go with a man."

"Like a drag queen in New Orleans?" Winnie asked.

"Something like that. They are often entertainers and are not looked down upon, but when Losi went to the mainland to study art he began practicing the gay lifestyle. That is not accepted here, not by the churches, not by the *'aiga*, the large family groups."

Beneath Adam's tan skin, a faint flush of red appeared. "Jesus. Sorry. When he told me he'd follow me to the University of Oregon and become a cheerleader, I thought that was just another one of his jokes. I mean, the Sinners have a gay punter and he is an all right kind of guy, but that way of life would never be accepted in the village."

"Losi came here with a young man when I'd barely taken over this church. Inexperienced and unmarried myself, yet they came to me for counseling. I told them what they did was a sin. They must give up their feelings for each other or return to California and never return. Still, they told the family and were cast out. Losi returned to the mainland with his lover. When his lover left him a year later, he committed suicide. I did not have the right words to help him, and he chose that man over his family ties."

"I'm so sorry," Winnie murmured.

Anguished, the pastor said, "He's not the only one. We lose our youth to despair, always expected to obey and give to those older and care for those younger without any thanks. The *'aiga* is all and the individual nothing no matter what they achieve."

Winnie shook her head sadly. "I can think of one person who doesn't follow the party rules."

Looking pained, Adam said, "Me."

"No! I was thinking of little Lita, Pala's sister."

"She is another kind of problem," the minister agreed. "Her father has beaten her several times for being indiscriminate, but that kind of treatment makes her more defiant. She laughed when Lila tried to speak to her. I suspect she'll be another one who leaves with the first man who offers to take her away from the village."

"What about Sammy Tau who sits on his butt doing his *musu* thing while everyone else works and thinks he is better than Adam?" Winnie persisted, not believing Adam could feel badly about himself when he was so successful at what he did.

"Sammy has given all he has, which wasn't much,

to attain status as junior *matai*. After he marries Pala and climbs to the top, he will get the best of everything. He wants what Adam has, fame, luxury, a beautiful woman, wealth, but he hides that by claiming to live the *fa'a Samoa*. Adam has given us funds to put new roofs on both churches and last year, computers for the school. Sammy belittles that by saying he should give more, give all to the village. He does not have the heart of a good *matai*."

The rain let up and allowed a ray of sunshine to race across the still heavily laden table like a golden mouse giddy with the abundance. Davita clapped his hands and the serving girl appeared to take away the food and stow it in two big baskets for the guests to take home.

"I am sorry our conversation was not more lighthearted, Winnie, but rumors circulate in the village. If you plan to be involved with a Samoan man for any length of time, you need to know the facts of life here. It is not the Garden of Eden it appears to be." The reverend walked with them to the door of his mansion. "I hope to see you in church."

"We will be there." The men embraced in farewell. The servant loaded the baskets onto their arms and the couple walked back to the Malala home as a cloud of steam rose over the jungle-covered sides of the mountain and the overflowing stream emptied its latest burden of water into the sea. Giving up, Winnie carried her shoes.

They arrived at the Malala house in plenty of time for the evening prayer service at six. When a boy clanged on the used propane cylinder serving as a bell, the village loungers and even Sammy Tau went inside for devotions. For ten minutes, Winnie participated in prayer ending with a hymn sung by Ela in a contralto voice rich as coconut cream. A dinner of steamed fish, taro, fresh fruit, and tea party leftovers, more than enough for Winnie, followed. Afterwards, she and Adam sat on the porch in the two rockers and enjoyed the evening ocean breeze along with the drop in temperature, though it remained as warm and humid as Louisiana in August.

"You know I could build my parents a bigger, better house, but no one can go to two stories without insulting the *matai* and the church. Only they are allowed a mansion," Adam remarked.

"Your parents seem perfectly happy with what they have." Winnie cooled herself with a fan of woven palm fronds. "There is something to be said for that."

"They will never want for anything, but if I send them a special gift, they give it away."

Winnie, catching on, nodded. "The *fa'a Samoa* at work."

"Exactly."

Ela came to the door and beckoned her son to come inside. "No, Winnie, stay and enjoy the evening air. I must talk to Adam. Do you need anything to drink? Noa can open a coconut for you to drink the milk. Very refreshing."

"No, I'm fine, thank you."

Within the house, windows wide open to catch that same breeze she enjoyed, mother and son conversed in Samoan, quietly at first, then rising in heat and tempo. Always so friendly, so even-tempered, Winnie wondered why they argued. She pretended not to hear. Using an app on her iPhone, she peered into the lowering dusk and matched the stars coming out so close to the equator, bright Canopus and the False Cross caught in the dense net of the Milky Way. Amid insect and amphibian noises from the rainforest, the soft rush of the waves on the sand, and the whine of the occasional mosquito she slapped with her fan, the village quieted for the night. One late stroller sauntered by the house, stopped, and climbed the porch steps. Uninvited, Pala seated herself with slinky grace on the floor by Winnie's feet.

"All alone?" she inquired in a perfectly melodious voice. "Adam does not keep you company?"

"He is inside. I notice Sammy is not with you either." Winnie flattened another annoying mosquito with one brisk swat.

"No, I only see him in the company of my family to protect my reputation. Besides, he is *musu* right now. A divorced woman like you has more leeway in your behavior."

"How do you know my marital status?"

Pala inclined her head toward the open window. "Because they argue about you. Ela says women in her church group noticed the two of you go off into the bushes last night. Now, they wonder what you and Adam do under her roof."

"We haven't done anything under her roof."

"But Adam says you are a divorced woman who can do as she pleases and not some shy village maiden. I am not particularly shy, but I am careful of my actions."

"So I notice."

"Ela says he should be looking for another village girl to marry, not running around with a fast *palagi*.

Adam claims you are not *palagi* but have black blood. I don't see it in you myself. I am darker. He thinks you should be respected because you are a nurse. Fine, Ela says. She does not want to lose him to a scheming mainlander, nurse or no nurse, because then he will never come home."

"Thanks for the running commentary." Winnie wished she'd accepted that offer of milk in a coconut. She could use the shell to conk the very helpful Pala over the head and shut her up, but that would probably break several village taboos. Across the way, she thought she saw Lita flitting between the houses with a young man in pursuit. "Maybe you should run along and see if your sister is in for the night."

Pala's voluptuous lips flattened across her teeth. Winnie half expected them to roll back into a snarl like the local dogs. Adam burst from the house, and her snarl curved into a pleasant smile. "You see I am keeping your guest company, Adam."

"Yeah, thanks." He unrolled a mat tucked under his arm and returned inside. A minute later, he bullied a single mattress onto the porch and threw it down on top of the mat. Adam took a wad of mosquito netting from under his arm and snagged it on a ceiling hook probably intended to hold a basket of ferns or flowers. "Now no one has to wonder where I am sleeping!"

Winnie pushed up from her rocker. "If my presence here is causing trouble, I should leave tomorrow."

Pala answered her sweetly. "Oh, no one travels on a Sunday. It is a day of rest. You must stay."

Adam glared at his former fiancée. "Pala, do you need us to escort you home?"

The village maiden rose as fluidly as the night mist

on the mountain. "Not necessary. You know there is no crime in the community. Sleep well." She left, hips pumping under a tightly wrapped lava-lava.

"Pala graciously translated what your mother said. Really, I should go back to Pago on Monday and let you enjoy the rest of your visit with your family."

"I seldom enjoy my visits. Last year, my parents arranged my marriage to Pala. I went along with it and what a mess that became. I am beginning to feel slightly grateful to Sammy for taking her off my hands." Clearly intending to sleep in full view of the village, Adam folded himself onto the mattress and unbuttoned the shirt he had worn to the tea party. "You should go in and get to bed. We have church in the morning."

Winnie wanted nothing more than to slip under the mosquito netting, nip his slightly sulky full lower lip, and lay down with her head on his now bare chest. But, remembering the no PDA rule in force in his hometown, she said goodnight and went to sleep alone.

Chapter Twenty-Four

The improvised church bell sounded early beckoning worshipers to the LMS service. Winnie donned her white ensemble and walked between Noa and Adam to the sanctuary. Unsurprisingly since Ela sang in the choir, she left earlier after admiring Winnie's wide-brimmed hat with its cheerful sunflower. Before leaving, she put out fruit and cakes for the family, but Adam warned Winnie to eat lightly.

"We will probably be invited to Sunday lunch, the *to'ona'i*, with the church leaders."

"If it has a fancy name, this must be another feast. I'm not sure how many of these I can handle before I become as big as your mother." Winnie had refrained from mentioning his mother's size before the unkind words spoken during the argument and engraved in her mind by Pala, though in the morning Ela had treated her with perfect courtesy.

"My mother's girth is widely respected. No one in my family goes hungry."

The terse way he answered made her shut her mouth and quietly enter the snowy stream of Samoans in their whites on the way to church. In a custom-made linen suit complete with a vest but worn open-collared without a tie, Adam made a magnificent appearance, larger than life. He'd subdued his wild hair with a leather thong and topped it off with the most elegant of Panama hats. She did not envy Pala walking beside Sammy who looked as rumpled and dumpy in his clothing as an old-time Louisiana politician.

While the church seemed overly embellished to Winnie and she understood not a word of the service, she did enjoy the soaring voices of the choir whose music rose majestically to the high rafters. The singing reminded her of the Rev's AME church in that respect. As they left the building, the rotund minister and his wife, who matched him like part of a set of salt-and-pepper shakers portraying two chubby bakers, issued the dreaded invitation to the Sunday lunch. Of course, they accepted.

The entire congregation left one church and hiked to the other for the next service. As they prepared to enter Reverend Tomanaga's sanctuary, Adam called out to Pala and Sammy, who walked slightly ahead in the midst of her family. "Since I will not be at your wedding, I want to present you with an early gift." Adam held out the keys to his newly purchased Jeep and dropped them into Pala's upturned palm.

Even her perfect mouth could think of nothing to say but, "Oh!"

Sammy Tau grabbed the keys and pocketed them in his lumpy suit. "Very generous of you, old friend." With no more thanks than that and a scowl on his face, Sammy nodded for his fiancée to enter the church and turned his back on them.

"I'll say that was generous," Winnie muttered. "Exactly how are we going to get back to Pago Pago now?"

"Someone will take us or we'll ride the bus like

everyone else," Adam answered shortly and stomped inside to take a seat.

Noa gave her an apologetic smile. "He is irritable this morning, probably from sleeping on the porch or from not getting what he wants." The smile changed to a small, suggestive grin. "It is never good to argue with Ela."

Speaking of the devil, or perhaps God's ambassador, Ela joined them, freed from her choir robes. As massive as her son in her whites, she wore a hat of such feathered grandeur and complexity Winnie's Nana would have been envious on a Sunday morning in the States. In fact, Winnie could almost hear Nana's voice saying, "If you keep giving it away, that man will never marry you."

Marriage to Adam. It never entered her mind before now, that kind of commitment. Maybe sitting beside him in church brought on the thought. She tamped it down, considering what he could have had in Pala—beauty, great status, and the approval of the community and his family.

The order of service pretty much followed that of the LMS church. Again, Winnie enjoyed the voices of the choir and understood little until Reverend Tomanaga announced he would give the sermon in English out of deference for their visitor. He spoke of the need to forgive in order to keep both the family and village at peace, aimed directly at Adam, no doubt.

When the pastor began to read out loud the contributions to the church, he did not catch Winnie off guard as the previous minister had. Noa beamed when half the proceeds from his fish sales were mentioned. Adam had put a hundred-dollar bill into his envelope, Winnie a twenty, though nothing was expected of her as a visitor. That gained her friendly smiles.

Lastly, the pastor held up a set of car keys and scanned the congregation for an explanation. Sammy Tau rose and in a booming voice announced, "An early wedding gift that I give to the church, a new Jeep." Many clapped.

Sitting across the aisle, Winnie watched Pala's mouth drop open, clamp shut, and resume its serenity. Beside her, Adam stirred.

He stood leaving a large gap in the row. "I want to donate a proper bell tower to each church. They will not fit in the collection plate."

The members of the congregation, and the *matai* who served as deacons, chuckled and showed thigh-slapping approval. Casting a triumphant stare on Sammy whose face had darkened with anger, Adam resumed his seat. Winnie suspected if he had been playing poker, he would have said, "I'll see that Jeep, and raise you a million bucks."

She whispered in his ear, "Where did that idea come from?"

"My generous nature."

She could not deny that. He'd built an entire beach for her and left it for handicapped children to enjoy, but she strongly suspected his hatred of Sammy Tau propelled this offer. So much for absorbing the peace and love message of the sermon. Both men ignored it. The service ended, and on to another spread of food that made Winnie wish for a dress with an elastic waistband. No wonder every one of the big eaters preferred a lava-lava for most occasions. The rest of

Sunday, she spent in a heavy meal-induced nap swinging gently in a shaded hammock because any other action on the holy day was frowned upon by patrolling *matai*.

Chapter Twenty-Five

Monday morning Winnie kept her promise to the village nurses to let one of them have the day off. Good thing she made her own plans because Adam had risen from his bed on the porch and gone to the communal garden to spend his day hoeing weeds and picking vegetables and fruits. She passed Sammy Tau back in his *musu* position on her way to the clinic. He spared her no greeting, not that she minded.

Helping with well-baby checks, Winnie soon learned her lectures on infant nutrition went unappreciated. In Samoan eyes, a fat baby meant a healthy baby, no changing their minds. She administered scheduled shots and kept her mouth shut about the rest. Her fellow nurse whose meals and housing the village provided waved her back to the Malalas for lunch. Adam had not returned from the plantation, though it appeared most of the gardeners were done for the day judging by the number of people lounging up and down the street. Noa encouraged her to help herself to anything in the house. His wife had gone to an aerobics class at the church hall. Now, that would be a sight to see—so much jiggling flesh bouncing to some lively exercise tune. Frankly, she still felt full from Sunday lunch and only nibbled her meal.

As she prepared to return to her volunteer work,

Adam arrived bearing a huge basket overflowing with taro, breadfruit, and a few purple eggplants, as well as carrying over one broad shoulder a bunch of bananas big enough to feed every monkey in the San Diego zoo. Winnie doubted if most men could have lifted his burden let alone hauled it back to the village. Ela, her lighter skin heavily flushed from exercise, came up behind him and immediately began berating her son.

"What did he do wrong?" she asked Noa.

"Again, too much food for our household. She says he must offer it around the village. His excess embarrasses her."

Still, Ela rooted in the basket, choosing some choice taro and breadfruit, claiming the eggplants as well as removing a hand of bananas from the bunch for their dinner before waving Adam away to distribute the largess. He failed to meet Winnie's sympathetic eyes as he went, but she noted he did pause to sling a few bananas into Sammy Tau's lap. If the word the *musu* man uttered meant "thanks," it came out sounding more like a curse.

Not knowing when Adam would return, she went back to her work at the clinic, but the only crisis of the day involved a cut requiring a tetanus shot and a bandage provided while the other nurse conducted a class in diabetes management. The disease flourished in the village since the introduction of junk food into the Samoan diet and their great regard for size and feasting, trim Nurse Talo told her.

"Country people," Talo snorted. "They like fleshy women, and don't want to change their ways. I'm far too thin for the men around here. Frankly, I am surprised Adam Malala prefers you over the local women, but then, he has been more exposed to American culture." Again, Winnie wondered if Adam would ultimately decide to follow his mother's wishes and take a village bride, but she did figure the lack of interest in Nurse Talo had more to do with her sharp tongue than her build.

Her companion killed the last few hours of the day paging through a lurid movie magazine that certainly reinforced the idea of foreign women being loose. As the regular afternoon rain poured down, her fellow nurse yammered on about getting her free day off tomorrow thanks to Winnie. She planned to be at the head of the trail waiting for the earliest bus in the morning to go get her delicious scoop of American civilization. Talo pumped Winnie on opportunities for nurses stateside and hinted she wouldn't mind seeing New Orleans, showing no less enthusiasm for the idea when Winnie revealed she currently lived with her sister three hours from the big city. Relieved when the day ended, she went back to the house and helped Ela make a large chop suey with rice for dinner, which Adam ate with little appetite, a first for him since they'd met.

In the evening, Winnie sat in the porch rocker again, and Adam, head lowered in his hands, hunched on the front steps not saying a word. "You're not going all *musu* on me, are you?" Winnie asked.

His grin flashed in the twilight. "Where did you learn about *musu*?"

"From your mother and the living example of Sammy Tau. I really don't understand how one man can choose not to work and you do and get chewed out for it."

"You see, I work too hard. I show ambition and pride in what I accomplish. Here, this is wrong. Maybe my mother is correct. I am too accustomed to the cheers of the crowd, to having fans and plenty of money to fit in here anymore. Maybe I never did. Looking back it seems those six boys sent to Pago Pago for school were the ones who were different. Davita had an early religious vocation that made him stand out. Sammy and me excelled at sports, Pisa and Pati at schoolwork. Poor Losi, how he could sing and dance as well as paint. The *matai* sent us out into the world where we could use our talents—and send money home."

Winnie's rocker creaked lightly against the porch floor. "That seems very calculating."

"Or very wise. The village benefits, and we don't upset the *fa'a Samoa.*"

"To be honest, I don't think I could live the *fa'a Samoa* either." She hadn't meant it as anything more than a sympathetic comment, but Adam's head snapped up.

"Who asked you to?"

"I didn't mean that in any special way. I know I am an outsider here, one who doesn't fully understand. Your people are generous and hospitable, the islands gorgeous especially in places like this where the old ways hold, but I feel so out of place. I should leave soon and let you figure out what you want to do without my hanging on you."

"You don't hang on me. Winnie, you anchor me to the wider world. You should go inside now before I am tempted to forget my good intentions and take you for another romp in the bushes."

She leaned toward him from her rocker. "I would

like that."

But, one of the younger *matai* who took turns patrolling the village approached before she could deliver a forbidden kiss. He carried a little boy sporting a huge shiner that closed one of his round dark eyes. The child's nose ran with snot down to a split lip.

"*Malo,* Adam. Raro Ulu got a little heavy-handed with his spare the rod and spoil the child beliefs tonight. Your family has plenty of room. Can you take him for a while?"

"Sure, my mother will see to him."

The *matai* walked right in to deliver this unexpected guest. Winnie, wide-eyed, said, "Does this happen often?"

"Often enough. A parent can chastise a disrespectful child, but the child belongs to the village. The chiefs move them around or the child might go to another home on its own. Someone might just scoop him up and house him. Our friend, Lita, could move out and stay with someone else, but I suspect she enjoys embarrassing her sister no matter what the consequences."

Winnie shook her head in wonder. "As a junior *matai*, Sammy Tau does this, walks around saving little children? Maybe I should have more respect for him."

"Save your respect. I know Sammy too well. He was lazy in his football training, cut all the practices he could and still stay on the team. I'm surprised he had the ambition to steal Pala. When his turn comes to patrol, he most likely finds a hidden place to sleep."

"I'll go in and make sure the child has nothing broken."

"I think you should. I really think you should."

****

Tuesday, Winnie reported to the clinic early knowing Nurse Talo would be on her way to Pago Pago by now. Lua, the second nurse, thanked her profusely for the day off. Her courtship had progressed to the point of wedding planning, and Samoan weddings evidently put the biggest Hollywood bash to shame. Two gowns were required, one for the ceremony and one for the reception, and at least a three-tiered cake with side cakes for the important guests. Lua shared all the details until they were interrupted by the entry of Lila Tomanaga leaning on her husband's arm. They arrived in the Jeep despite the short distance between the minister's mansion and the clinic.

"Her pains began a couple of hours ago, not too strong yet," Davita told them.

"We will take good care of her, pastor." Lua steered the pregnant woman to an inner room and waved him back to caring for his flock.

"Do we call someone to take her to the hospital?" Winnie inquired.

"No, no. We have a birthing room. Women have been giving birth for a thousand years on this island—and without clean sheets and an IV drip. I have my midwifery license. We just keep her comfortable until the child comes."

At first, they entertained Lila with wedding talk, and she recounted hers to Davita, a grand thirty-pig affair with a multitude of fine mats traded between the families. That topic ran thin around noon when Winnie took a short lunch break. Leaving the house, she nearly tripped over the battered boy playing happily on the Malala's porch with another child, his older brother who had decided to move in as well. A little girl napped on Adam's mattress. No explanation about her. At this rate, they would be up to the Lorena Ranch child count in no time at all. She went back to her duties stunned again by the ease and yet the deep responsibilities of the *fa'a Samoa.*

As Lila's labor progressed, Winnie rubbed the rippling belly with fragrant oil and massaged the woman's back to ease the pain. Some of Davita's female relatives came to visit and talk above the tightening mound in the bed. They got in the way but did provide a distraction.

Dinner came and went with Lila existing on ice chips to suck. She progressed slowly into the night. Winnie stayed by her side. Lua showed her patient how to breathe as the pains intensified, but the last hour came punctuated with outright screams.

"Good, let it out if you need to," Lua encouraged.

The shrieks did not comfort Reverend Tomanaga, haggard in the waiting area, but at last his eight-pound son came into the world at 2:35 a.m. He thanked Lua and Winnie, but his wife most profusely. The nurses cleaned up both the mother and baby and settled them in for the rest of the night. Lua intended to stay at the clinic until morning when she thought Lila could go home. She encouraged both Davita and Winnie to leave and get some sleep. They went out into the night together.

"Allow me to escort you to Adam's house," the pastor offered most gallantly.

"It isn't that far and even the village dogs know me by now," Winnie answered, seeing how wrung out the man was as if he'd gone through labor himself.

"Besides, you have virtually no crime here." Still, she let him walk beside her under that vast arc of the Milk Way through the silent village.

"Oh, we have quick-tempered men and domestic disputes, but rarely anything else. Still, I've heard rumors lately that a *moetotolo* might be on the loose."

Winnie laughed at the strange word. "Is this like a *loup-garou* in Louisiana? A werewolf tale to keep children in their beds at night."

"Hardly. The term does come from olden days when everyone slept in open-sided *fale*. The *moetotolo* is a night creeping rapist who molests young women in their beds."

Winnie raised her eyebrows skeptically. "Seems that would be hard to do with an entire family sleeping in one room. Wouldn't the woman cry out or at least report the rape after it happened?"

"Well, there used to be much more honor attached to virginity, so a girl might not want to report such a thing and spoil her chances at a good marriage."

"Not so much today."

They neared the Malala house where Winnie expected to see Adam snoring on his outdoor mattress for the sake of her own honor. The web of mosquito netting held nothing. He must have given up and gone inside for a better rest. She turned to thank the pastor at the foot of the steps when screams tore open the peace of the village and people ripped from slumber stumbled outside to search for the source.

At first, Winnie turned toward the clinic thinking Lila might be suffering complications, but no, the solid walls of the clinic would have muffled any such cries. The piercing shrieks issued from the direction of the beach. She and Davita ran in that direction with the rest of the crowd, not knowing what they would find. The screams stopped very suddenly leaving the rescuers without a direction. Several *matai* bearing clubs large enough to crack a skull shouted to the others to return home. They would search the beach.

Davita said, "We should leave this to them, Winnie. The *matai* handle most of the problems in the village without going to the police, and this might turn out to be nothing but the young people playing a prank."

"I don't think so. Adam is out there somewhere. Those screams belonged to a woman. He would have run to help and could have gotten injured himself. I might be able to assist medically."

"Then, I will stay with you."

In the distance, they saw the younger, swifter *matai* closing in on a distinctive clump of coconut palms slanting against the night sky and headed in that direction. Of all the senarios Winnie might have imagined, finding Adam crouched with a bloody coconut clutched in his hands over the still form of Sammy Tau did not number among them.

Chapter Twenty-Six

Adam Malala was a hero on the football field. He should have saved the girl and subdued the bad guy, not been found kneeling by the corpse of his former friend, murder weapon in hand. No, Winnie would not believe it.

"Let me through. I'm a nurse. I'll check for vital signs."

The blood-fouled coconut rolled from Adam's fingertips as she knelt to dig for a pulse in the rolls of Sammy's fat neck. No throb there or in his wrist. She could see the damage to the broad face, the nasal bone smashed with such force it must have penetrated the brain, and more blood from a contusion on the top of the head matting the short, curly hair. She'd seen enough accident victims in the emergency room to know Sammy Tau had gone to meet his ancestors.

"He's not breathing."

Adam made a motion, his big reddened hands crossed as it he would perform CPR on the flabby unmoving chest. Winnie shook her head. "Head trauma. He's gone."

The *matai* consulted. Finally, the two largest bearing clubs stepped forward to take Adam's arms and raise him to his feet. Winnie knew with his size and spectacular physical condition, he could have thrown them off easily and run into the jungle. He did not take that chance.

"I found Sammy like this when I ran toward the screams. I was far down the beach. If I had been quicker…"

"No, you wouldn't have saved him. The head injury was too severe."

The guards hustled Adam away from the body, and Winnie followed back to the village where they led him to a storage building full of hundred-pound sacks of rice waiting for distribution. Passively, Adam arranged a few of the sacks into a bed and stretched out as the *matai* watched cautiously.

"Winnie, tell my parents where I am and what's going on. Don't worry. Get some sleep."

The door shut behind the prisoner. A boy ran up to the guards with a flimsy lock to secure it. Winnie protested.

"Can't you let him go home? I mean where is he going to run with no transportation? Adam is too famous to hide. This is simply ridiculous. He would never murder anyone."

Suddenly, the men did not understand her English. They stared out into the night like carved wooden tikis on either side of the door. Pastor Tomanaga spoke from behind her. Spending too much time on writing his sermons, he seemed a bit breathless after running across the beach and returning.

"This is beyond the power of the *matai*. The police are being summoned; a group of men will stay on the beach to keep the crabs off the body and try to prevent the tide from taking the evidence. There is nothing we can do for Adam before morning. Rest, and thank you again for your help in bringing my son into the world. One soul enters. Another leaves. The ways of the Lord are mysterious, but I do believe Adam is innocent and will be vindicated." Once more, he escorted Winnie home.

The Malalas sat waiting on the porch rockers. Ela's chair creaked heavily beneath her weight. By the look on their faces, they already knew.

"Sammy Tau is dead, and my son will be taken away when the police come. More shame for our family." Ela pushed up from her seat and went inside.

Noa remained. "Sit with me. We will wait and see."

Winnie collapsed into the rocker, and without realizing it, rocked herself to sleep. She woke when a police cruiser and a coroner's van passed on the lava rock and shell road in front of the house. The vehicles returned an hour later, one surely bearing Sammy's remains and the other hauling Adam in the backseat. He raised his manacled hands, the dried blood rusty on them, and managed a brief, confident smile as he left for Pago Pago, not in his Jeep or by village bus, but in the back of a police car.

****

Ela set out a banana porridge made from the very fruit Adam has picked yesterday for their breakfast. The three children, now part of the family, gobbled it down, but Winnie could not eat.

"Shouldn't we go into town to see if Adam needs any help?"

"The *matai* will take care of it." Ela turned away

Not long after, the police returned to the village. Imposing men dressed in plain khaki lava-lavas with a matching uniform shirt of the same color complete with epaulets and heavy sandals on their feet, they stood by the old gas cylinder as a boy banged on it to get the attention of the villagers. Winnie joined the crowd along with Noa who hadn't taken his boat out that morning.

One of the *matai* spoke up. "He is asking the woman who screamed in the night to step forward and give her story to the police," Adam's father translated. "Also a young man with feet much smaller than Adam Malala's who was near the scene of the crime."

"That's good, isn't it? They are looking at other people," Winnie whispered.

But, no one in the crowd moved. One of the officers added details. Judging by the footsteps running away from the body, they sought a young woman still light on her small feet. The merry girls who had decorated Winnie with garlands huddled together like baby chicks when a hawk darkens the sky with its wings. None came forward. Because of the silence, all would have to be interrogated. The authorities set up a table and chairs in the church hall and began their interviews. The young women deferred to Winnie who had been herded into the hall along with them.

She told her tale of sitting up with the pastor's wife, the unimpeachable truth of walking back to the house with the reverend and hearing the screams exactly like everyone else. Yes, Adam was missing from his bed on the porch. She saw him next, coconut in hand, by the body. He wanted to perform CPR, she added, but she'd declared Sammy Tau dead. Unable to stop herself, Winnie blurted out that she and Adam were in a relationship, and he had never hurt her despite his size. The cop nodded and sent her away. She needed to do more for Adam.

At the infirmary, Winnie questioned the returned and refreshed Nurse Talo about catching a bus into the city. "Very easy. Walk to the main road and flap your hand up and down when a bus approaches. They will pull over. Have correct change or else the stop will last forever as the driver tries to find change to return to you. One should be by around ten, more or less. All of Pago Pago is talking about the murder, you know."

Lila and the baby had gone home. Briefly, Winnie thought about borrowing the Jeep, but driving it up that treacherous dirt lane to the main road and then surviving Samoan drivers made her stick to the bus idea. She went to the house and removed some cash and a credit card hidden in the lining of her suitcase. The new little girl in residence had helped herself to Winnie's Sunday hat and paraded through the house with it atop her tight pigtails. Winnie traded her a length of lava-lava cloth for the return of the chapeau, which she hung on a high hook out of reach of the small, grubby hands. The boys, it appeared, had gone to school. For now, Noa watched his temporary daughter while Ela went on one of her missions. No fresh fish tonight. She doubted she would ever fully understand the *fa'a Samoa*.

Other than her Sunday clothes, she hadn't brought much other than lava-lavas and *puletasi* to the village. The rest of her clothes remained stored at the hotel. She washed up quickly and put on a clean cloth and her shoes. If she hadn't gone entirely native, her body had, now more tanned, the waves of her gold-streaked hair untamed in the high humidity. Her clear green eyes stared at this woman in the small bathroom mirror, the one who had wanted an adventurous fling with an easygoing Samoan hunk and now found herself willing to defend a complex and conflicted man from a murder charge. Adam might not have gotten past the point of having a casual affair, but she knew she'd gone far down the road to loving and caring what happened to him.

Wishing she had a good pair of athletic shoes instead of the stupid slides on her feet, she set off to climb the mountain road and arrived wilted at the top with fifteen minutes to spare. Then a half hour to spare, forty-five minutes, an hour. At last, one of the *'aiga* buses tooled down the road blasting Samoan rock music and resembling in its many wild colors a hippie mini-van from the Sixties. Winnie flapped her arm as vigorously as a blue-footed booby trying to take off into the sky. The outrageous vehicle already full to the point where a young man in the back sat on another young man's lap stopped to let her aboard. An older man near the front offered Winnie his seat and lacking another space, simply stood in the aisle.

They bucketed along only a few miles when the bus stopped to load a granny with a small pig on a rope leash. Immediately, the man next to Winnie offered up his seat. As they jolted off, the pig sniffed Winnie's feet and after nearly losing its footing to a dip into a pothole, sat on her toes with a contented porcine grin. As they lumbered on a few more miles, one of the men in the back rapped on the ceiling for the bus to stop. Everyone standing in the aisle got off to let him disembark. The bus reloaded, paused next to pick up two girls going into the city for a day, as they told

Winnie when they stacked themselves into one spare seat. The granny and her pig got off halfway down the mountain, though the beast showed some reluctance to leave Winnie's feet, and she had to assist by shoving its curly-tailed hams from the bus. Great, now her hands smelled like pig, too. At this rate, the passengers would not reach the city before night.

Finally, they rolled into Pago Pago and most of the passengers got off one place or another. Winnie worked her way to the driver and asked about the nearest stop to the jail. She hesitated before adding, "The one where they took Adam Malala."

With a broad grin, he said, "I hear about that this morning. I take you there. Go lotsa times."

Not sure if he'd been in jail many times or simply dropped visitors there, she still appreciated this courtesy upon arrival at the building. "When will you be going back up the mountain?"

"I stay in Pago tonight. Maybe in the morning. You wave when you see me."

Okay, vague enough. She thought she had adequate money for a taxi to the hotel and could simply put her room on the credit card. Right now, hot, hungry, and tired in mid-afternoon, she overcame the temptation to go there immediately. Adam must come first. The police had taken him bare-chested wearing nothing but the loincloth he used for sleeping. He'd need clothing, a lawyer, bail. She trudged up to the top of the steps only to be nearly bowled to the bottom by a man exiting in a gray business suit complete with necktie above and a matching lava-lava below.

"*Tulou*," he apologized, grabbing her elbow to keep her from falling.

She looked into the man's lustrous dark eyes and said simply, "Adam."

"Winnie, how did you get here?"

"Bus, quite an experience. I thought maybe I could bail you out or bring you some clothes. I see all of that has been done." He didn't need her, not really.

"Yes, I called an attorney first thing. He brought my suit from the hotel. The team lawyers are on their way from New Orleans, too. News travels fast in the computer age. I understand my arrest is already up on Yahoo and Google."

A dark and lean nervous man wearing whites pushed through the door. "Don't linger here. The piranhas are gathering." He pointed to the once deserted base of the steps where photographers swarmed from shaded nooks to catch a shot of Adam Malala leaving jail. Beyond them, a pre-ordered cab waited. Adam tucked Winnie under the protection of his arm and threw a few light blocks at the paparazzi to get all three of them inside the taxi. Of course, his only comment was "no comment."

He took Winnie's hand and raised her fingertips to his lips. She snatched it away. "Don't! I have eau de swine scent on them. I had to help push a pig off the bus."

He shook back that magnificent hair and roared with laughter, his white teeth brilliant against his dark skin. "Oh, Winnie! Thank you for coming. Thank you for making me laugh."

The lawyer could not spare a smile. "No laughing when we get out of the cab. I want you sober, serious, and sad about the loss of Sammy Tau when you emerge. You know the press will follow us."

"Right." Still, he reclaimed Winnie's delicate, pig-scented hand and covered it with his much larger one, not releasing her until he had to run interference again with a few photographers who divined where they headed. Maybe her presence, her support, did matter.

As soon as the doors of the hotel closed behind them, Adam went into conference with the humorless attorney, and Winnie reclaimed their suite with its wonderful hot shower and a flush toilet that did not have to be personally recharged with a bucket of water. She lavished herb-scented shampoo on her hair and washed her general grubbiness down the drain. A cream rinse helped tame her hair, and she dried it wrapped around a brush with the complimentary hairdryer. How living in the village made her appreciate small luxuries.

She padded into the bedroom wrapped only in her towel and found Adam stretched out in the bed covered only by a light sheet. His suit and formal lava-lava hung on a chair. The chunky gold Rolex he had retrieved from the hotel's safe passed the time on a night table. He appeared to be sound asleep, and she should not wake him after all he had suffered the previous evening. Winnie tiptoed toward her suitcase to take out fresh clothes.

A strong arm whipped out, caught the edge of her towel, spun her back to the bed and into Adam's clutches. He drew her naked under the covers. "I missed sleeping next to you." He buried his face in her fragrant hair. "And this." He teased her lips open for a deep kiss. "This, too."

His fingers traced the curves of her upturned breasts and tickled their way down her centerline to the place where she already throbbed for him. "These and this most of all." He rolled above her, keeping his weight balanced on his muscular forearms. She drew him in by crossing her legs over his tattooed hips. They started out as slow as a Samoan afternoon and ended more like the tsunami that had hit the islands a few years ago. On cue, the daily storm poured from the sky as Adam poured his seed into Winnie. She clenched around him, holding him in, not wanting to let him go now or ever.

When they parted at last, Winnie lay with her head resting above his great, booming heart while Adam stroked her hair and curled it around his fingers. "You aren't going to ask me outright if I killed Sammy? I heard you defending me to the guards last night, and it felt good, that one person believed in my innocence. But how can you know so certainly? I mean, I play a violent sport. Hell, I told Joe, the Rev, and even Macho I wanted to kill the man. Someone will find out and add that to the argument I had with Sammy the day I came home. They will say I had motive, jealousy over Pala."

Winnie shook her head against the strong wall of his muscles. "Adam, when I watch you play football, you cross that field and take out an opponent with athletic joy. You are the first one, like the Rev before you, to offer that man a hand up after the hit. I witnessed your gentleness with Teddy, your happiness in creating a beach out of a piece of scrub land. When I heard you talking to Pala, I did feel you might still want her, but later you said you were glad Sammy would have to live with her, not you. No, you didn't kill him over a woman. You did not kill him at all."

"I want to tell you what little there is to tell. I could not sleep that night. My mother's words bothered me. I walked a long way on the beach considering if I wanted to live the *fa'a Samoa* with another village girl or stay stateside and marry a wonderful *palagi* woman."

"Did you find your answer?"

"I was close when I heard the screams and this whole mess began. I cannot go any farther until my name is cleared."

She wanted to say yes, he could. Yes, she would marry him in sun or in rain, but held back and simply told him what he always told her. "No worries. Get some rest. Sleep on it."

"Tomorrow, I will contact Davita and ask him to bring your things here. I know you are uncomfortable in the village."

"About as uncomfortable as any black woman everyone mistakes for white can be, but I want to go back for a few days and see if I can find out anything to help."

"Lovely Winnie." He kissed her hair. "The police have questioned everyone. What can you do?"

"Whatever it takes to clean up this mess so we can get on with our lives."

He laughed softly. The next sound she heard from him was a light snore. Men could do that, just go to sleep. She could not. The rain outside continued to fall hard. On the village beach, it would wash away Sammy Tau's blood and wipe out those feminine footprints.

She recalled the flitting form of a girl running in the night on the evening Pala had so viciously translated the argument that hurt her feelings. What young woman was bold enough to meet her boyfriend by the banyan tree, then offer herself to Adam? Perhaps, Lita meant to lure Sammy Tau away from her sister and show her up by marrying a *matai*. Maybe, one of her other lovers had killed Sammy when he found them together in that small coconut grove.

Then, she had to consider the rumor of a *moetotolo* roaming the village. Sammy might have had more courage and integrity than she gave him credit for, done his nightly rounds and caught the man in the act, only to be killed. The girl, ashamed of being raped, had fled and feared to speak up about it.

Adam had to stay in Pago. She could return to the village and with the eyes of a foreigner see what the rest of the villagers might want to ignore.

Chapter Twenty-Seven

Winnie squeezed a lime wedge over half a papaya and prepared to eat the healthy part of her breakfast. Samoan pancakes, more like donuts, and a cup of the rich, chocolatey *koko* waited for her attention. No wonder so many people wore lava-lavas; they easily adjusted for weight gain. Still in her robe, she sincerely believed she would have to face an extra five pounds or more when she put on her mainland clothes again. Maybe the trek up the mountain road yesterday had melted some of the fat off her hips and thighs.

Across the small table in their suite, Adam polished off a platter of eggs, corned beef, and hash browns washed down with coffee. Not an extra ounce showed on him, but then, he'd been hauling in fishing nets and hacking down weeds in the plantation. The telephone rang. Winnie assumed the call would be from Adam's lawyer or the pastor, but being closer, she picked it up.

Damn, her sister had figured out how to make an international call. Like any prudent traveler, she'd given Mintay the name of the hotel where they would be staying, though she'd strayed far from there during her trip.

"God, baby sis, do you know you are all over the internet? Thank the Lord Nana doesn't own a computer and Mom and Dad pretty much ignore Yahoo and

Google. For now, you are labeled Adam Malala's unidentified island companion, but that won't last long. The tabloids will offer some bucks to discover your name. What on earth happened down there? Adam accused of murder. I do not believe it."

"Me neither."

"Hurray for you. Is Adam with you now? Rev wants to speak to him."

This would not be good. Reluctantly, Winnie handed the phone to Adam. "The Rev, and I don't mean Davita."

She could hear the blast of her brother-in-law's voice from across the table. "Whatever kind o' trouble you got brewing down there, you'll be putting our little sister on the first plane out of Samoa. She don't need this, you hear me good."

Adam nodded. "I will do that."

"Give me that phone." Winnie snatched it back. "Now you hear *me* good, Revelation Jeremiah Bullock. I am way over eighteen and no one can tell me what to do anymore. The last time I followed my family's advice, I married Doug and that did not work out so well. Like the GI's in World War II, I am in the islands for the duration. I'll be home when I am good and ready." She disconnected before the sermon could begin.

Adam smiled at her over a small arrangement of red ginger blossoms. "You've come a long way from the woman afraid to exceed the speed limits."

"I think I'm reaching a hundred miles an hour and not slowing down."

Another ring of the phone let them know that both the lawyer and Davita had arrived. Winnie ducked into the bathroom to throw on one of her sundresses and sandals and came out ready to return to the village.

"Are you sure you want to do this?" Adam asked again.

"I'll be back to stand at your side in a few days if I don't find out anything. I'll even ride the bus with a whole herd of pigs if I must."

He kissed the top of her head, maybe not what he really wanted to do, but with the minister and lawyer standing there, kept it simple. Winnie made two requests of Davita on their way out of town—the first that they stop to pick up a baby gift for his wife and son. Knowing Lila would nurse and that the baby in this climate would wear little else than a diaper, she settled on a mobile of bright fishes to hang over his bed, a very modest offering at best, but Davita approved because a fish often represented Christianity. The new parents had settled on the name Sa, which meant sacred or holy, a good moniker for a preacher's boy.

She also asked him to stop for some groceries, a large sack of rice, and a case of the ever-popular corned beef to present to Ela because her household had grown by four since Winnie's arrival. "You are catching on to ours ways, Winnie. Accept graciously and give generously," Davita said as he helped stow the supplies.

"Yes, I believe I am." Cautiously she steered Davita to news from the village. Did the people really believe Adam to be guilty?

"Those that know his good nature from childhood say no. Others side with Sammy's 'aiga and recall only their recent bad blood. If Adam is found guilty there will have to be a huge public apology from his family to prevent more violence."

"I understand that now. Have you heard anymore about the *moetotolo*?"

Davita shook his head. "No, probably what you first thought. Someone might have started the rumors to keep the young women in at night."

"Who told you these rumors?"

"Oh, my wife. She thought I should know and wondered if any troubled parishioners had come to me about it, but none had." He swerved to avoid one of the overloaded buses careening down the center of the road, then set the Jeep back on course with steady hands.

"I suppose if someone confessed to you, you could not turn them in."

"We are not Catholic, Winnie. I would go to the *matai* and then the police if I knew who committed such a crime, but none have been reported."

At length, they came to the rutted road and the jungle-obscured sign pointing to the village. Winnie asked to stop at the parsonage to see Lila and the baby. Davita dropped her there and went on to deliver the food to Ela. Winnie found both of her patients thriving. Lila sat in a well-padded rattan chair and had the baby at her breast under a light shawl. She drank her own concoction of *vaisalo*, the cooked grated coconut meat and milk mixed with arrowroot starch supposed to be good for new mothers and whatever else ailed a person. She offered a cup to Winnie who took it to be hospitable and prolong the visit. Once little Sa had completed his meal and gone to sleep, Winnie presented her gift to Lila's delight and slowly sipped her thick drink.

"Thank you so much for your good care of me

during my labor. I was terrified, but tried not to show it. You have very soothing hands."

"Thank you. One of the things I enjoy about caring for people is lessening pain. I learned a lot from Lua that night as well." Winnie took a deep cleansing breath herself and continued. "I don't mean to spoil your joy, but I am so concerned about Adam."

Lila nodded. "We all are."

"Not some perhaps, but that doesn't matter. I wanted to ask about the *moetotolo* stories and who told you."

"Oh, my husband and Pala asked me to speak to Lita about her wild ways. Having a softer manner, they thought I might succeed where they had failed. Lita thought the rumor was aimed at her, to keep her from going out at night, but the other girls lacked her spirit and were very nervous. This all began before Adam returned. At least he cannot be accused of coercing young girls."

"He never would."

"No, I thought not. I got to know him when he and Pala became engaged and did not like seeing what was happening between my friend and Sammy. He pursued her from the moment Adam went back to the States when he was meant only to keep other men away. Gradually, she listened to him. Pala is devoted to the old ways, almost obsessed. Perhaps, Sammy was a better match for her since he aspired to be a *matai*, but I often thought Adam would never raise a hand to her and would treat her well. I was not so sure about Sammy."

Winnie took a small mouthful of her *vaisalo,* not wanting to know how many calories it contained. "He had a violent streak?"

"Not that I noticed in my time here, but the same people who remember Adam's easy nature recalled that he and Sammy were like different sides of the same coin when they played sports. Adam took his bruises well and blamed no one. Sammy would be sure to hit anyone who gave him an injury harder the next time. They all thought Sammy would be the one to go on to a big football career, but Adam worked harder. He had ambition that went beyond the needs of the village. To Pala, this was not a good thing. Sammy curbed his temper around her."

Winnie stood to go. "I appreciate your telling me this. Could you direct me to where Pala lives? I would like to give my condolences."

Lila described the house and its location in the village, and Winnie went to make her next call. The island princess sat on her gleaming brown haunches outside a squat light blue concrete block house with louvered doors and windows no different from any of the others. She wore only a simple white lava-lava and wove the fibers of the pandanus plant into a lengthy mat. Her fragrance drifted in the light breeze making Winnie wonder if she oiled those glistening thighs daily. Pala certainly possessed the whole feminine Samoan package, but Winnie had one thing this perfect woman did not possess—faith in Adam.

Winnie sat down cross-legged beside her and fluffed out her sundress. "I wanted to say I am sorry for your loss."

Pala continued to weave. "Why? You did not like Sammy. He told me he tried to apologize to you for his insult that first day but you would not accept his words."

Winnie still didn't have all the Samoan customs nailed down, and so she simply said, "I will not speak ill of the dead. My grandmother taught me that," instead of "your boyfriend hit on me." She admired the mat. Drawing on the information from her travel guide, she asked, "Is that an *ie toga* in progress?"

"Yes, a fine mat. I was making it to present to Sammy's family at our wedding. Few of the young girls want to learn the craft anymore. Now, I will give it to them at his funeral."

"It is lovely like its weaver. When you are ready to move on, you will have no trouble finding another husband." Might as well grease Pala up a little more.

The *taupou* nodded as if this compliment were her just due. "Yes, my family already talks of the possibilities, but first we will have a big *fa'alavelave* and put on a grand event for Sammy's funeral. We will use the wedding goods as our gifts to his family since he was a junior *matai*. It will take a while to accumulate more."

"I hope I might still be here to pay my respects at the funeral. When will it be held?"

"Two weeks, probably. Relatives must come from all over and the gifts assembled."

"I see." Enough of the island small talk. Winnie got to her point. "Is Lita at home or is she at school? I'd like to speak to her as well."

"Lita at school, ha! Why do you want to see her?" Pala raised her dark eyes from her weaving and pinned Winnie with a suspicious glare.

"I know Lila Tomanaga tried to get through to her about her bad habits and failed. I thought I might help."

Not Lita but Adam.

"You, a divorced woman who wants only a rich husband regardless of his lack of values. How could you do any good?"

Winnie swallowed that remark more bitter than raw cocoa. "I could tell her where I went wrong." Her first wrong step, marrying Doug, who used her to get through medical school, just as Sammy would have used his marriage to the *taupou* to gain status. She should tell Pala she'd gotten a lucky break, but held back again.

Pala did not answer. She carefully set her work aside, rolled her mat, and took it inside the house. At first Winnie thought she'd been left to swelter in the sun without an answer, but the *taupou* returned. "She has been staying with her friend, Alisi, since the night Adam killed Sammy out of jealousy."

"Innocent until proven guilty. We are in *American* Samoa, you know," Winnie rebuked. "I do not believe jealousy was the motive."

"Because Adam has a skinny *palagi* woman instead of me?" Pala released a harsh laugh.

Once more, Winnie curbed her words. "No, because Adam did not do the crime. Are you going tell to me where Alisi lives?"

"No, I intend to take you there. Anything I can do to set my sister on the right path I will do."

Pala set off leaving Winnie. to follow her undulating hips. Determined not to be led, Winnie caught up and took Pala's hand in the friendly gesture often seen among the village girls. Pala stared at her as if she wanted to chew that hand off at the wrist, but Winnie held on and they continued through the village to its far end nearest the deserted stretch of beach. Outside another square house, Pala called her sister.

The sulky teenager poked her head through the open doorway. "What do you want?"

"The *palagi* woman wants to talk to you."

Pala made a move to enter the house, but Winnie dropped her hand and said, "Alone."

The interior seemed dim after being outside in the bright sun, and the air was stuffy despite all the louvered windows being open to let in air. A better day to be on the beach than cooped up here, Winnie thought. Alisi, a round-faced girl she remembered from the *fiafia,* sat on a mat where she and her friend had been pursuing movie magazines and digging into large bags of potato and breadfruit chips that weren't going to reduce the size of the plump belly under her lava-lava. A couple cans of Coke rested among the snacks.

"None of my business, but shouldn't the two of you be in school?"

"School is boring. I dropped out and got a GED last year. Alisi doesn't feel well so I'm keeping her company." Lita threw herself down carelessly and began paging through the magazines again.

Despite the evidence piled around them that she could hardly be sick and eat all that junk, Alisi asked politely, "Would you like a drink, some food?"

"No, thanks, just some conversation." Winnie noticed a shadow outside one of the open windows. She swore when Pala's youthful beauty faded and she'd had a few babies to expand her figure, she would become the village eavesdropper. Well, let her listen.

"Lita, no matter what anyone says about you, I believe you are a very clever girl."

239

Beneath the heavy eye makeup and red lipstick, teenager smirked. "Maybe."

"Lila Tomanaga told me you heard rumors about a *moetotolo* being on the loose but did not believe them."

"I was wrong." The girl looked sidelong at her friend who stared into the open can of Coke as if it contained holy visions. "The *moetotolo* existed. He caught Alisi out one night and forced himself on her, threatened her if she screamed or told. Now there will be a baby. Soon everyone will notice. Tell her, Alisi."

The other girl kept her eyes lowered and shook her head.

"You can speak now. He can't hurt you." The pregnant teen stayed mute.

"Alisi wasn't the only one. I know of at least two other girls. He said they were bad to be out at night, and he had needs, great needs that were not being met. Since they were already corrupt, no one would believe them if they accused him. He was strong. They did what the big *matai* told them to do. They couldn't get away."

"But you did. Isn't that right, Lita?"

The girl shrugged in a world weary way. "The boy I walked with on the beach ran away. Afraid the *matai* will beat them, they always do. He left me behind for the *moetotolo* to take."

"You screamed and fought because you are braver and bolder than the others"

"Yes! Lila Tomanaga told me God would forgive me and look after me if I gave up my wicked ways. I guess He did. When the *moetotolo* tried to cover my mouth, he knocked me against the palm tree. One of the coconuts fell and hit him right on top of the head. He collapsed. I didn't know whether he was dead or not, but I wanted to make sure he never hurt me or my friends again. I bashed him as hard in the face as I could with the weapon God put in my hands and ran away. I haven't gone with a boy since because God protected me from a rapist."

That would be all of three days of celibacy, but Winnie did not point out this fact. "Just to be perfectly clear, the rapist was Sammy Tau." She thought she heard a small gasp outside the window as she pronounced the name.

Lita gave her a sly smile and raised her voice. "Yes, my sister was going to marry a *moetotolo*. I saved her and the rest of my friends, too."

"Why did you let people believe Adam Malala killed Sammy?"

"I offered myself to him and he rejected me. I would have made a better wife for him than Pala or you. I want to get out of this village, off this island. I want to live it the States and have lots of money, not stay here and preserve the old ways. Besides, I knew Adam would be let off. I read the magazines. Famous people never get convicted. But I would be. Don't expect me to go running to the police to confess. Alisi won't tell what she heard and my sister will be too embarrassed to speak about it."

"You were defending yourself—and it could have been death by coconut, strange as that seems." Now who was grasping at straws?

The unfortunate Alisi giggled when Winnie said that until Lita poked her in the belly with a finger across the display of chips and soft drinks. "Yes, death by coconut. That's what it was. I bet Sammy Tau died before I hit him. Do you think there will be a reward for information, enough to get me off this stinking island?"

"Maybe. I will have to ask Adam's lawyer, but it would be better by far to confess now. Otherwise, people might think you were paid to make up a story." Clever, not stupid, Winnie thought again, and let her words sink into the girl's calculating mind.

Lita cocked her head and considered. "I can tell them where I scratched Sammy on the cheek and bit him on his fat breast. I will give the police the name of the boy with me that night. He is part of Sammy's *'aiga* and does not want to come forward to bring shame on the family."

The teenager took a long drag on her Coke as if it contained fortifying alcohol. Maybe it did. "Besides, God saved me. Maybe if Pastor Tomanaga went with me to the police, I would not be put in jail. Later, Adam might give money to the *matai* for a scholarship on the mainland. I know I am worthy of such a scholarship."

Well, no, Winnie thought, but the *matai* would be glad to be rid of the poor example Lita set for the village girls, and that might be enough incentive. "I'm sure you are."

"What colleges do you have in New Orleans?"

Winnie's mama did not raise an idiot child. "I think you would be happier on the west coast. Maybe in Los Angeles where you might see movie stars from time to time." She had no desire to drop in on Adam one day and find Lita and half a dozen of her girlfriends staying at his place because island hospitality demanded it.

"Movie stars, I would like that."

"Me, too!" the excited Alisi said. "I mean I could visit after I have my baby."

242

Winnie began to see how things worked in the village, slow and roundabout, but in the end, everyone got what they needed. "When will you go to Reverend Tomanaga, Lita?"

"Today, tomorrow, pretty soon."

Winnie dearly wanted to wipe the makeup from Lita's face and frog-march her to the parsonage right this minute, but she knew haste was not the Samoan way. "Sounds good," she made herself say. "Thank you."

Outside, Winnie saw no sign of Pala and walked back to the Malala house alone. Her welcome was not as warm as it had been with Adam around. She guessed fish and guests stank after three days in Samoa as well as anywhere else. However, she helped Ela squeeze the grated coconut to make a corned beef *pulasami* for dinner. When the children returned from school, she assisted them with their simple arithmetic problems, let them practice their English on her, and generally kept the little girl out from under Ela's big feet. Being useful, one of her strong points, Winnie figured.

The day passed painfully into evening as if the sun walked carefully across hot coals. An older couple, both of substantial belly size, came to visit Ela and Noa, and passed a few polite words with Winnie on the porch before going inside to hold a lengthy conversation in Samoan. The children nested for sleep in Adam's makeshift bed, which they seemed to prefer to all other places. She gave up waiting for his return and went inside for the night.

Winnie decided to spend the next day at the clinic close to the parsonage where she might notice if the Jeep left with Lita in it. Eventually, it did. She wished she could stick out a thumb and hitch a ride into Adam's arms, but knew her influence over the girl's confession would not help his case one bit. The afternoon rains came with extra force since they had skipped a day and had to make it up. She watched the water cascade from the sky, another kind of waterfall that only made her think of Adam and their visit to *Nu'uuli* Falls.

Lua embraced her shoulders. "Do not worry. The *matai* and the Sinners will not let Adam go to jail."

"The Sinners, sure. They would hate to be out a cornerback, but the *matai* seem to think he is guilty the way they locked him up."

"Things are not always what they appear to be here. Have patience."

Borrowing an umbrella at the end of the day, she reluctantly went back to the house where she now felt unwelcome. Ela's mood had changed like the weather. She hummed as she prepared the evening meal. Somehow, that made Winnie more uneasy than her suppressed hostility. What was going on? What did no one tell her?

Chapter Twenty-Eight

Winnie visited Lila and her baby the next morning and discussed what she had learned from Lita. "I was a help then in saving Adam. I am so glad," the new mother said. "Davita told me some of this, but not the details. I must pray for the soul of Sammy Tau."

She invited Winnie to stay for a bite to eat, and when the phone rang, was much more forthcoming than Ela. "Adam is free. They are coming home this afternoon."

"I should go tell his parents."

"I am sure they know already. He would have called them first."

But not me. Why hadn't Adam asked to speak to her? Winnie lingered with Lila and the baby until late afternoon when she thought the Jeep might arrive based on her other trips to Pago. Her timing proved to be correct. As she neared the house, the bright yellow Jeep rolled down the rutted road at a very sedate speed to keep from running over or leaving behind the adults, children, and dogs running beside it and following. A cheer went up when Adam stepped down from the vehicle.

Taboo or not, Winnie raced toward him. She half-expected him to stop her at arm's length, but he did not. Adam folded her into an embrace and accepted her jubilant kiss. When Winnie opened her eyes again, she noticed just over his broad shoulder Ela's face harden into lines of disapproval that aged her ten years. Beside Adam's mother, Noa smiled with unadulterated glee. Other people made up the welcoming group on the porch, the couple from last night and Pala, all of them displaying deep frowns. The old childhood threat about ugly faces freezing that way came to Winnie's mind.

Lita emerged from the backseat to be engulfed by her hugging girlfriends including the pregnant Alisi. Davita turned off the engine and got down. He suggested a prayer. The crowd bowed heads and fell silent. He thanked God the truth had come out and freed an innocent man, that His mighty hands sent the coconut to bring down the guilty, but also asked them to pray for the soul of the departed. Amen.

Ela clapped her hands to draw attention. In a clear, strong voice, she announced, "Still more good news, my friends. The wedding between my son and Pala will go on as planned in May."

Pala stood there between her parents doing her blushing maiden routine, eyes downcast, hands folded in front of her, but she raised her tawny lids just enough to send Winnie a very smug look. The woman must have hotfooted home after Lita's confession and babbled to her parents. No sense in grieving over a rapist, back to Plan A. Oh, they would send Sammy off with a church funeral, condolences to the family, and a hearty meal, but the gifts for such a corrupt man need not be lavish. On with the wedding!

Winnie's knees weakened. Adam's arm held her close. He answered in an equally loud, firm voice. "No! The engagement was broken. I will not marry Pala. I want Winnie."

"You refuse to honor the wishes of your elders?" Ela asked.

"Yes."

"Then you are not my son." She turned and moved back into the fine house that son provided for her. Noa hesitated, came down the steps first to embrace his son and whisper a few words, then follow his wife inside. Pala, shielding her face with her hands, dashed into the crowd to be trailed at a more dignified pace by her outraged parents. Her mother kept repeating the same phrase as she went among the people. Adam translated it as saying, "My daughter has many other offers."

Lita, standing nearby, laughed cruelly and commented, "Yes, from old, fat men. I guess I should go with them, but they aren't going to thank me for what I've done. Adam, you must get me out of here soon!" Hips swaying more provocatively than Pala at her best, the lesser sister went after her family.

Adam put a hand on Davita's sleeve. "After we gather our things, will you take us back into the city?"

"Of course, my friend, but I think you should stay and work things out with your parents."

"If they had bothered to consult me, this could have been done in a more private manner. My father says he understands and has no quarrel with me. Once he was forced into a marriage, too, and never found the courage to leave because my mother's family was so powerful. That answers a few questions I've had all my life. I cannot bend on this. Let's get packed, Winnie."

Since they'd come to the village with little more than lava-lavas and Sunday clothes, that task took no time at all. Winnie found her cell phone forgotten on the bedside table. It held a message about his being freed thanks to her efforts. Whether he called her first or second no longer mattered. Adam had chosen her over Pala.

Like a good son, Adam muscled the mattress off the porch and back into the bedroom before they left, but got no thanks for the job. Ela stayed in the kitchen and refused to speak to him. Noa did see them off and tacitly gave them his blessing. Soon they would be on their way to Hawaii again, then Louisiana. Thank God and death by coconut.

Chapter Twenty-Nine

The tickets for their departure lay on the small hotel table with the vase of red ginger. Not easy to get at the last minute, Adam had scored the last two seats in first class for the flight by uprooting the Sinners' lawyers who had arrived only to find their services were no longer needed. He put them up at the same hotel and told them to enjoy a few days in the islands at his expense. The heat and humidity had the attorneys out of their suits and basking their pale bodies, alcoholic drinks served in a coconut in their hands, by the pool within hours.

Adam and Winnie made love in the morning and left the sheets rumpled on their last day in Samoa. He let her have the use the bathroom first since Winnie wanted to make a last minute excursion to the stores for family souvenirs. Adam planned to shower while she shopped, and she knew he would spend almost as much time drying his hair as she did, though he didn't give a damn about frizz. At the moment, he lingered over another mammoth Samoan breakfast, liberally dousing some fried plantains with ketchup and perusing a newspaper with an article about his release. Yes, the headline did read "Death by Coconut Declared."

She left for a couple of hours and purchased *puletasi* for her mother, grandmother, Mintay, and Nell, lava-lavas for her niece, Riley, and all of Nell's girls. Knowing better than to present any of Joe's sons or her nephews with a skirt by any other name, she got the boys a whole fleet of small, carved Polynesian canoes she thought they might like to race in the swimming pool. For Joe Dean Billodeaux who inadvertently brought her and Adam together, she selected an 'ava bowl to sit on his bar. Then, realizing the extant of her purchases, found a suitcase that would hold the lot. One good thing about traveling first class with a Sinner, no worries about extra baggage.

Another matter did niggle in her mind—she hated being the cause of a rift between Adam and his family, of severing him from a way of life he admired but found too confining. As he held her in his arms the previous night, he kept assuring her the decision to make his life entirely in the States had been a long time in coming. Meeting her only sealed the deal.

His father had confirmed what he long suspected, that his mother had gotten pregnant and married into a lesser 'aiga than her own. Ela's only hope to regain lost status rested in her son, his marriage, and his future. He possessed a fortune, much to give away and become a *matai*, enough to raise himself up to the territory's congress, the *fono*, with the presentation of many gifts.

"Bribes, you mean?"

"No, lovely Winnie. Generous gifts for which I expect no return. It is how we gain status."

"And votes?"

"Well, yes, but I have no desire to serve in the *fono*. I will always send gifts and money home because it is our way even if I never return. Do you understand?"

"I can accept that."

She hoped he had no regrets later and would encourage him to visit once the bad feelings died down. Look at her, making plans about a future with Adam Malala when he had not proposed or even said directly that he loved her. He wanted her more than Pala. That would have to do for a while.

****

Adam polished off the plantains and had a second cup of coffee, so much weaker than the kind served in Louisiana. No need to hurry if he knew anything about women and shopping. Winnie wouldn't be back for hours. He tossed his confining robe on the unmade bed and headed naked to the bath on the other side of the suite. A light rap sounded.

"Done shopping already? Forget your key?" He wrapped a towel around his waist just in case the knock came from someone other than Winnie and went to answer.

Pala stood on the other side of the door. Her long hair lay tangled in a provocatively sensual way, and she wore a fresh red hibiscus flower possibly plucked from the hotel's shrubs behind one ear. Though she had creases in her lava-lava from a long drive, her skin smelled of fragrant coconut oil, not pigs or other people on a bus.

"How did you get here? They aren't supposed to give out my room number at the desk."

She stepped inside the room and quietly closed the door. "Lila let me borrow the Jeep. I told her I needed to get away after yesterday's embarrassment. As for the other, one of my aunties is a maid here and very pleased I came to visit for a short time."

She placed a hand, so good at weaving fine mats, preparing *'ava,* and moving gracefully in the *siva* dancing, on his cheek. Her fingers moved down his tight jaw and roamed over his chest, the very first time she had touched him intimately.

"I was very foolish to listen to Sammy and want to apologize. I know our parents should have asked you about resuming our engagement. I told them they must."

Adam felt a tightening in his loins. She was a beautiful woman after all and standing very, very close. He stepped back. "Thank you for the apology. I appreciate it. You should go now. I need to get ready to catch my flight."

Pala stepped near again. "I came to offer myself to you. Our wedding is only a few months away. What does it matter? Sammy kept saying that to me, and I would not have him. Maybe I sensed what he did with other women. Maybe I did drive him to it just as my turning from you forced you into the arms of the first *palagi* woman who came along. I know that you used this Winnie only to defy your mother and show her you are a man who makes his own decisions. We can still have all we were meant to have on our own terms." She unknotted her lava-lava and let it drop to the floor, but her use of Winnie's name broke the spell.

Adam backed toward the bathroom. "Pala, you are delusional. Don't make me drop kick you naked into the hallway. Now, I am going in here, locking the door, and when I come out ready to leave the islands, I want you gone. Understand me? We are over. In fact, I think we never were in any real sense. No love, no affection, no trust in each other, just a physical attraction on my side and a desire for status on yours. Love, affection, trust, I have that with Winnie. Go, I don't want to lay hands on you."

He did as he said, clicked the lock, and braced his back against the door for a moment. Close call, very close call as if the spirits of the island were trying to lure him back again. Adam turned on the shower and waited for the steam to rise. He got in and washed Pala's touch off his body.

****

Wanting very much to break something, Pala stood still naked in the center of the suite. She stalked over to the breakfast table intending to fling the vase of flowers against window with the ocean view, possibly breaking both. She would trash the room and see that her auntie reported the damage done by the self-centered American football player. Then, she noticed something else sitting among the dirty dishes—a folder containing airline tickets for Adam and the *palagi* woman.

Pala withdrew Adam's ticket and ripped it into tiny pieces. He needed to stay. Winnie Green needed to go. Simple as that. With her rival out of the way, Adam would accept her offering of her greatest gift, her virginity. She would no longer be humiliated and scorned, but soon become the wife of a famous man who might become a *matai* or even serve in the national *fono* to govern the islands. Let him have other women back in the States. She would stay here and pave the way with gifts for his new career when he retired from sports.

Now, how to go about driving the *palagi* woman away? If she found Adam in bed with her, that would work, but he'd been very clear about not wanting to see her when he returned from the shower. Pala recalled the old wedding custom that had fallen into disuse, of the bride and groom going into an enclosure during the ceremony and having intercourse to prove the virginity of the bride with blood spilled upon a clean, white sheet. She would have passed that test and been proud of it! Her mother told her some women bled more, some less, and a bit of chicken blood often came in handy. She swiped her finger through a scrim of ketchup on the edge of Adam's plate and stared at it thoughtfully.

Leaving her lava-lava where it lay, Pala kicked off her sandals and went to the unmade bed. She sniffed. It smelled of a man and woman together and still had a damp spot in the center. Centering herself just above that dampness, she smeared the ketchup on the sheet and drew the top sheet up between her breasts, but left both them and her legs exposed. She only had to wait and hope Winnie Green returned shortly. After some time, the shower stopped blasting and the roar of the hairdryer replaced that noise. Pala nearly missed the faint click of the key card in the lock, but when Winnie entered the room, she was fully prepared.

****

Winnie smiled at the sound of the hairdryer, that curly mane of his, his single vanity. "Adam, stop primping. I know I took too long, but the cab is waiting and our suitcases are in it. You need to finish dressing, grab our tickets, and go."

A low seductive voice spoke from the bed across the room. "He is not going with you. I offered myself to him. He took my virginity, and now we will marry as planned because Adam Malala is a man of honor. He

254

tore up his ticket, you see. Yours is still on the table."

Pala dropped the sheet from her body and flung it back to expose a russet stain between her legs in the exact spot where Winnie and Adam had sex that morning. The lush body of the young woman adorned only with the ropes of tattoos on her thighs lay there naked as a Samoan goddess, the very spirit of the islands incarnate, summoning Adam back to his village and his way of life.

"Yes, I thought Adam was a man of his word. Evidently, a woman can be wrong about men more than once."

Pala inclined her head as if agreeing with this statement entirely. "I win. You lose. Go home, *palagi* woman."

Winnie experienced the same numbness she'd had when Doug announced his decision to leave her for another woman. Only her feelings for her ex-husband had atrophied by then from his lack of interest, her fatigue working long hours. Her love for Adam was so fresh and new, so easily bruised and damaged by this revelation. Of course, she came in second best compared to that lush creature in the bed.

Did he expect her to get into a cat fight with Pala over him? Or had he planned to come down to the desk, meet her, explain, and hand her the ticket to get home? He might have perfect timing on the football field, but it failed him now. Winnie took her ticket, went to the cab, and left Adam's baggage behind.

Chapter Thirty

Adam emerged naked from the bathroom in a small cloud of steam like one of the old gods, hair wild, his tattoos showing courage and manhood. Wrapped in a bed sheet, Pala stood near the balcony doors and held out her arms to him. "Take me. Your other woman is gone."

"What the hell, Pala! I told you to get dressed and get out of here. Where are my clothes, my ticket? Where is Winnie?"

"All gone. I have a sheet here with your semen on it and the stain I showed her marking the loss of my virginity before she left."

Adam tore the sheet away from her body and examined the smudge. "Are you so crazy you cut yourself? I mean football groupies do some loony things, but this tops it." He wet a finger, ran it across the patch of red, and popped it into his mouth. "Yeah, I thought so, ketchup."

"We can make it real now." Pala held out her arms again.

"That will not happen. Just tell me where my clothes are."

"Out there." She pointed a finger to the balcony.

Adam shrugged into the hotel robe, always too tight and too short on him, doubled the stained sheet over and wrapped it around him lava-lava style because no way was he going to leave it with Pala and whatever she might try next. He went to reclaim from the landscaping the clothes he'd laid out for his trip. His khakis and a red Sinners shirt hung on some bushes halfway down the cliff. He found his black boxer briefs tenting a vivid red ti plant and one of his athletic shoes in the driveway. Finally giving up, he pounded up to the desk and simply asked the clerk for help.

"Oh, Miss Green left your suitcase with us."

"Thank God for small favors."

"Will you be staying on with us?'

"No. Call a taxi. I'll need it as soon as I change my clothes which I'd like to do down here if you have a private space."

"Is there a problem with your room?"

"Yes, pest infested."

The clerk's eyes widened in horror. "Not bed bugs!"

"No, only someone crazy as they are. I need a young woman removed and sent on her way."

"So sorry about this. One of your fans?"

"Not anymore."

He dressed quickly in the manager's office, even packed the damned sheet, but the cab came in Samoan time at a very leisurely pace. At the airport, he explained that his ticket had been lost. The very flustered woman behind the counter repeated Winnie's words. "Miss Green said you decided to stay and would not be in need your ticket. I am so sorry, but we gave it to the first standby passenger, and they have already boarded. We can put you on tomorrow's flight."

"How about removing that standby's ass from my

seat because I need it?"

"Oh, oh, we can't do that. The door is closed on the aircraft. I am so sorry about this misunderstanding."

"Yeah, so am I." No sense in taking out his frustration on a woman just doing her job.

Adam moved to the window overlooking the runway and watched Winnie's plane taxi away from the gate. He wondered if she could see him standing there through those tiny windows. Not wanting to see Samoa again, she probably had her shade drawn against the burning tropical sun and any view of him.

****

Having no desire to watch Tutuila island shrink into the vast Pacific, Winnie drew down the window shade. At least, she traveled home in style with a spacious seat that would recline into a comfy bed for sleeping on the long journey—if only the man sitting next to her would simply shut up and leave her alone. He'd already asked her name, pressed his business card into her hand, and expressed his happiness at securing a last minute seat and such a lovely woman to sit next to him. Lovely, a word Adam used so often when describing her. She had no desire to hear it on this man's lips, this Dexter Sykes, photographer.

Shorter than she and going soft through the middle, Sykes wore his thinning brown hair combed back over a small bald spot and regarded her with round, brown eyes that except for being bloodshot held some puppy dog appeal. Nana would have used the term "hound dog" eyes. You stay away from those hound dog kind of men, you hear me Winnie? Time to start listening to Nana again.

Still, Sykes examined her rather shrewdly. "Yes, I

just completed a big swimsuit assignment on Ta'u Island. Great beaches, beautiful babes, but, oh brother, all that rain delayed my departure by days. Missed my flight from the ends of the earth. Really deserted over there. You ever do any modeling? You look familiar."

"No, I'm only a nurse. I was visiting with a friend and helped out at a clinic for a few days. Now I'm on my way back to New Orleans." Enough said.

"Me, too! I have a studio there. You got the bones for modeling. Good hair and eyes, kind of an exotic look about you. Exotic sells. You ever want a portfolio taken, I'm your man."

"I don't think so, thanks." Winnie immersed herself in the flight magazine crossword.

A couple hours into the journey, the attendants served a hot meal in first class. Winnie selected the fish. Sykes dug into a very small steak and seemed compelled to engage in dinner conversation.

"Poor suckers back there in tourist class only get sandwiches, dry ones. I've gone that route often enough, but I'm doing real well financially. Why, you ask?"

Winnie hadn't asked. She held up her cup for a refill of white wine.

"Because I got luck. I'm always in the right place at the right time. I mean the gig to go to Samoa and do a photo shoot paid, but when I get stranded in Pago Pago on my way back, the Adam Malala business boils up, one of the Sinners players accused of murder. Hot damn! I had time to kill so I staked out the courthouse and got the money shot of him coming out the door with some island honey. You follow football?"

"Not much." Winnie concentrated on her meal and

hoped with her hair held back by a colorful scarf and wearing white slacks and a tailored blouse she bore no resemblance to the frizzy-headed "honey" in the soiled lava-lava.

"You gotta know Adam Malala. He has all that hair. Wish I did."

"Yes, he's done some commercials."

"Right! For a coconut cream rinse and shampoo. You think he was really guilty? I mean that story about death by coconut is pretty thin."

"I understand such things happen. I do believe he is innocent."

"Remember the Connor Riley/Stevie Dowd business back a few years? I took that shot right after he sacked her on the football field. Those two really moved my career along. Confidentially, I slept with Stevie before Connor came along. We used to be partners."

"Really?" The Stevie Riley she'd met long ago at Mintay's wedding now had two cute little children and a handsome ex-Sinner husband—who would probably like to rip this guy's head off and run it in for a touchdown for saying those words. Or, Stevie might do it herself, she had that kind of attitude, one Winnie lacked.

Winnie's eyes must have registered her disbelief because he quickly added, "I had more hair then and wasn't quite so wide around the middle. How about you, Winnie? You with anyone?'

"Not anymore. Divorced, I mean."

"Nothing wrong with that. How about I buy you breakfast or lunch or whatever when we get to Honolulu? Though, if you are sitting here in first class, nurses must be making some pretty good change these days."

"My friend paid for the ticket. Look, in Honolulu I have to arrange the rest of my trip back to New Orleans. This fare only takes me to Hawaii. I guess we were going to stay over a few days, but I want to go directly home. I don't have time for fancy dining."

"Not fancy, just breakfast, maybe in the terminal. I figure I'm sitting in this friend's seat. You break up with some undeserving guy?" The hound dog had picked up the scent.

"Let's just say he went back to his old girlfriend and leave it at that."

"Vacation breakups are the pits," he said, deeply sympathetic.

The steward came to take their trays and hand out headsets for a movie. Winnie took the offer gladly and after that accepted a blanket and pillow to curl into with her face turned toward the window. The next thing she knew, hot facial towels to refresh her after the long flight were being handed around. After landing, she managed to outdistance Dexter Sykes with her longer legs, but he came up behind her in the ticket line.

"What do you say I treat us to first class all the way back to New Orleans?"

"I'm sorry, I can't accept that."

"Okay, for the pleasure of your company I'll ride in the back with the rest of the cattle."

"Please don't do that."

"Come on, you can tell me all your troubles. How about some eggs and bacon? I can tell you I am tired of corned beef and taro."

Because Dex would only follow, she submitted to a

breakfast where the eggs came with little purple orchids as garnish and tall glasses of pineapple juice filled in for orange. He insisted on buying her a lei, prepackaged, inspected, and sealed to take out of the country to cheer her up.

"Was your breakup bad, honey?"

"No, just sudden, unexpected. I really do not want to talk about it."

They caught their late flight to L.A., another overnighter, then a layover in that city where the photographer asked her to pose with her lei on by a clump of small palms outside the hotel where they stayed overnight. No harm in that. She left the lei for the maid after he tried to talk himself into her room that evening. Oh God, another three hours of Sykes tomorrow before she got to New Orleans. She placed a call to her sister and asked for a ride to her house. If anyone could scare off a pesky photographer, that would be the Rev.

Sykes dogged her all the way to the luggage pickup at Louis Armstrong International Airport where the Rev waited, black and as mountainous as the place where Moses wrote the Ten Commandments. His clerical collar dug into his neck like a choke chain on a pit bull holding him back from violence, but he said in his deep, ministerial voice, "Are you following my sister-in-law?"

Dex snapped his fingers. "I know you! Rev Bullock. I used to do some sports photography at the Sinners' games."

"And I know you, Mr. Sykes. You are the man who took immoral pictures of my friend, Stevie Dowd, and had them published." His big eyes rolled toward Sykes' camera bag.

"No immoral pictures in here. No, sir. Simply a pleasure to have Miss Winnie's company as we traveled. Got some calls to make. Have to run." With a cell phone plastered against his ear, Dexter Sykes trotted off so fast his rolling luggage tipped over in his haste. He dragged it several feet before pausing to settle it on its wheels again.

Winnie exhaled. "Thank you for getting rid of him."

"Oh, baby sis, I don't think we did you any favors. Now Dex knows you are related to us. I figure he is adding up all the numbers right now in his head, and they aren't going to come out in our favor," Mintay said.

"Let's get on home." The Rev seized both her bags and led their group to the black Escalade with the cross on the rear. He did not ask about Adam for quite a few miles, just let her babble about her big adventure, how she bought souvenirs for everyone, and had probably put on ten pounds eating Samoan cuisine.

"No, you look wonderful, all tan and healthy," Mintay claimed, obviously pretending not to notice the signs of stress. She'd chosen to sit in the backseat with Winnie and let her husband be their chauffeur.

The question had to be asked. "Exactly why did Adam let you travel all this way alone when lowdown dawgs like Dexter Sykes could get after you?" the Rev asked. "Your face was all over the internet when you came out of the courthouse with him. The least he could do is see you home and protect you from paparazzi."

"Oh, he did protect me in Samoa. It's just that he decided to stay and marry his virgin. Well, I guess she isn't anymore. I found her in his bed. I mean who wouldn't prefer a beautiful young woman like that over me? Second best again. Please don't tell anyone I'm back yet, not Nell or Joe. I need a few days to get over this." More like forever, she thought.

Then the tears came. The three of them could have floated all the rest of the way to Versailles, the gated community where the Rev and Mintay lived in a substantial home beside the golf course fairway. Her brother-in-law stopped at the guardhouse and rolled down the window.

"Anything I can do for you, Reverend Bullock?" the white-haired security man asked as he raised the barrier.

"Yes, put the name Adam Malala on my no entry list."

Chapter Thirty-One

Adam accepted he wouldn't catch up with Winnie on the road, but he knew where to find her. He did his layover in Hawaii and took care of his business there. Then, he took a night flight to L.A., a day flight to Dallas, and right on to the Lafayette airport, the nearest one to Winnie. He handled the whole affair as if he were on the football field picking out his target to tackle, taking the most direct route with the most wallop at the end. Just before his plane left for Louisiana, he placed a call to Joe Dean asking for a ride and a place to stay. No problem. Now, Winnie remained his only concern.

****

Joe Dean put his phone aside. He dipped the edge of the second of his grilled cheese sandwiches into the last of a bowl of tomato soup and bit off the corner. Sitting next to him at the kitchen table with a smaller version of the same meal, Nell asked, "Who called?"

"Oh, Adam, back from Samoa. He wants a lift from the airport. I guess he plans on staying with us again."

Nell stifled a small sigh. "Doesn't he have a place in New Orleans?"

"Sure. Maybe he likes our company or wants to lie low after that mess in his hometown. I won't blame him for not wanting to stay in the islands longer. He can have the same cabin. Maybe he'll roast another pig for us."

"We don't need another roast pig. We need some time to ourselves. Thanks for making lunch. It's nice to come home from the clinic and have a meal waiting."

"I know the way to a woman's heart."

"More than one. When do you have to pick up him and Winnie?"

"Hour and a half. Doesn't matter if I'm a little late getting there."

Joe polished off his second glass of milk and got up to fill a mug with coffee from the pot on the counter. He palmed a handful of some kind of healthy cookie that didn't taste too bad from the jar and offered one to his wife. She looked directly into his deep brown eyes as she accepted it. They'd been married long enough it seemed they really could read each other's thoughts or at least their desires.

Corazon shopping for groceries, Knox doing something around the ranch, the discreet Brinsley polishing their rarely used silver service in the dining room, Nurse Wickersham taking one of her vigorous constitutionals around the property, and all the kids in school—they had a good hour to go upstairs together before leaving for the airport. In this family, you had to be quick. Joe took Nell's hand.

The van pulled up chock-full of Winn-Dixie bags to haul inside. The ever useful Brinsley appeared in the kitchen to help. Knox materialized at the door with the first armload of sacks, and Corazon's round figure rolled into the room waving a tabloid. "You must see this. Everyone must see!"

She spread the paper on the kitchen table. The same photo of Adam and Winnie leaving the courthouse they'd already seen on the internet filled the left hand side, but the headline read, "Malala Cleared of Murder. Coconut Conked Rival."

"Sure, same as before only now he is innocent which we all believed anyhow," Joe said, unimpressed.

"No, no! At the bottom. You see what he did to our Nurse Winnie."

An inset showed Winnie decked out in a lei, backed by palm trees, and captioned as "Malala's Jilted Island Honey." Nurse Wickersham entered and asked what was going on.

Nell held up her hand. "Let me read it aloud."

"She stood by her man, but Adam chose another. Malala's island companion has now been identified as Winnie Green, a divorced nurse from New Orleans and sister-in-law of retired NFL player, Revelation Bullock. Returning to the mainland alone, Green revealed to our informant that Sinners' cornerback Malala chose to reclaim his former fiancée believed to be the cause of a deadly quarrel resulting in the death of Sammy Tau. When a witness to Tau's unfortunate accident came forward, Malala was released from custody only to reaffirm his wedding in May and hand Green a plane ticket home. 'I do believe he is innocent,' the faithful and lovely Miss Green said."

Nell tossed the tabloid onto the table. "Poor Winnie, dumped by two men within a year. She must be devastated."

"Despicable," Nurse Shammy said.

"*Si*, de-vastated and what she said," Corazon agreed, jerking her head in the nurse's direction.

"Another one of my best players with his head screwed up by women!" Joe folded the newspaper and sent it sailing across the room.

"Now, now," Brinsley intervened in his cool British voice that made all things seem reasonable. "Miss Winnie is from Shreveport, not New Orleans. There could be other errors in this article. We should not jump to conclusions until we have heard from both parties."

Knox Polk squeezed his plump wife's shoulders. "Now you quiet down. Like the Brit said, we don't know the truth yet. Anybody heard from Winnie?"

"She'll be at her sister's home, I'm sure. I need to go over there," Nell decided.

"Hold off on that. Adam is on his way here, and the Rev, minister or not, is going to want to take a piece out of him for scratching an itch with his sister-in-law. With all those church dinners under his belt, I don't think he can do it. He might have a heart attack. Jesus, Mary and Joseph, what a *cochonnerie*! I guess I need to handle it."

"You should since you thought it was a great idea for Adam and Winnie to have an affair," Nell agreed, and all the other women chimed in along the same line.

"Hey, like you and Mintay weren't drooling all over Adam and saying how Winnie needed a fling. I'm going to the airport to pick up Adam and straighten this out. Corazon, those groceries need to be put up. Brinsley, the silver won't polish itself. The rest of you, do what you do." Joe found the truck keys, scooped the tabloid off the floor, and went out the door. At least, the airport would be quiet and free of accusatory women. He almost hoped Adam's flight would come in late.

No such luck. The plane arrived right on time and debarked a smiling Samoan without an ounce of guilt showing on his broad, brown face. Joe shook his hand and gave him a friendly back slap. "Nice to have you out of jail and back in the States again, but we do have a problem."

"Winnie?"

"*C'est vrai.* And speaking of the truth, you better take a look at this." Joe offered his cornerback the tabloid.

"Winnie told the press this?" A big man never looked so hurt.

"I can't say how they got their information. Those lowlife paparazzi are everywhere."

"Is she staying with the Rev and her sister?— because I have to see her and explain. I know we pass their place on the way to yours. Drop me off there."

"That might not be the best of ideas right now. What is your explanation?"

They made their way from the terminal to the short-term parking and slung Adam's suitcase into the backseat. Adam climbed in the shotgun seat and closed the door before answering. "She found Pala naked in my bed."

"A naked ex-girlfriend in your bed, that one is always hard to explain."

"Winnie saw her and took off. We were supposed to come back together. I planned to give her this in Hawaii. Bought it in Honolulu where they have more selection than in Pago Pago." Adam reached into the pocket of his black Sinners' jacket and opened the ring box.

Joe whistled. "Nice rock."

"A ten-carat canary yellow diamond with two white brilliants on the sides. Think she'll like it?"

"Sure, if she doesn't cram it down your throat first. According to that rag, she thinks you are marrying Pala after all."

"No way! That is one crazy Samoan bitch. She rubbed ketchup on a bed sheet to show Winnie I took her virginity."

"Crazy like a fox and hard to disprove."

"I brought the sheet with me. I mean close up you can tell it is ketchup."

Joe shook his head. "Won't work. Could be any sheet."

"Well, it has other stuff on it—like my DNA."

"One thing I know about women. Lab tests aren't romantic. They want to feel your innocence in their hearts. At least she still believes you didn't murder Tau."

"I didn't, but I'm glad you weren't called to testify since I said I wanted to kill him. That wore off when I realized he'd be stuck with Pala for life while I had Winnie. Hey, this is that gated place where the Rev lives. Pull over!" Adam made a grab for the steering wheel. Joe elbowed him in the side, but did turn toward the little guard hut.

"If you are sure you are ready. Honestly, I think I'd tell Nell your story and let her run some interference first."

The elderly guard approached the truck. "Oh, hello, Mr. Billodeaux. Who is that you got with you?"

"Adam Malala, my cornerback."

"Then sorry, I can't let you in. The Reverend's orders."

"I can take him," Adam whispered.

"He is carrying a gun, and you are a pretty big target." Joe put on his best comradely grin. "I'll come back after I drop Adam at my place."

"Good idea."

They circled round and came out on the highway again. Adam pointed out a break in the fence where a stream funneled through the golf course. "I could wade through there and get to the Rev's house."

"Sure, huge brown guy with wild hair wades onto the golf course of a gated community. If that guard doesn't shoot you, someone else will, so I'm not stopping. We need to get Winnie out of there and away from the Rev who is probably pretty pissed at you."

"I'll just call and ask her to come over." His attempt went to voice mail.

"Don't leave a message! We won't be able to get her to our place if she knows you are here. Right now she probably figures you are still in Samoa sipping out of coconuts with Pala and you called to make your breakup official."

"You're the quarterback. What's the next play?"

"We lure her to Lorena Ranch. Let me think about it."

They left the highway and took the back roads home, turning in at the gate right behind the van full of school children and passing Teddy as he labored along on his crutches with Nurse Shammy wheeling his chair in the rear. Teddy shouted, "Hey, Adam!" as they passed.

Joe grinned the way he did when the Sinners were about to execute a trick play. "There's our key player, Teddy. Winnie is very fond of him. We use him as a diversion and then you take her down."

"I don't like using a little kid to get what I want."

"Teddy will be in on it, like that night he and Stacy spied on you, but this time to do a good deed which might make up for the other."

Joe parked the truck and Adam got down, wading into the crowd of children waiting to greet him. Macho and Titi raced around the corner of the house and barked. Knox Polk merely leaned against the van and waited to see what came next like a village elder.

"Your family makes me feel like I'm still in the islands," Adam remarked.

Stacy was the first to ask, "What did you bring me from Samoa?"

Teddy puffed up beside her and blew a lock of sweaty blond hair out of his eyes. "Did you see, Adam? I walked the whole danged way up the drive on my sticks. I been working out." Still, the boy fell back gratefully into his wheelchair. Freed from his crutches, he held up a fist for Adam to bump.

"How's it going, my man? I think you grew since I saw you last."

"Great! I got new boots and a bigger chair so I only look taller. Wish I was. Daddy Joe and Mama Nell are going to adopt me. I already picked out my new name—Teddy Wilkes Billodeaux. I'm getting rid of the Bear part because people tease me. I hope my mom won't mind. I still worry about her, you know what I mean."

"She left you in a safe place with good people because she loved you. Now she has to take care of herself."

"I guess so."

Adam squatted by Teddy's side. "I need your help to plan a surprise for Miss Winnie."

Teddy glanced all around with his big blue eyes. "Where is she? Mama Nell said you went on a vacation together."

"We did, and I got her this ring, but she doesn't know it yet." Adam flashed open the box again.

Jude, always quick on the uptake, squealed, "It's an engagement ring!"

Dean and Tommy rolled their eyes, and Dean remarked like a college guy whose best friend just succumbed to marriage, "Another one bites the dust."

The girls mobbed around Adam and Teddy to get a look. Stacy leaned in coolly appraising Adam's taste. "It seems to be of very good quality and will be attractive with her skin tones."

"Thanks, Stace. Always good to know you approve. Now listen, Miss Winnie doesn't know I'm here. She's visiting her sister for a few days. We need to get her to come to the ranch. I want to give her the ring on our beach by those palm trees where we…like to hang out together."

Stacy snorted but didn't dare say a word when Joe gave her the eye. Dean and Tommy poked each other with their elbows. Joe shot them a settle-down frown. "We need all of you to keep the secret that Adam is here waiting for her. And we want a way to get her out to the beach without suspecting anything. Any ideas, team?"

Teddy raised his hand, wiggling his fingers like a star pupil with the right answer. "I know, I know! I can say I want to show her how I can walk on sand with my sticks. She'll want to see that. Then, I lead her to Adam.

He can crouch down in the bushes and jump out at her."

"All good except that last part. We go with Teddy's plan." Joe clapped his hands. "Snack time."

The children trooped into the kitchen where the healthy cookies and glasses of milk lined the table. They dug in and completely ignored the tribunal of women who glared at Adam, arms crossed under their breasts. Nurse Shammy moved to join Nell and Corazon and hurried to impart the news.

"I do believe Clive was right about the misinformation."

"Clive?"

"Ahem, Mr. Brinsley. He is always impressively clear-minded. Adam wants to marry Winnie. He has a gorgeous ring to present—if we can get her to come here."

Corazon's posture softened. She held out a plate of cookies. "Welcome back, Mr. Adam. You want a snack? They got coconut in them."

"Yes, please." He hunkered down among the children and poured himself a large glass of milk from a pitcher on the table.

Joe moved to put his arm around his wife who had relaxed her stance, too. "Tink, we have a plan, but we need you to do your part. Call Winnie and invite her over here tonight."

"Are we certain she is at the Rev's?"

"Considering that the guard wouldn't let Adam into Versailles, I'd say for sure. Grab a phone and work your magic, Tinker Bell."

"Don't call me that," Nell answered automatically, but she picked up a cell and punched in a number she'd dialed so often she knew it by heart.

Chapter Thirty-Two

"Hi, Mintay. Heard anything from Winnie lately?"

"She's here," the doctor whispered. "You read about her and Adam in the tabloids, I'll bet. Dexter Sykes, you remember him always photographing Connor and Stevie and making a buck off of them. He sat next to her on the plane and put the story together, even conned her into posing for that picture. Anyhow, she doesn't want to see anyone or go anywhere. It's not good."

"Maybe not as bad as you think."

"You'd have to be here and know her better. With all that attention from Adam, Winnie was finally getting her confidence back. Now she's returned to thinking she is always going to be second best."

"She needs some distraction. Bring her over tonight to visit with the children. Tell her Teddy wants to show her his new skills." Nell met Joe's eyes. He nodded.

"Well, she did bring a whole suitcase full of souvenirs for your kids. You should see Riley in her lava-lava. She could be an island girl."

"Tell her to wear it when she comes along tonight. We'll have a little welcome home party and won't mention Adam at all."

"I'll try. In fact, I will insist she gets out. See you

275

around seven."

Nell offered a thumbs-up to everyone in the kitchen. As she disconnected, they gave her a round of applause.

****

Winnie sat in Joe's vast den and distributed her gifts from Samoa. Her sister, the brainy one who always made the right moves and married a wonderful guy, had been correct again. She needed to get out and get on with her life. She'd taken a fling with Adam far too seriously. If only she hadn't gone to his village, witnessed his conflicts, she could have gone on believing that he was nothing but a happy-go-lucky guy who never worried about tomorrow. She hoped he'd made the right decision to embrace the *fa'a Samoa* and tired to wish him well. She wasn't quite there yet, her sense of being used again to defy his parents still far too strong. As for Pala, she hoped the woman swelled up as fat as Adam's mother in the coming years. The village maiden must have pursued Adam to the city, and that she could not forgive.

She presented the *'ava* bowl to Joe and told a little about the ceremony, grossed out the kids with tales of flying foxes, eating octopus tentacles and fried worms, and showed the girls how to wrap their lava-lavas. Teddy sat in his wheelchair right by her side proudly holding the best of the carved wood boats she'd brought for each boy. Choking only once when she described the *fiafia* where Adam danced for her and her alone, she lightened the moment by revealing he'd performed in a skirt of shredded leaves as a general part of the entertainment. That brought groans from the male sector.

"I don't know. It could be very sexy," Nell said, regarding her husband speculatively.

Joe Dean held up his hands as if stopping her mind from going there. *"Mais cher,* Cajuns dance but never in leaf skirts. Can't wait to tell the team about it though." He got the chuckles he wanted, especially a great, booming laugh out of the Rev who knew about locker room razzing.

"Miss Winnie, Miss Winnie," Teddy pleaded as soon as the laughter died down. "I want to show you how good I can walk with my sticks now, even in the sand. Let's go to our beach right now."

"That's great Teddy, but I don't think so. It's dark out and getting late."

Teddy threw his new mama a desperate look. Nell caught it smoothly. "Please Winnie, it would mean so much to him. Afterwards, we'll have cake and punch and get the children to bed. The lights are on along the pathway, and it is a beautiful spring night."

"Okay." She could endure a little heartache for Teddy's sake. She shook her finger at the rest of the children. "Don't eat all the cake while I'm gone." That sent them into gales of giggles, heaven knew why. The Billodeaux children had been very easy to entertain all evening.

Nurse Shammy and Brinsley went along for the walk. They stayed at the edge of the beach when Teddy got out of his chair and took up his crutches, easing his paralyzed lower legs along the paved path and then cutting off at a place that held too many memories for Winnie.

"You're doing so well. Now let's go back. Don't go any farther."

Lynn Shurr

Teddy pushed on laboring against the sand, disappearing behind a clump of too familiar bushes. "I said come back!"

Faintly, she heard Teddy call, "I can't. I'm stuck. I fell down."

Nothing else she could do but go after him. Maybe it was better she face the place where she and Adam first made love and put it out of her mind forever. She rounded the bushes. "Adam," she said.

Teddy hurried to backtrack though his shoulders ached badly. He found Nurse Shammy and Brinsley waiting for him on the path and fell into his chair with relief. "I think I did a good job and made up for being bad before," he told them.

"Yes, it is never too late to make amends," Nurse Shammy said.

Brinsley carried the crutches as Teddy whizzed ahead eager to tell the rest of the family about his success. The nurse and the butler followed more slowly. The night did hold all the promise of spring, rebirth, and renewal along with the faint scent of honeysuckle and the song of one mockingbird still seeking a mate. Brinsley took his companion's hand.

"A lovely evening for a stroll, Edith."

"That it is, Clive."

They entered the kitchen where Corazon finished piping the words, "Happy Engagement, Winnie and Adam" on a very large, multi-layered hummingbird cake before she glanced up and noticed the clasped hands. "Do I need to add two more names?"

"Oh my, no! Clive—Mr. Brinsley merely helped me over the oak roots." Nurse Shammy's gaunt cheeks flushed, and Brinsley's pale face reddened.

The butler seized the huge silver bowl of pineapple and ginger ale punch with its floating ice ring of strawberries. "I shall take this into the dining room."

Nurse Shammy fanned her face. "Hot flash." She regarded the message on the cake. "What if she refuses the ring?"

Corazon held up a spatula. "Then we scrape it off and still eat cake. I don't go to all this trouble for nothing. But me, I think we gonna have a party real soon."

Chapter Thirty-Three

Standing by their palm trees, Adam Malala wore only his lava-lava wrapped up like a loincloth despite a slight chill in the spring air that puckered his nipples. Winnie swore he'd oiled his body and tucked a sprig of coral azaleas from Nell's landscaping behind his ear simply to remind her of the night he'd danced for her at the *fiafia*. He began to move, making those strong, graceful gestures again, still powerful without the music. Experiencing emotions as potent as an aphrodisiac, Winnie yearned to go close and trace the lines of his intricate tattoos right to his center where all the designs led.

Instead, she summoned up her best nurse-with-a-naughty-patient voice. "What do you think you are doing? Why are you here and not with Pala?"

He continued to sway, coming nearer. "I am courting you, not Pala, never Pala. I dance only for the woman I love."

Winnie made herself pretend she didn't hear that last statement. Much as she disliked Pala, what Adam had done to her was wrong. "Yet she was good enough to take to bed in the time it took me to buy some souvenirs. She valued her virginity, Adam. How could you take it and kick her aside?"

"So many questions. Sometimes you think too

much, lovely Winnie. You mistake ketchup for blood on a sheet, lies for truth, and yourself for second best. Pala wove a spider's web to destroy you, and my pretty *palagi* moth flew right into it. She came to our room to tempt me. I told her to go and locked myself in the bathroom. I regret I did not put her out more forcefully, but I don't care to manhandle women."

He danced so close now she could feel his body heat and a weakening in her knees demanding she lie down in the sand with this man, this gorgeous man. Winnie made a last effort at resistance. "You expect me to believe that?"

"You believed I did not kill Sammy Tau, went out and looked for proof. I brought the sheet if you need evidence that I did not make love to Pala. A test will show I lay with you only—and confirm a messy ketchup stain." He brushed his body against hers, lifted her long hair, and kissed her neck.

Her arms went around him, and she breathed against his bare chest. "I feel as if I am stealing you away from paradise and your family. You might be unhappy later."

"I left that particular paradise behind when I went to college. By agreeing to marry Pala, I made my last effort to go back there and please everyone but myself. We'll create our own paradise somewhere else, Winnie."

Adam slid down the length of her body and knelt in the sand at her feet. Her breasts throbbed with his absence. He took the small box from a fold in the lava-lava and offered her the yellow diamond. "I planned to buy this in Honolulu and offer it to you by a waterfall on Maui to remind you of our time at *Nu'uuli*, but you ran away. Winnie Green, will you stand by me and make me your husband?"

Winnie went to her knees in front of him and cupped his broad face. "Yes, Adam Malala, I will." She tugged at his tightly wrapped lava-lava until it fell free.

He pressed his erection hard between her legs while he fumbled with the annoying buttons of her blouse and the zipper of her slacks. "When it comes to clothes, the Samoan way *is* better," he complained.

****

In the cabin where Knox Polk operated the surveillance screens that guarded Lorena Ranch from intruders, Nell said to Joe, "Time to turn this off, and not a word that we wired the beach area while they were gone. I am fairly sure her answer is yes."

"I'll say. I've seen Adam's naked butt and those tattoos in the locker room but really don't want the expansion team part of him burned into my brain." Joe flicked off the monitor. "Knox, how about you go over to the house and tell everyone the party starts in a half hour."

"Be happy to do that." Knox sauntered out with a knowing smile on his usually serious lips.

"Let's see, Mintay and the Rev are watching their kids, ours, and Corazon's boy. Corazon, Brinsley, and Nurse Shammy are protecting the refreshments from our horde. We have maybe twenty free minutes," Nell said thoughtfully. "I have to say that particular kind of Samoan dancing is very arousing."

Joe put his hands on his waist and rotated his slim hips. "Maybe I could manage some naked zydeco, sugar. I know for a fact Adam never locks his cabin. I'll bet the sheets are still clean."

"Twenty minutes, no more. I'll have to put clean linens on the bed."

"You know one of my favorite sayings. When you see an opening, take it. *Allons*!"

Chapter Thirty-Four

Professors Edwin and Sondra Green stiffly occupied the large, overstuffed couch in the Rev's spacious living room overlooking the Versailles golf course. They did not allow their backbones to relax against the comfortable cushions. Winnie's beloved Nana sat with them. The women's hands lay clasped tightly in their laps, and her father's fingers dug into the soft upholstery. They said, "This is certainly a surprise" and "We wish you the best" and "How happy you seem, Winnie," but their eyes broadcast the message, "Our little girl has gone native."

Sitting cross-legged and barefooted on the floor and leaning against Adam's muscular, tattooed thigh, Winnie admitted to herself she enjoyed their discomfort. Late onset rebellion, she realized. Intentionally, she wore a lava-lava that exposed her darker skin and a flower in her untamed hair, frizzy with Louisiana humidity. Adam refused to meet her parents in Samoan dress. He tied back his hair, put on a red Sinners polo shirt and shorts that exposed only the lowest part of his tattoos. Nana could not take her eyes off of his body art, though she would have been to first to say staring is the height of bad manners.

"I thought we should just have a simple service at the Rev's church and a nice party for our close friends afterwards," Adam said.

"Since Winnie is a divorced woman that would be most appropriate. She should not wear white," Nana commented, posture perfect and impeccably dressed as if she planned to go to church directly after meeting Adam.

"But, I said since Adam is an only child and never been married before, his mother will be upset if we don't do the full *fa'alavelave*. That's a gift exchange ceremony. I mean she has been storing rooms full of fine mats and canned corned beef since last year anticipating his wedding. Ela was very upset when we left Samoa and would not come to the phone when we called to tell her about our engagement. When his father told her we wanted to have the ceremony in Samoa, she finally relented."

Nana's eyes, green like Winnie's, projected a look of horror. "You plan to serve corned beef at this *lavelave* affair?"

Adam gave her his dazzling smile, and the elderly woman softened her posture a little. "No, Nana, we will also have roasted pig, lobster, chicken, taro, and chop suey. Maybe macaroni and potato salad, too."

"Yes, you can't lack for starchy foods at a Samoan feast," Winnie agreed. She did so enjoy watching the faces of her slim, health conscious family as they digested all this information.

Only the Rev, sitting off to one side with Mintay, smiled. "Sounds real good to me."

"We realize your family doesn't have any fine mats to trade, but a couple dozen bolts of good cloth will make up for that. Maybe we could substitute some good perfumes to exchange for the fragrant oils," Adam continued.

"Wait, wait! We are moving along entirely too fast," Dr. Edwin Green asserted with arms crossed over his narrow chest. "What about the other woman those scurrilous papers said you intended to marry? For all we know, you might have another wife in Samoa."

On the verge of laughing, Adam grinned wider than ever. "Oh, we gave up having two wives or more when the missionaries arrived. Shortly after we returned to the States, my father tells me Pala accepted the proposal of a high ranking chief who has been widowed for a year and has six children to raise. Two are nearly grown, but the others need a mother. The *matai* claims he is still young enough to give Pala six more of her own. He has a great belly and a very fine two-story house. They will marry in May and plan to have a thirty-pig reception. We want to have our ceremony in June and must have at least forty pigs. You need to supply a wedding gown for the reception, but my mother will pick out a few for the church service, and Winnie can choose the one she likes for that."

The hands resting in Dr. Sondra Green's lap twisted together. "We do want to honor your customs, but you have to realize we are college professors, not millionaires. Why, traveling to Samoa will take a large chunk out of our budget already."

"No worries. Joe Dean Billodeaux plans to charter a jet to fly his family to the islands. You are welcome to ride with him and any of the Sinners team who want to attend," Adam assured them.

The Rev held up his big hand as if he were going to bless his congregation. "Put me down for twenty pigs and a dozen bolts of cloth. As long as there is a

Christian ceremony first, I want our family to do this up right."

"Our friend, Davita Tomanaga, is the Methodist minister. He will perform the service." Adam squeezed Winnie's hand.

"Won't the LMS minister be upset?" she asked.

"Not if he is a guest of honor and gets his own cake. My mother will take care of the cake, three tiers at least with a dozen smaller ones for the *matai* and other honored guests to take home."

"Oh, my, what shall I wear?" Nana worried.

"The *puletasi* I bought for you and Mama. You will look marvelous. You always do."

"I will give you a check for all your obligations. You have no extended family to chip in. Just don't let on to my mother I paid for your part," Adam told them.

Slowly the shock wore off and other questions surfaced. Sondra Green's usually smooth brow wrinkled above her wire-rimmed glasses. "Winnie, where do the two of you intend to live?"

Adam answered for her daughter. "We want a house with a beach and palm trees, maybe on an island, with a big guest house for visitors."

"In—in American Samoa?"

"I was thinking Florida."

"Oh, that's wonderful! Not so very far away."

Winnie covered Adam's large, dark hand with her long, slender fingers. "If we have children—"

"When we have children," he corrected.

"I want them to know their Samoan family and way of life. I think we should spend two months of the year on the island."

"Her idea," Adam said.

"I also want them to be able to fulfill their dreams and ambitions and enjoy individual achievement. They should be educated here."

"You've given this a great deal of thought," her father said. "That is good, very prudent."

"Winnie has. I haven't gotten much beyond the wedding plans yet." Adam snapped his fingers. "I almost forgot. The bride must perform a traditional dance in her second wedding gown to open the reception."

"You know I don't dance well! I'll be embarrassed with Pala looking on, she does it so perfectly. No, I can't." Winnie covered her face already imagining her clumsy disgrace.

Adam parted her hands and lowered them. "We will find an instructor for you. Whatever you do will please me more than any dance of Pala's."

"What we have here is a good start to a marriage." The Rev did stand this time and offered a blessing.

Chapter Thirty-Five

The blessing must have helped because in the slightly drier season of June in Samoa, no rain fell on the numerous white canopies that shaded the wedding guests behind the Malala home. Reverend Tomanaga conducted a very traditional Methodist service in both English and Samoan, the choir's voices soared in the flower-festooned church, and as the bride and groom left the church, the new bell in the tower rang joyously proclaiming that Edwina Green and Adam Malala were man and wife.

In a bedroom of the house, Nell and Mintay helped Winnie out the wedding gown chosen from three offered by Ela. All of her mother-in-law's selections resembled huge piles of whipped cream and made Winnie feel like one of those Barbie dolls trapped inside a wide skirt of cake as she tried them on. She'd started to choose the least elaborate, but seeing the disappointment on Ela's face settled on the second with its three-tiered veil and short train. Her friends assured her that with her slim figure, she could carry it off, and perhaps she had.

Now, gratefully, she shimmed into the dress she'd chosen with her mother, sister, and Nana—a simple silk sheath of the palest yellow that showed off her narrow hips and upturned breasts, but was covered in swirling patterns of tiny pearls, crystals, and sequins that caught the light as she moved. Winnie took her hair down, brushed it out, and crowned it with a simple headpiece made of the plumeria blossoms Adam always said she resembled. With that last step taken she was as ready as she ever would be to dance in front of hundreds of guests.

Mintay patted her shoulder. "You go, girl. Show them what you can do."

With her usual hard work ethic, Winnie had perfected her one dance. She swayed in time to the music provided by the hired band from Pago Pago and displayed her graceful arm movements and subtle footwork. No, she would never be as good at this as Pala who sat looking a little green beside her three-hundred pound, middle-aged husband. Pala's *matai* hinted during the congratulations at the church that he believed his wife already carried a child. Perhaps she did and that accounted for her ill expression, but Winnie believed envy had something to do with it, too. No matter, tonight she danced only for Adam, and by the look on his face, she did her dance well.

The feasting began with overflowing plates delivered by rank first to the ministers and *matai,* the elders, the school principle, the owner and coach of the Sinners, the rest of the team, and so on down the line. Ela had chosen Brinsley in his immaculate white linen suit to serve the most important guests. He, Nana, Corazon, and Shammy filled in as elders for Winnie's family and did their job impeccably. Winnie's nephews and niece and all the older Billodeaux children were pressed into service to serve the other guests as was traditional. Even Teddy, a towel on his lap, managed to wheel out one plate at a time. Only Stacy balked. Brinsley reminded her that sophisticated people learned the customs of others when in their country and that settled the matter. Easily half the food slid into containers to be taken home before anyone chowed down.

Well up to the task, the Rev gave a long congratulatory speech and blessed the couple. The incredible five-tiered cake covered in Samoan designs and connected to islands of smaller cakes by little bridges disappeared into mouths and baskets. The parade of gifts began with the women of Ela's family shaking out the fine mats to be admired. The wives of the Sinners, Nell, Stevie, Cassie, Precious, Sharlette and more, unrolled the bolts of cloth and paraded them around. Their hefty husbands, Joe and Connor, Howdy, Calvin, Asa and the rest of the Sinners team, persuaded to wear red shirts with black lava-lavas, carried the uneaten pigs adorned with spikes of red ginger on planks. Bottles of fragrant oil were exchanged for some very nice perfumes selected by Nana. Winnie felt part of a new, larger family and grateful to all of them for their help.

The dancing began and would continue well into the night. Precious Armitage, in a brilliant orange and gold floral dress boogied by with her cumbersome husband, Calvin, and said, "I tell you, these are my peoples. They know how to eat and how to par-tay."

Winnie glanced around for her new husband and found him gone. Leaving the shade of the last canopy, she scanned the beach for him and experienced a small frisson of worry as memories of the night Sammy Tau died flooded her mind. It receded like the tide on the village shore when she noticed him crouched by Teddy's wheelchair watching a game of *kirikiti*, a Samoan form of cricket the bored children started as the heat of the day waned a little. Getting their wedding finery dirty, Dean, Tommy, Jude, and Xochi participated. Teddy and Stacy sat on the sidelines. Having abandoned their shoes in a little pyramid on the shore, quiet Annie supervised the triplets and Knox, Jr. wading at the edge of the water. Dean used the three-sided club to wallop the rubber ball into the waves. Stacy jumped up and did an impromptu cheer as Winnie joined the group.

"I wish I could do that," Teddy said wistfully. "But it's okay. Daddy Joe and the ice hockey team in Lafayette are going to sponsor a sled hockey league for kids like me at the arena next winter. It's so cool even Dean and Tommy want to do it, but they won't be allowed. You'll come see me play when you can, won't you, Adam?"

"I will. Winnie, too. I figure without you and Stacy I might never have gotten to know my bride so well, never brought her here at all, but we had to get away from you brats." He tousled Teddy's hair to show he teased.

"We're completely forgiven, then?" Stacy asked. She jumped suddenly to her feet and shouted, "Way to go, Tommy!" as her cousin caught a piece of the ball with the club and sent it sizzling like a hard line drive. Primly, she sat again and rearranged her skirt. "I'm trying to be more of a team player, but I really don't care for sports very much."

"You're trying. That counts for a lot," Winnie told her. Despite Samoan customs, she slipped her hand into

Adam's and his strong arm came up around her waist pressing her close.

****

Joe Dean Billodeaux moved behind his wife who watched the little scene on the beach a short distance away. Never one to obey rules, he nuzzled her neck and rubbed against her *puletasi*-clad backside.

Nell poked him with her elbow, but not hard enough to hurt. "We're not supposed to do that here."

"Do I look like a Samoan, me?"

"Maybe in that lava-lava, but our kids certainly do all barefooted and playing in the sand in their wedding clothes."

"Let them have fun. Wait until they see the fire dancing later. This is a once in a lifetime experience and worth shutting down Camp Love Letter for a week."

"It is," she agreed. "Romantic, too, with the palm trees and the beach and the blue water. If only we didn't have those helicopters buzzing around."

"The sun is going down. They'll leave soon. Hey, Knox did a great job securing the road and patrolling the perimeter with his off-duty policemen for any paparazzi who tried to sneak through the jungle." Joe pointed to his ranch manager, clad in khakis and a bush hat, who still ranged along the expanse where the mountain met the beach with his troops. "He said it reminds him of 'Nam, not romance."

"That's sad, but I think Brinsley and Shammy are making the most of the trip."

Far down the beach, the older couple walked side by side. Observing proprieties, the butler had his arms tucked behind his back.

"You think those two are bed-hopping?"

"Joe! No, Shammy is a former nun and Brinsley is far too proper."

"Still, I think we have another wedding in the works and probably a permanent butler and nurse at the ranch now."

"With the size of our family, we need all the help we can get."

"At least this Samoan romance was easy to bring off before it screwed up the football season. We just had to let our kids send them running to the islands to get away together."

"Oh, you're taking credit for this happy ending, are you? I don't call it easy transporting ten children, one of them with special needs, to Samoa for the celebration. The Rileys, the McCoys, and nearly everyone else had the sense to leave theirs at home. They are having second honeymoons, but us, no!" Still, Nell relaxed against him and wiggled her backside in just the right place.

"Tink, it's not a wedding without a whole lot of kids running around."

"Correction, it's not a Cajun wedding without a lot of kids."

"True, and right now all those kids are occupied and I'll bet you me, the bedrooms in the house are not."

"What, no lovemaking under the palms?"

"Not after what happened to Sammy Tau. Come along with me, and I'll show you what paradise really is. Sugar, you know I always keep my word."

A word about the author...

Once a librarian, now a writer of romance, Lynn Shurr grew up in Pennsylvania Dutch country. She attended a state college and earned a very impractical B.A. in English Literature. Her first job out of school really was working as a cashier in a burger joint. Moving from one humble job to another, she traveled to North Carolina, then Germany, then California where she buckled down for an M.A. in Librarianship.

She found her first reference job in the Heart of Cajun Country, Lafayette, Louisiana. For her, the old saying, "Once you've tasted bayou water, you will always stay here" came true. She raised three children not far from the Bayou Teche and lives there still with her astronomer husband.

When not writing, Lynn likes to paint, cheer for the New Orleans Saints and LSU Tigers, and take long road trips nearly anywhere. Her love of the bayou country, its history and customs often shows in her books.

You may contact Lynn at www.lynnshurr.com or visit her blog, lynnshurr.blogspot.com.

Other Books by Lynn Shurr
A Trashy Affair
THE SINNERS SERIES
Goals for a Sinner
Wish for a Sinner
Kicks for a Sinner
THE MARDI GRAS SERIES
Queen of the Mardi Gras Ball
Mardi Gras Madness
Courir de Mardi Gras